I0831700

Paradosso Dell'Amore

By Jordan Hampton

Printed in the United States of America.

ISBN 978-0-692-16445-7

Published by DeWayne Jordan Hampton

Fayetteville, NC

Subject Heading: FICTION: ROMANCE—GENERAL/FICTION: ROMANCE—FANTASY/FICTION/ROMANCE/ACTION & ADVENTURE

Quotations

"We always believe our first love is our last, and our last love our first."

– George W. Melville

"I have decided to stick with love. Hate is too great a burden to bear."

– Martin Luther King, Jr.

"Love never fails."

– 1 Corinthians 13:8a, TNIV

To My Future Wife

Hey there,

I struggled to figure out what to do here, actually. I didn't know whether to write a normal dedication page with a lot of the names of the people who mean a lot to me or just do one of the cheesy one-liners that a lot of authors put in their books, but I did know that I wanted something unique. That's why I made up my mind about talking to you.

I'm no good at this, you know; but I still wanted to let you know that I think about you. A lot more than I admit, actually. If we're being honest, this entire novel came about because I was thinking of all sorts of possibilities of what our life together could look like. I'll admit that my imagination took over at some places, but there's a verisimilitude to it. Those tender moments, honest conversations, the witty banter, even those moments where we fight or come on hard times and have to pull each other along, I look forward to it. I guess to be more accurate, I just look forward to you.

I don't think that our life together will be perfect, and I know that I have a lot of rough edges that need smoothing over, but even now, before I know who or where you are, I know that I don't want to spend my life with anyone else. I spent my time writing this book thinking about the way I wanted to love someone else, and how I wanted to be loved, and what came out was this time-transcendent love letter to you. You're worth every word between these pages and so much more, and I recognize your value even in the distance.

For now though, enjoy this story and know that I'm working my way to you.

Love,

Jordan Hampton

Chapter One

"And now, for the moment you've all been waiting for," the master of ceremonies called into the microphone. The man of the hour stared out at the crowd from behind the curtain with a scowl that he desperately attempted to mask. He shook his head. This should have been a joyous occasion for him like it had been so many times before. It was a moment that once upon a time epitomized his every dream, but this instant that should have been alive with color for him only emanated the saddest shades of gray. "It is my honor to present to you," the announcer continued as she began to step out of the way of the table that sat at the front of the bookstore, "the one, the only, David Masters!"

As his name echoed through the room and the crowd of fans cheered for him, he walked across the stage and took the microphone from the MC. He lifted his hand with a hollow smile on his face.

"Thank you," he started in his best attempt at sincerity, but the enthused congregation of assorted admirers were all too fixated on his presence so that none noted his uninterested tone. "Eight years ago, I stood in a bookstore like this in my hometown of Edgehaven, Arizona and pulled every book I could off the shelf." He paused to take in the soothing creams, darker yellows and browns of his surroundings, the shelves upon shelves of books galore that would only serve as an appetizer to whet the palate of a man of his literary yearning, the heavenly aroma of coffee in the air, the warmth of the room that so wonderfully contrasted the chill of the outside. He inhaled deeply, and for but a moment it was as if the color that had previously been drained from his entire world returned in a moment of wondrous vitality and awe-inspiring power. "You see, I wanted to dive into worlds I'd never even thought imaginable, but more than that I wanted to be just like the writers whose works I loved so much. Now, thanks to all of you and the support you've given my stories and me, we're here in New York to celebrate the fact that something that we all cherish is now on display for the entire world to see. Again, thank you so much." He passed the mic back to the MC and took his seat at the table lined with towering rows of *Death by Knight*, the Medieval drama that served as his passion for the last year.

He smiled as he glanced down at the lustrous gray knight's helm half shrouded in shadows. It was one of his most sinister cover designs, but it had a pull about it that made a person question what it was that hid behind that mask. The crowd became a single-file line that divided the store through its center, and David withdrew his favorite pen from his pocket in preparation for the many autographs that he'd no doubt be asked to sign.

As the hoard of people before him felt their hearts rev with the anticipation of even a brief conversation with their literary hero and the room wherein they stood swirled with the intoxicating aroma of adoration, he still felt his senses overwhelmed by the sudden mundanity of the occasion. His heart sank as those who admired him passed through the line and received their autographs with smiles on their faces, disappointed that no matter the effort he put in he remained incapable of reciprocity. There was no excitement in him, no longer any joy now that the project that occupied his time and his mind proved finished.

His hand began to cramp from the writing, and so he made conversation with the people as they came up to the table in an effort to slow down. Much to his surprise he enjoyed hearing of their different professions, their ordinary lives devoid of book tours and press releases, and more so the fulfillment they all enjoyed. David briefly looked over to the curtain to the left of the table on the stage. Nico Alaimo, his manager and best friend, stood on the phone with his wife and peacefully smirked at something she said. The author, whose heart now desperately longed for a change of pace, returned his focus to the people that awaited his signature in their books.

"I'm sorry, everyone, I have to take a little break but don't worry," David spoke loudly enough for the remainder of his fans to hear. The exhaustion that he felt, both literal and figural, seeped through his tone as water through a thin towel and as he continued he hoped that no one would notice. "I'll be back in five minutes, but please, indulge in the works of my contemporaries as you wait." As if on cue, the store clerks assumed the floor with eyes that hungered for a curious expression, and David briskly made his way to the restroom.

The author paced the floor frantically with his hand against his temple. He didn't know why it upset him so, to hear of the lives of others and to see the people he cared for happily taken care of, but at this point he didn't care. He stopped and slammed his palms against the edge of the sink as he gripped it. He stared into his solid brown eyes and ran his fingers through his curly black hair. *Is this all I have to look forward to,* he asked himself. He turned away for a moment and contemplated a swift kick to the steel trashcan, but decided against it. The fans would think him frustrated with them, and profits aside he sincerely wished to spare their feelings.

He redirected his eyes to the mirror again and surveyed his smooth chocolatey complexion, the pools of deep brown that glistened in the lights that rested upon the ceiling, the full lips, and despite the obvious beauty in him he could only see failure. Failure to make something of his life, to find a reason beyond himself to continue to press onward, to be satisfied, and though the casual attire with which he clothed himself and the fine car he drove spoke to others of his obvious successes, he yearned for something more personal, something more… *real*.

He glanced at his watch, and after he calmed himself and donned the showman's smile once more, he pressed onward to resume his post at the table. The line reformed, and as he took his place behind the table his eyes locked with those of a most peculiar woman. She spoke, but rather than her words the only thing that filled his ears was the sound of a nagging familiarity. He knew her. Certainly they'd crossed paths somewhere before… hadn't they?

"I'm sorry," he politely interrupted as he squinted suspiciously at her. Her skin was sun-kissed, though her ethnicity proved a mystery, and her hair was a silky dark brown, topped with a black fedora with white pinstripes. She wore a black cashmere sweater and a pair of dark blue jeans that exhibited her style and perfectly complemented her elegant figure. Her lips were as luscious and red as newly ripened cherries in the amber gleam of the summer suns that were her eyes, but looking past her obvious beauty he couldn't shake the alarming sense of intimacy between them. "Have… have we met somewhere before?" The sound of his own voice filtered into his ears, and rather than the smooth tone that he'd hoped for he was horrified to find that it was shaky and borderline terrified.

The young lady chuckled and offered a friendly smile.

"Only in my dreams," she told him, and his eyes went wide with the statement. Before he could ask, she offered her hand to shake and said, "Eva Gallows. It's certainly a pleasure." He took her hand, the stunned expression still blanketed over his face and eyes still firmly affixed to this Eva.

"The pleasure," he started, and upon the realization that his voice had risen in octave decidedly started again with more… masculinity, "The pleasure is all mine. How long have you been a fan of my work?" She chuckled again at his expense, and he couldn't believe how flustered he was over this stranger.

"Actually, not that long," she said with a moderately embarrassed look.

"Really? Well nevertheless I'm thrilled to have your support now. And why not take a free copy of *The Night at Raven's Rock*? It's a psychological thriller that I think you'd take interest in." He surveyed the table for a moment and picked up a copy of a book with the ominous cover of a woman dressed in all white that stood upon the edge of a cliff on a moonlit night. Eva smiled, but shook her head.

"Thank you so much," she started in reply, "but I've actually read a few of your books and they just seemed… What's the word? Overdone." The statement sent shockwaves through his body. David Masters had made his peace with the possibility that someone somewhere would dislike his writing style, and surely enough time did prove him right in the matter, but for her to dislike it, her of all people, it drove him mad. Still, he quelled his initial urge for emotional response and merely raised his eyebrows.

"Overdone," he inquired. "Care to elaborate?" She raised her eyebrows at the calmness in his voice, but then again, he was a professional and would probably be used to polarized opinions about his passion projects.

"Well take *The Night at Raven's Rock* for instance. The overall premise is good. After all, I feel like time-loop fiction is among the most compelling if done correctly, but this is relatively generic. I mean, the characters of Jesse and Amanda are so hollow, and from a dynamic sibling duo I sort of expected more out of them because it is the road less traveled. I mean, he's your typical hero. He does good for the sake of doing good, and while in real life there's nothing wrong with that, in terms of literature it's kind of boring." He watched her intently as she spoke, and refused for even a second to turn away. There was something in the way her eyes sparkled with intensity as she dissected the book in his hand, how she expressed her opinion so directly and yet so politely. Or perhaps it was how her brow furrowed as she made a conscious effort to remember what was displayed within the pages of the tome in question. It was as if in literature, perhaps too in some incomprehensible play written by the angels in heaven, they were somehow connected. He couldn't help but smile as she scratched her head. "Maybe it's just my preference, but I like a little grit in my hero. Even when faced with the choice of killing the beast that murdered half of his social circle and terrorized his sister he decides to let him run off into the forest, only to have him come back and kill Jesse to start the loop over. I have to give you points for creativity and sticking to the integrity of your character, but I just found him hard to fall in love with, is all. And don't even get me started on the damsel-in-distress sister who can't seem to do anything for herself or figure out where she's going, for that matter, despite having gone camping with this group of people once every year *at that location* since the age of sixteen. But I suppose the language of the book also makes it hard to truly enjoy it."

"I'm sorry but what was wrong with the language?" David asked the question excitedly, but whether he wanted the answer or merely to watch her brain at work was, at this point, a mystery to him. His eyes shifted to the people in line behind her, and rather than displeasure that she took up so much of the author's time, they were just as intrigued as he was to see the end of this exchange.

"Well it seems a little forced at points" she reluctantly admitted, now fully aware of the intensity of his stare. She felt the temperature of the room rise, and was surprised that the bashful man who could barely master the tone and octave of his voice now spoke volumes with such little dialogue. "More often than not, you switch between pretentious and common diction so much your readers are bound to get whiplash. I don't know, it just seemed like there were two different versions of you working on that book. One was this deeply sophisticated, mentally stimulating and personally challenging individual, and the other was this choppy, generic, uninspired manipulator who just wanted to prey upon the tired leftovers of Hollywood flops reheated for another tasteless meal." David's smile grew all the wider as her words filtered into his ears.

"You've quite the tongue on you, Ms. Gallows," he told her, and she blushed. "Have you ever considered a career as an author?" Her eyes went wide with humor at the thought and she rapidly shook her head as she waved him off.

"Oh, absolutely not. I'm the type of person who can tear into a good book, dissect it, and then tell you exactly what I like and hate about it, but when it comes to writing from the core of my ideals I think I just lack the heart to pull it off," she responded honestly, and then she clasped her hands over her mouth as her eyes locked back on his. "Oh my gosh I'm so sorry. Now that I think about it, I just sort of told you how you should do your job."

"There's no need for apology," he responded comfortingly and released a little bit of a laugh. "Actually, if more people did what you just did I might just improve as a writer. So, if you don't mind me asking, what changed? If you didn't like *Raven's Rock* so much then why pick up *Death by Knight*?" She noted the way his eyes narrowed with genuine fascination, and took in his smooth appearance. For but a moment, she felt the connection that he'd earlier insinuated and internally struggled with throughout their encounter, but then shrugged and set her copy before him so that he could sign it.

"Well I'm not entirely sure. I think the main point of interest for me was that it seemed different from your typical story, and I was right, because it sharply contrasts your other works. It's the song of a tortured soul," Eva responded, and her enrapturing amber eyes locked onto his soothing chocolate browns, "burdened with passions and thoughts unexplored, all of which are tantalizing to him and expressly forbidden by the oath of chivalry that he's pledged his life to uphold. And we're made to feel bad for the character of Sir Alan Conway because shortly after he adjusts to his duties under Lady Aileana and gradually builds up affections for her as her personal knight, he encounters Aria, the free spirit who makes him question his entire way of life. And so, he's split. Does he walk the righteous path of knighthood in service to Aileana, or does he abandon the mundanity of it all to pursue a different reality with the carefree rock to the glass of his present known as Aria? He wants more than what he's settled for, but which path should he take to get it? He dies either way, but will he suffer death in happiness, or will it indeed be Death by Knight? The realism in the language and Conway's character make me wonder, are you just as torn as he is?"

David sat in total silence, and the smile that once decorated his jaw slipped away to leave a desperately riveted expression in its place. She saw so clearly through him, deep into the recesses of his heart. He was speechless. The line behind her remained silent as he scribbled the last few words of personal inscription and autographed Eva's copy. Their eyes remained locked for moments longer as this inexplicable bond they'd earlier experienced seemed to intensify, but then an alarm erupted from the smartphone in her pocket.

She pulled the device from her side and unlocked her screen.

"I'm sorry," David spoke now. "I didn't mean to question you so much." She looked up at him as a smile crossed her lips, and gently brushed her dark brown hair out of her face and tucked it behind her ear.

"Really, it's nothing," she assured him with gentleness in her voice, "I just have a last minute rehearsal before a concert tonight." She turned away from him for just a second, but with a glance back to him she looked into those entrancing brown orbs of his once again. She pulled out a pair of tickets from the same pocket as her phone and laid them before the writer. "You should come. Your manager, too." David looked over to Nico, who now stood smiling at him with eyebrows raised in intrigue. He shook his head at the manager and faced the front once more, but to his dissatisfaction all that remained of Eva Gallows was the light scent of honey and brown sugar, as well as the tickets she left on the table.

His brow furrowed as he attempted to refocus on the task before him. After all, he had a duty to his fans. Nevertheless, it did little to take his mind off of her. In fact, he longed for the ending of the present engagement so as to hurry to the location of this concert. His mind went wild with the possibilities. *Could she be in a band,* he wondered, *or perhaps a dancer for some pop star or worse, a rapper?* He realized that his facial expressions had run out of control as a fan walked away in stitches.

"Still thinking about that woman, aren't you," asked an elderly gentleman with soft gray eyes, a thinning hairline and a gentle smile. "She's a little spitfire, I'll tell you what." David smiled at him as he nodded in agreement.

"That she is. It's been a long time since anyone's given me that kind of feedback," he mused aloud. He took the old man's book and autographed it without delay before he handed it back. The old man chuckled.

"I can't blame you for being in a rush to go see whatever show she's putting on, son. If I were your age and a woman that rockin' came a-knockin' at my door I would…" The old man laughed a bit before he waved his hand. "Never mind. There are children present. All I can say is go get her, Tiger." The man walked back towards the door and out into the city. It was all David could do to restrain his laughter, and after a brief pause he resumed his signing as scheduled. Three more customers remained in his line, and with each he spoke politely as he fulfilled their desires and signed their books.

"Thank you so much," the final customer whispered as he handed her book back.

"You're most welcome. Please, enjoy your night. It was a pleasure meeting you," he responded. The customer squealed with delight as she pressed the book into her chest and all but skipped out the door.

"It's a good thing cleanup is on the staff of the store," Nico said as he approached the table and sat in the chair beside his client. "So, where are we going? As I understand it, a certain someone managed to score a pair of tickets from a pretty girl tonight."

"Hold on," David chuckled. "How do you know that *we* are going anywhere tonight?" He pulled the tickets from his inner breast pocket and looked for an address.

"I reiterate, favorite client of mine," Nico insisted with a smile, "where to?"

"The address on the tickets say, '881 7th Avenue…'" David's voice trailed off as the pistons in his brain started to fire with unprecedented speed. Nico pulled out his phone and input the address into his GPS.

"David, that's Carnegie Hall…" Nico muttered. "This woman is performing tonight at one of the most world-renowned concert halls in history!"

"I know," replied the author as an uncontrollable smile slithered onto his face. He checked his watch and compared the time of the moment with the time on the ticket and in an instant his expression changed. "We're late."

“Well then we should probably get going,” Nico said matter-of-factly as he pat his friend on the back. David donned a puzzled expression as he rose from his seat, and as if he anticipated it, Nico, who now walked towards the door with phone alight in the palm of his hand, looked back at his longtime friend. “Looks like the driver doesn’t mind a little bit of a detour on the way back to the hotel.” David clapped as he advanced towards the manager, to which the young Italian gentleman bowed. “Thank you, thank you. You’re too kind, really.” With a playful shove out the door, the two ducked into a black limousine parked just on the curb in front of the store. “Driver,” Nico all but shouted, “to Carnegie Hall!”

“We’ll be there in no time, sir,” answered the driver. David’s heart jumped into his throat, and with a smile he sat back in his seat as the car pulled onto the busy road.

Chapter Two

As Eva's fingers elegantly struck the black and white keys of the piano, David and Nico walked in and were shown to their seats by a young usher. David found himself captivated by the passionate rendition of Beethoven's *Appassionata* that she so masterfully performed. He could feel the amount of pain and pleasure, joy and anguish, sorrow and elation that the legendary composer poured into this single piece, and as she moved through the first movement of the sonata with the skill and composure of he that did compose it, he became immediately fixated on her. Just as she had seen his soul in *Death by Knight*, he could hear the powerful trembling of her essence being spilled before those who sat dumbstruck by her display.

There it was again, that sparkle in her beautiful amber eyes, that furrow in her brow that filled him with wondrous inquisition. What is it that she contemplated as her fingers moved about the keys? What hidden memories lurked within the shifting melody that filled the listener's ear? No, surely it was a ridiculous question to pose as he needed only listen while her soul spoke to him. Amid the tranquility of her life there were bursts of uncontained intensity. She longed for some sense of solitude within her own mind, and did what she could to make the most of it all, but the fear of some unforeseen disaster still persisted in the back of her mind despite her best attempts to rid herself of it.

Sweat dripped down the side of her face and her breathing became irregular, but not to the point of alarm. No, Eva merely immersed herself, the entirety of who she was in the music. She allowed it to flow through her, to control her so that it was no longer a spectacle centered on her, but a display of unquestionable love for one's art. The frequent shifts between fortissimo and pianissimo, between crescendo and decrescendo all echoed her sincerity as much as they did that of the man who first composed the work, and before long all fell quiet for but an instant.

She continued, though much slower and softer than before. David was well aware that the second movement had begun and as it did, she looked relieved upon the stage. Her breathing stabilized and her wrinkled forehead instantly smoothed. She was as tranquil as the celestial hosts of which she was the envy, and as she gradually encountered the eighth note embellishments to the original theme of the movement, her smile grew all the wider.

David truly enjoyed seeing her in her element, and was delightfully taken with her talent. The flow of the music began to speed once more, but whereas the tone of the first portion of this piece proved dichotomous at best, this part maintained its peaceful and uplifting disposition. She slowed once more, and the sudden silence made his heart beat faster, because it was at that moment that David realized that it was now time for the third movement to begin.

This was the movement that he listened to on repeat as he labored upon his recent book. This music that represented raw intensity and endless contemplation, that conveyed in its notes the conflicts of a man's tortured soul, was the perfect theme for a protagonist afflicted in much the same way. Hearing it again made David recall just how twisted Alan became on the inside, how he longed, neither for the right nor the left as the work neared its conclusion, but for a way to escape it all. More than that it reminded him of how his own life had turned out, how he was tired of the interviews and the acclaim, how he felt the sting of his own loneliness as each day dragged on longer than he'd wished, how he hoped that something would happen to transform the reality in which he survived, and how frantic he became with every passing second.

Another similarity, it would seem, that he had with the beautiful woman in the sultry black dress upon the stage who now swayed with the power of the music. No matter how hard he tried to look away, to come up for air, he could feel his eyes grow all the more fixated on her, and gradually he drowned in her very existence. All the questions he'd asked himself since their meeting earlier at the book signing resurfaced.

Who is this woman, he asked himself, *and why do I feel so drawn to her? And what does she think of me? Am I reading too far into this? Am I* that *dissatisfied with the way my life turned out that I can no longer separate fiction from fact?*

Despite the tempest that raged within his head it was the music itself, this monstrous melody that sparked his inner turmoil, that also served as shelter from the storm. It was the frantic pace, the moderately dark tone and pronounced passion that compelled him to find an answer to those questions that plagued him through this concert.

Her playing slowed once again into a brief lull with minor build up, and as if the sweetest taste rested upon her tongue she closed her eyes as if to savor it, and then resumed her play with just as much power as before. She allowed it to take her to a place that even her soul on display could not reveal, and with eyes still closed her face seemed almost pained and yet… satisfied. In this moment, she was naught more than an ethereal being who transcended all time and reasoning. She *was* the song, and it was her. The repeats rang throughout the auditorium, and the eyes of the members of the audience were glazed over with euphoria as the tempo of the music once again picked up, and as the final flurry of notes rang into the atmosphere and with them the ending of the piece, Eva took her place center stage and bowed before the audience.

She was met with thunderous applause, a standing ovation well deserved, and as she stood upright she took a moment to survey the crowd. David watched her, this queen of the stage, as she waved to her adoring fans. She turned, then, and at the moment their eyes met he all but stumbled at the spellbinding beauty of the honey yellow hue only magnified in majesty by the luster of the stage lights. The crème colored walls adorned with golden accent served as the perfect backdrop of this magnificent creature, whose very breath seemed so melodious as to incite him into dance, and elegantly contrasted the darkness of her dress.

She bowed before the audience once more, and the scarlet curtains drew shut. A sinking feeling penetrated the heart of the young author as this vision of beauty, this very proof of God's existence and marvelous power gradually disappeared from his sights. David, who in his short lifetime had never experienced anything quite like this, nor encountered anyone such as her, reluctantly left his seat and made for the entrance of the concert hall.

"What a talented young lady," Nico commented over the clamor of the departing crowd. David remained silent. There were no words to describe what he had witnessed, what he'd felt. No, the only justice he could do to show his appreciation for her performance was simply allow the echo of the sonata to linger in his ear and truly relish in every perfectly stricken note. As they traversed the audience at sluggish pace, a hand reached out to touch David's shoulder. Startled awake from his dreams of music and the muse who played it so smoothly, he turned to find that the young usher who had earlier led them to their seats returned.

"Mr. Masters," he started with an apologetic expression, "I'm deeply sorry to have caught you by surprise, but I was informed before tonight's show that you might be in attendance and was subsequently instructed that should you arrive I was to bring you backstage." Nico turned to notice that his friend was no longer in tow, and walked back toward him through the crowd in the way a fish might swim upstream.

"Hey, is everything alright," asked the manager. David looked in the direction of his friend's familiar voice, and upon the sight of the sleek black hair and goatee, the hypnotizing hazel eyes, and smooth crème-colored skin that shaped perfectly around the sharp features of his face, the author momentarily blanked on a name. He was still under her spell some twenty minutes or so after the curtains had closed, and so he stared much longer than he should have. *My word,* he contemplated, fully embarrassed that he'd forgotten the face of a man that has been in his life for most of it, *just what does this woman do to me?*

"Nico," he finally said aloud. Nico crossed his arms in disappointment as his eyebrows raised in disbelief.

"C'mon, Masters. You've known me for how long now?" David shook his head remorsefully as his friend spoke.

"I know," he replied, "I'm sorry. The usher was just telling me that we've been invited to go backstage." Nico's mouth fell agape as his lips curled into a smile.

"You don't say…" spake the agent as he slapped his client on the back. "It seems like you made quite the impression at the bookstore."

"Please, stop," David begged as he rubbed his temple. Nico slung his arm around his best friend's shoulders.

"Stop what, buddy?" His grin grew all the larger as he uttered the words and stroked the hairs of his goatee. David's eyes focused on Nico now, and he removed the arm that his friend had wrapped around him.

"You've got matchmaking eyes right now and you know it," he replied with an annoyed look on his face. "I already told you. Right now, the only thing that I need to focus on is my career." Nico rolled his eyes.

"Not that again… look, if that were really the case then you wouldn't need me here. And I'm not saying this as your agent or your manager. Hey," he said in a tone that dripped with concern. David looked him in his eyes. "I just don't want you to work yourself into a coma. It just seems to me that forming a new relationship is a good way to keep that from happening." David groaned.

"Fine," he conceded and slid his hand into his pants pocket. "I suppose I could at least give it a shot. Shall we be off, then," he asked as he turned his attention back to the usher, who smiled and waved his hand in the direction of the stage.

"Right this way." The population of the room continually decreased, and within mere moments they stood before a white dressing room door behind which could be heard the heavenly hums of an artist accomplished. The usher knocked, and the stirs in David's stomach pulsed in unison with the accelerated beat of his heart.

"Come in," she called from the other side. David took a deep breath, and as the usher opened the door the hallway began to move.

"A Mr. David Masters here to see you, madam," spoke the polite young man, and before long he made his way back through the concert hall to resume his duties for the evening. She turned briskly in her chair and caught sight of her invited guest as he walked awkwardly into the dimly lit room. Her heart skipped a beat as he offered a smile, but nevertheless she exhibited the utmost calm. After all, what sort of stage performer would she be if she allowed her excitement to throw her off before the crowd?

"You were wonderful," Nico said as he filed into the dressing quarters after David. She bowed jokingly with a slight giggle.

“Thank you, sir,” she responded in jovial tone, “it’s always a great feeling to hear that your hard work is appreciated. I don’t believe we’ve met, though.”

“That’s right,” Nico realized aloud. “Please, forgive me. When you met David at the bookstore I was on the phone with my wife. Nico Alaimo. Charmed.” She smiled at him and extended a hand.

“Eva Gallows. It’s a pleasure to meet you,” she told him as they shook. Like a majestic falcon locked onto her prey, her eyes shifted to meet those of the man who, as much as she hated to admit it even to herself, excited her beyond all imagination. He panicked, and were his skin light enough surely she would have seen him blush.

“Marvelous job,” he managed. She placed her hand on her hip and simply stared at him as she tucked her hair behind her ear. “It would seem that I have yet to recover from it.”

“I see. Well, since you questioned me at the signing earlier I have a few questions of my own,” she told him. She couldn’t resist. Since he walked into the room she could see the nerves with which he battled so clearly, the excitement in his eyes that mirrored her own.

“Do you now,” David asked, now totally calm. She stalked the room with her eyes firmly locked on him. He turned to face her as she paced about. “What did you want to ask me?” Nico, fully aware of the situation slowly moved towards the door and placed his back against it as he watched the two converse with the utmost intrigue.

“How much of it were you able to see,” she opened. She squinted her eyes in curiosity as he smiled and placed his hands in his pockets.

“We came in just as you were starting the *Appassionata*,” David answered in full confidence. She raised her eyebrows and her grin expanded.

“You know classical music?”

“Of course,” he responded. “There’s something to be said of classical music and writing. I feel as though they go hand in hand. The range of emotions that one experiences in such works would help them to create a multitude of scenes in a wide assortment of tones.”

“Really, now? And what, may I ask, is your favorite piece to listen to while you work?” He gave a brief chuckle as his eyes locked onto hers.

"The very one you ended your show with tonight," he told her. His stare became mesmerizing to her, piercing, as if she suddenly became transparent to him. "In the first movement Beethoven conveys a melody that is equal parts beauty and beast, one that clearly defines the contrast of joyous serenity and excitement with this powerfully ominous foreboding. It changes frequently between brutality and docility, but what I think he was going for is the idea that these dichotomous concepts are also complementary." Her eyes went wide, and in an effort to maintain the façade of her calm she broke the eye contact as she paced all the more.

"Very interesting thought, Mr. Masters. Would you care to elaborate?" she questioned with a flair of sultry curiosity in her tone. He shook his head and laughed a bit before he eagerly refocused his vision on her.

"I feel as though I've suddenly stepped into a college level musical philosophy class," he mused. She looked at him again with a wide smile in place and a lustrous gleam in her eye.

"Grad level, sweetheart. So I ask again, would you care to elaborate?" Nico's eyebrows raised as he supervised, and as a result he decided to take his seat in a nearby chair.

"Well, what I mean is that through life we all experience moments of both joy and anguish, and what we tend to find to be most pronounced is the pain, or more accurately, the scars that those darkest moments leave. That isn't to say that the darkness in our lives overshadows the light, but at the same time neither does the light overshadow the darkness. They coexist, trading off with one another, changing like seasons, and because of those extremely well-exemplified shifts in tone within the first movement, Beethoven hooks his listeners with the one thing no man can truly avoid: his reflection."

"So I see. But then what do you make of the second and third movements?" She did her best to conceal her smile, but as they conversed the illusion of her calm gave way under the gravity of her glee. He barely noticed, though, or rather, he just didn't care so long as she would smile at him just a little longer.

"The second movement exhibits a primarily tranquil vibe. To me it represents the seasons of contention in a person's life, where things couldn't possibly get any sweeter, any more ideal than what they are. As for the third, it's a sharp contrast in that it portrays more darkness, more ferocity. Whereas the middle movement is more reflective in essence, the third is far more tumultuous and emotional. For me it hardly affords me any time to think. That said, there is still a beauty about it that makes the third movement the most appealing to me."

"So wait… the reflection of pain is most beautiful to you," she begged. He nodded.

"Absolutely. Without pain, it is impossible to know pleasure. If we are not stretched, it is impossible for us to build endurance and grow stronger. Without pain, simply put there can be no beauty. It makes me wonder, Ms. Gallows, what tremendous pain have you experienced to be able to play that piece with such mastery?" She froze as a chill ran down her spine.

"What makes you so sure I went through any at all," she asked as the smile that previously graced her lips slowly receded. David slowly paced towards her, and the look on his face was as sober as she'd ever seen on a man.

"Your expression," he all but whispered to her. "The way your eyes intensified on stage just before you closed them and lost yourself in the melody, the way you don this pained look on your face that radiates of pleasure, the way you sway with every motion of your hands as if wrapped in the winds of a hurricane." Her fingers twitched at her sides as he spoke to her, as though at the mere mention of her mannerisms the music once again flowed through the foundations of her being. She found herself alarmed by the way his voice soothed her, and even more so by the way she watched him so carefully as he stared, not through her, but at her. He could see her essence now just as clearly as she could see his through his novel, and somehow she felt that it brought them so much closer together. *No,* she shouted at herself internally, *this is ridiculous. There's no connection here. After all, you just met him.*

"How can you—"

"You're an artist," David interjected before she was afforded an opportunity to finish. "The nature of art is not only to provide observers with release, but to exhibit the very soul of the artist." Eva fell speechless, powerless to even move beyond his sight. With every waking moment she could feel some otherworldly force as it pulled them closer together, and no matter how desperately she wished to fight it off she knew that something about it just felt right.

"David… Mr. Masters," she started, but David held up his hand.

"Please," he assured her, "David is fine."

"Would it inconvenience you at all if we continued our conversation over dinner?" The second the words left her lips Eva realized just how forward she was.

"What did you have in mind," David inquired with a welcoming grin.

"I know a great diner on Broadway that sounds great right about now," Nico interrupted. David and Eva both turned their attention toward him, and Nico smiled with the screen of his phone visible to them. "It's still open and it's only ten minutes away. Trust me, they've got the best cheesecake in town." After an exchange of looks between the author and the musician, the latter nodded and walked back over to the vanity at which she sat upon the gentlemen's entry.

"So I guess it's settled then," Eva half sang, "we'll go to Papa's Diner in Time Square and we can continue to get to know each other. Just give me a few minutes to get out of this dress and when we get outside I'll hail a cab."

"My dear," Nico said in his best British accent as he twisted the ends of his moustache, "as generous an offer as that is, it is most unnecessary." The accent dropped when she giggled. David rolled his eyes and paced over to the door. "I've already let our driver know that we would probably be getting something to eat on the way back." David glared at him to which Nico could only offer a sagely smirk.

"I'll only take a moment, boys, if you don't mind," she spoke. They left the room, and the moment the door closed behind them David playfully punched his agent in the shoulder.

"You planned to have us taken to dinner in advance," David asked. Nico's smirk transformed into a toothy grin as he shrugged.

"I have no idea what you're talking about," he stated slyly. "I just told the driver that we would be going to a concert and that we'd grab a bite after."

"Sure you did," David agreed in all sarcasm. Before the debonair Italian could open his mouth for a response, the door to the dressing room opened and out came Eva garbed in the same sweater and jean combination as before.

"Shall we," she inquired of her company, and before an answer was given she walked down the hall and toward the exit with the boys in tow. Carnegie Hall was empty now, and in a couple of minutes they exited the building to find that the limousine had maintained its position in the front. David took to the door and opened it for the lady in their midst. "What a gentleman."

"After you," he said as he extended his hand for her. She took it with a look of surprise on her face as she lowered herself into the car. Nico followed her into the backseat, but David stood completely petrified. His eyes were glazed over, and despite the shouts of his friend and the rumble of the engine behind him, it was as if he'd slipped out of this reality entirely. Nico looked over to Eva, only to note that she was as frozen as David now. He stepped out onto the sidewalk and took hold of his friend, but as soon as he came in contact with David's hand the entranced author felt a sudden burning sensation course through his entire body.

The calm air of the late autumn night began to swirl, and the movements of the other people on the sidewalk slowed rapidly until they stopped altogether. Sound filtered out of the world around him, and only Nico's voice remained. David and Eva's eyes glowed a bright white and yellow respectively, and as the hues of their orbs intensified the surrounding buildings, streets and people drained of their color.

In the next instant David and Eva dropped where they were, completely unconscious, and the world around them returned to its normal state. The people that previously walked the sidewalk now gawked in horror at the man who collapsed to the pavement, and Nico became frantic as he shouted for help.

Chapter Three

"Eva?" David screamed her name as he awoke under clear blue skies in a long spread of land. The light of the sun momentarily blinded him, and as he placed his hand upon the ground and moved to stand he felt… tremors. He surveyed his surroundings, and desperately tried to remember what had happened before he wound up there. *New York*, he thought, *Carnegie Hall… we were on our way to dinner when…*

As he reached his conclusion the tremors beneath the soil grew stronger, and with every vibration of the ground came the sound of armor-clad footsteps as unknown forces approached. His survey of the landscape became more frantic. The ground was in shambles, with burn marks and disheveled patches here and there where the earth beneath the grass had been unceremoniously exposed. A rocky incline lay off to his left, and in a panic he scrambled for the opening in its base. In fear he pressed his back against the wall of the opening and watched in suspense for the oncoming army.

The pounding noise of weighted steps against the earth grew louder by the second, and with it grew the ferocity of his beating heart. *I need to figure out where Nico and Eva are,* he contemplated as he reluctantly protruded his head to expand his range of sight. There, just crossing over the horizon, was a vast army of knights whose swords stood upright within their grips.

"Steady," came a deeply masculine voice from behind him. David jumped, and turned to see a pair of terrifying white eyes that glared through the grate of a knight's helm. Around him stood a hoard of troops, all clad in armored suits darkened by the shadow of the stone, swords drawn and hunger in their eyes.

"Excuse me," David began when he saw that they refrained from attack, "but I'm a little… lost. You see, I'm looking for my friends, Nico and Eva. You wouldn't happen to know where they are, would you?" There was no response, and David became increasingly unsettled as the army around the corner advanced. He waved in front of the commander's face, but even then he remained unacknowledged. He checked around the corner once again, and noted just how far the advancing army had come in such a short time. The author, who felt alien to whatever was about to transpire, returned to face the intently focused military official at his back. "Please, if you would just tell me where to go I can get out of your way." The sound of stomps against the dirt and grass became louder still, and he knew that in a matter of moments the army without this poor excuse of a shelter would undoubtedly discover him. The thought crossed his mind that this was some sort of war reenactment, but the way the commander's eyes glowed with the animosity of a wild beast and his men shook with anticipation as if they were some wily pack of wolves told him that this was very, very real. "Look, I'm begging—" he said as he extended his hand to touch the breastplate of the intimidating knight, but was horrified upon the observation that his hand passed right through.

He opened his mouth to scream, but the thought set in that nobody around him would hear it.

"Attack," the commander released in a deafening roar, and at his beckoning the legion of soldiers passed through David and stormed their enemies. David, now fully aware that he was naught more than a specter, dropped to his knees and turned his head toward the battlefield. "Show no mercy, men! Bleed every last one of them! Under the orders of the king not a single one is to leave this place alive!" The savage soldiers released a war cry as they cut, slashed, impaled, maimed and decapitated the men who so unwittingly marched into their den. Blood splattered on the ground and against the rocky incline behind which David still hid. The commander of this vast militia maneuvered with unprecedented agility and poise as four enemy troops came at him all at once. This man so… at home on the battlefield easily evaded the strikes of his enemies, and dealt a lethal blow to each one before he confidently moved on. He turned around and, for a moment, admired his handiwork when an enemy soldier rushed him from behind.

Without missing a beat, the obvious war veteran inverted his blade at his hip and the fool who rushed him slid grotesquely down its length. The enemy grunted, and with the last of his strength he lifted his sword overhead in an effort to take out the man that would ultimately prove to be his demise. The commander, who now chuckled in almost sinister amusement, withdrew his blade from the other man's flesh and armor, and in one fell swoop severed his enemy's arms and head. The foolish assailant stood perfectly still for but a moment as his limbs continually distanced themselves from their trunk, and as the Commander calmly walked forward he pushed the body so that it fell out of his path.

The men that warred around him exhibited the same warrior's expertise that he did, and effortlessly cut down their prey. Another fool rushed the Commander, and without batting an eye or turning his head he merely raised his sword and impaled his oncoming attacker in his throat. He retracted the blade and slashed through the air to clear the blood from its edge as he kept moving. David's eyes followed this enigma of a warrior as he quite literally cut down all who dared oppose him, and before long the entranced author emerged from the rocks at the battlefield's edge.

What… what's happening? I should be horrified, he thought in all reason as he paced through the warzone and witnessed the savagery that he'd always opposed throughout his life. His heart raced more anxiously now, but what he felt was far from the deep-seated trepidation and sense of uncertainty that he'd experienced upon his awakening. No, what filled him now was an excitement he'd never known before: the thrill of battle. As the war-trained object of his observation marched proudly through a line of bodies slain and the fearful eyes of his enemies watched him as his soldiers executed them from behind, there stood one in his path that refused to back down.

"Aeridus," spoke the Commander. "Tell me, what would it have cost you to simply bow your head to the king? What do you stand to gain from rebelling against him and so abandoning Alaedrea?"

"You do not get to speak to me on the subject of *your* bastard king, knave," replied an irate Aeridus. The commander's grip tightened on his sword, and in the time it took for David to blink the seasoned combatant charged his adversary. Aeridus returned the gesture, and at the clanging of their swords the spectating novelist felt the shockwave resonate with his very soul. Something triggered within him, something that led him to believe that this was not the first battle he witnessed. In the distance he could hear bombs dropping and guns firing as presently as the clashing swords before his eyes. His eyes refocused on the battle for strength between the officer and his enemy, and just as he felt in his first meeting with Eva, there was something eerily familiar at work here.

"You dare speak ill of King Aradmus," asked the Commander as he spun to the side and extended his blade to catch the back of his enemy's neck. Aeridus narrowly ducked at the last second, and executed an attempted slice at the Commander's legs. The Commander, however, hurled himself over the hunched back of his enemy and rolled away from him before the traitor had time to counter. He quickly turned to face the rebel, who paced calmly and playfully swung his sword to either side of him.

"I dare speak what comes to mind, child. Your king is a self-serving tyrant and always has been," he charged once more, and again did blade pound against blade as the two struggled for the upper hand. It was then that the setting warped, and David caught sight of the war-ravaged streets of Normandy in wartime, where a man of his darkened skin tone fired on German forces as bullets returned his way. As the mysterious man turned to reload his rifle, the setting warped back to the previous battlefield of the distant past. The Commander and his rival Aeridus stood face to face, locked in a battle of strength and skill, and neither warrior felt so cowardly as to back down. "Once I take your life here on this battlefield, boy, I will march my troops over the borders of Alaedrea and execute your precious monarch before your people in the capital." The Commander's armor trembled from the intensity of his sheer hatred, and David the observer slowly became immersed in the man's rage. The Alaedrean chief succumbed to his emotions, and in a feat of strength that alarmed even himself, pushed Aeridus away. The two rivals ran at one another again, and when Aeridus thrust his blade forward for his opponent's midsection, the masterful Alaedrean slid feet first with his hand and blade upraised and poised to strike. Seconds before the Commander's blade met with the lower extremities of the enemy leader, an arrow dislodged the weapon from its master's grip.

The Commander looked in the direction of the shot, and saw that an archer arrogantly loaded his bow for another. The archer fired, and the leader of the savage knights rolled along the ground as shot after shot came for him until he was able to spring back to his feet. The Commander sprinted about the combat zone as the overly eager archer shot rapidly in his attempts to slay the rebel general's rival, but found himself unable to match the speed of his target. The Commander watched him intently as the arrow-master tried, though, and more importantly, he kept his eye on the decreasing number of arrows in his quiver.

David, who now moved for the center of the conflict, began to shake with delight at the evasive knight's wonderful displays of speed and power, and even laughed at the archer, who clumsily executed his companions in his pursuit of his enemy. David's eyes, like his unquestionable hero's, fell on the quiver, and quickly did he count the number of projectiles ready for use.

Five arrows remained, and in a reckless grab for the upper hand, the Commander darted in the way of the archer who readied another shot and pulled back the bowstring. He paused for just a second to take aim, but upon his release the Beast of Alaedrea instantaneously dodged to the left and continued his advance unencumbered. Four arrows left, now, and the overconfident Aeridus swung his sword on level with the Commander's chest just as the archer shot to his side to keep their target from evading the blow. The proper militant leader, who already proved as agile as he was tactical, utilized the momentum built from his sprint towards the archer to aid him as he flipped over the oncoming sword.

Three arrows, and as soon as the Commander's feet hit the ground he pressed onward for his mark. A slightly flustered Aeridus lowered his blade and stood watch as his foe undertook a dangerous task in warring against the marksman, who already lined up his next shot. He aimed carefully for the Commander's head, and with a well-timed jump to the side the archer once again found himself evaded. Two arrows remained, and David already knew that the white eyes of the commander hungered for the extermination of the pest before him. He gradually closed the distance between them, and the archer now shook with fear as he realized that impact was imminent. He clumsily shot another arrow, this time at the Commander's leg, but just as with all the times before he was so vexingly dodged.

David's eyes became wide with anticipation as he analyzed the scene. The Commander's soldiers scattered about the battlefield grew increasingly relaxed, as only a single of Aeridus' troops still drew breath. None of the ravenous Alaedrean army sought to spill the blood of the rebel leader, but only watched as their Commander skillfully evaded the last arrow at point blank range. The distance had been closed now, and the commander reached out his armor-clad hand to grab the front of the archer's helmet. With all the momentum behind him, he pushed the archer into the dirt and stabbed him with his own sword. The archer released an ungodly croak, and beneath the weight of his killer he fell motionless. Here it was, the confrontation that David couldn't have written better if he tried, and as the climax came in this warrior's tale he longed to know the Commander's true identity. Who was this man that filled him with such bloodlust that he dared step onto a battlefield, even as a phantom invisible to all others?

"The only one left is you, Aeridus," the Commander exhaustedly huffed as he regained his legs. The rate of David's pulse skyrocketed and Aeridus, now filled with an even mixture of hatred and fear, yelled as he rushed the Commander with sword upraised. Just as before, the commander ran into a slide and evaded the attack. As he slipped beneath Aeridus, he grabbed his adversary's leg and pulled him down to the ground. He stood up again and quickly kicked the weapon out of the cunning rebel's hand. "Coward. You fight an unarmed man… with a sword?"

"What you say is right," answered Aeridus in an agitated tone as he picked himself off the ground. "I will wring the life from your body with my own hands." The Commander and the troops that followed him only laughed at the asininity of his statement.

"Then move," the Commander beckoned. "I hate to have my time wasted." Both men ran at each other as the blood that pumped in their veins ran hot with raw animosity. Aeridus launched a stiff right hand but was easily blocked by the Commander, who locked his fingers down onto his opponent's fist. The insurgent adversary refused to give in, though, and attempted another strike with his free hand only to be blocked once more. The Commander unleashed a spine-chilling head-butt that brought Aeridus to his knees, and then followed up with a crippling kick to the chest. Aeridus slid across the ground, and just as he realized that the Beast moved to stomp on him, he rolled out of the way to stagger back to his feet.

The Commander threw a punch now, but was easily evaded and nearly floored by a right hand to the midsection. Aeridus aided him to the ground with a subsequent leg sweep and attempted a stomp to the chest, but the Commander narrowly managed a block with both hands. He did his best to push Aeridus off, but the enemy leader applied his full body weight to his connecting leg. The tactical leader of the Alaedrean knights grunted as he continued in his struggle, but in a stroke of genius he used his own body to roll off to the side with Aeridus' foot still in his hands. A loud crack resounded through the landscape as the rebel's legs spread farther apart than his body would allow, and as he sat there the Commander took the time to replenish the air in his lungs.

The troops around him cheered at the pained cries of their enemy, and David's mouth adopted a satisfied grin. He thought himself a fool for avoiding battle, for abhorring it as he had in the past, and now sought to embrace it. How he would in his daily life, though, was a problem to be worked out at another time. David watched intently as the Commander methodically paced towards his downed opponent. He stripped off the helmet of his enemy to reveal a man of pale complexion, jet-black hair, and dark green eyes that shifted with the movements of his nemesis.

“Finally it ends, Aeridus,” spoke the Commander with deep relief in his voice. The dark-haired individual spat blood upon the sabatons of the commander’s armor.

“You will all die,” Aeridus yelled into the fading lights of the now setting sun. The Commander drove the sole of his foot into his enemy’s face and pressed his head into the ground. Aeridus howled in agony as his skull began to crack and his face began to shatter under the pressure, and for a moment he squirmed frantically until the sudden thrust of the Commander’s leg put a stop to it.

“Not by your hand,” muttered the victor as he looked over the corpse.

“My lord,” shouted a messenger as he scurried through the bloodstained battlefield, “I bring you word from King Aradmus!” The Commander looked up at the boy, who now surveyed the piles of bodies that lay awkwardly in the field.

“Out with it, boy,” he ordered, which jolted the young man back to reality. The Commander shook his head as he once again surveyed the body of Aeridus.

"Y-yes, sir, your presence is requested at the palace at once!" Every eye in the field that still saw the light of day fell upon the young messenger, who now bowed before the Commander and took his leave. The Commander mumbled something under his breath before he began to pace towards the rocky crevasse from which they previously emerged.

"Eulic," he called out, and immediately one of the soldiers came and stood before him.

"Sir," the man shouted as he took a knee.

"Return to the encampment. Tend to the wounded and see that guards are posted at all entrances to the camp just the same as always. I must go and see to the needs of the king. I'll make every effort to be brief," the Commander instructed.

"Sir," Eulic responded in confirmation. As he gathered the troops and they moved in the direction of Aeridus' earlier advancement, the mysterious Commander marched through the crevasse of the incline and scaled its top. David followed him, and upon his arrival saw that the Commander headed for a lone brown horse speckled with white spots. He ran his hand gently along the mane of his steed, and as he mounted its back the scene went dark.

David, who up until this very moment had been enraptured by the allure of this mysterious character's adventures and uncharacteristically shared in his penchant for battle, suddenly felt a wave of calm that both soothed his mind and vexed his soul as he dropped to his knees in this fresh pool of shadows.

"Why have I been summoned, Sorin," demanded the voice of the Commander from the battlefield before. David watched in awe as the darkness in which he sat gave way to the staggering light of a long and glorious palace hallway. The walls and arches were pure white with solid gold trim and silver décor scattered about. The Commander, accompanied by a man with the same hazel eyes and black hair as Nico, hurriedly tread upon a floor made of marble and black onyx.

"It seems as though His Majesty the king has learned of an alliance between the Alaedrean insurrectionists and the Kingdom of Odelia," responded the companion. "The messenger that was sent to you was also tasked with confirming for the king whether or not Aeridus still breathed, and since clearly he does not it will only be a matter of time before a much larger war is upon us." The Commander, still fully garbed in his bloodstained battle attire hummed in vexation.

“I see…” he mumbled as the duo approached massive wooden double doors. Sorin stopped and bowed before the Commander before he turned to take his leave. The Commander took a deep breath as he placed his weary hands against the doors of the throne room, and after a moment’s pause he entered the presence of the king.

King Aradmus, who sat upon his golden throne surrounded by only the best warriors in all the Kingdom of Alaedrea, trained his steely gray eyes upon the young man with an expression of disgust written about his face. He stood, and David marveled at the shimmering crimson and gold of his robe, as well as the true length of his long white hair and beard. He was aged, but nevertheless a strength rested with this man the likes of which could only be seen in the Commander.

“Do you know why I have summoned you, Raebon,” asked the king as he walked towards the warrior. Raebon quickly took his place at the center of the room and knelt before him.

“I do. It would appear that a much larger conflict is on the horizon,” he returned. David was surprised to hear that Raebon’s voice was far more relaxed now than it had been at any point before, almost as if he found comfort in the presence of this intimidating monarch.

"Indeed, this is so. Romedor, king of Odelia will no doubt learn of his ally's defeat when the latter fails to return from the battlefield. Unfortunately, the negotiations with Britannia have fallen through, and if war does ensue (and undoubtedly it will), it will take everything we have to maintain our way of life," Aradmus explained.

"With all due respect, my king, why have you summoned me from the battlefield? Is it so that I might aid in the war effort from the capital," Raebon inquired. The king sighed and shook his head as he paced away from the young knight.

"Raebon," his voice became softer now, "you understand that you are the only heir to the throne, do you not?"

"I do," Raebon replied. David's eyes went wide with shock, but rather than fill his attention with the myriad of thoughts that penetrated his mind, he merely continued to watch. "Father, what is this about?"

"Raebon… I have brought you here, so that you might be put under the Kingdom's protective custody." The prince rose immediately, furious that the thought had even crossed his father's mind.

"You wish me to go into hiding?" Raebon almost screamed it, and the cool eyes of the king suddenly fell upon his son in a way that made him tremble.

"Yes," the ruler responded. "Regardless of what happens to us, Alaedrea must live on. *You*, my son, must continue to survive even if the rest of us perish."

"Father, what you speak is nonsense! Before your very eyes my training was conducted. You better than anyone should know that I would be of much greater use to our country on the battlefield!"

"You'll do as I say," shouted the flustered King Aradmus. His stern glare softened, and the tone of his son relaxed. "That's the last I'll hear of it."

"But Father—" Raebon began to protest, but the king held up his hand.

"You are dismissed, Prince Raebon." The prince's body trembled with irritation, but he understood full well that his father's word was law and exited the king's chamber without delay. He paced through the halls of the palace and came to its entrance. David followed him, now just as heartbroken as the young prince Raebon.

The prince picked up a rock as he neared a small hut in the village without the walls of his illustrious home, and tossed it into the window as he passed by on his way to a hill that overlooked the bustle of the capital. He took his place beneath the tree and watched the stillness of the night sky as he waited.

"You really must find a different way of getting my attention," came a feminine voice from behind him. He looked around, and there before him stood his muse, the angelic creature that prompted his ferocity on the battlefield, his love.

"Miria," he whispered, and she smiled gently. He turned his back to David and walked towards the woman before he removed his helmet, and placed a tender kiss upon her lips.

"I've missed you," she told him shakily. "To see you here, unharmed, it—"

"I know," he replied as he took her hand and pressed his forehead gently against hers. David approached the two, as the time had finally come to see the face of the savage prince, but what he saw was not the face of a stranger. No, the face that surrounded those war-hungry whites that he'd seen however long ago was none other than his own.

Chapter Four

Nico paced back and forth as he struggled to control his nerves. He had no idea how he was supposed to think straight with that incessant beeping in the background. He hated hospital rooms and always had, but his best friend lay unconscious mere feet away from him and he'd sooner be burned alive than leave David in such terrible condition. He stopped by the enormous glass window to gaze upon the glowing lights of the city as he reflected on the incident at Carnegie Hall.

Why did this have to happen, he wondered as he pulled out his phone and scrolled through the contacts. At the sight of her name he pressed the call button on his screen and held the device to his ear. He looked back to David, who remained motionless in the bed, and then in anguish returned his attention to the night sky and the lights below. *One little dinner date and you end up in the hospital,* he thought as the line began to ring, though his attempt to make light of the situation poorly masked the immense worry that he felt.

He tapped his foot against the floor and ran his perfectly rounded fingertips through his sleek black hair. The line clicked. She answered.

“Hey, Babe,” came the moderately concerned voice of his sweet wife Sierra from the other end. “What’s up, is everything okay?”

“David,” Nico started as he choked back tears. He took a moment, because for some reason the man who could speak to anyone had trouble relating what he felt to his wife.

“Nico,” she responded, genuinely worried now, “sweetie, what’s the matter? You’re scaring me a little bit. Did something happen?” Nico shook his head and looked up at the tiled ceiling as tears of agonizing uncertainty welled up in his eyes.

“It’s David, he….” He paced the room again, and considered his words carefully lest she not believe him. “Something’s happened to him and he’s in the hospital.” She audibly gasped.

“Oh my God, is he alright?”

“I…” he recalled the bright glow of David’s eyes, his petrified stance on the sidewalk outside Carnegie Hall, and how lifelessly his body collapsed to the ground. A chill ripped through his body as the fear returned. “Honey, I don’t know. He just collapsed on the sidewalk out of nowhere. We were on our way to dinner with a friend, and the next thing I knew he was…”

He realized that he became more overwrought as he tried to explain.

"It's okay," she reassured him soothingly. "Everything is gonna be alright, love."

"Except it might not, Sierra!" Things got quiet, and the only sound left was that accursed machine that beeped by David's bedside. A doctor came into the room to check on the duo, but after assurance from the unnerved agent the medic continued his rounds through the halls of the hospital. "I'm sorry," he started again as he slid his palm back and forth upon his forehead. "I didn't mean to yell at you, baby, it's just…" he grunted in aggravation. "How could I let this happen?"

"You can't blame yourself for this," she told him sternly. "You didn't know that this would happen and knowing the kind of man David is, he didn't either or else he would have told you." He hesitated to speak now. He knew she meant well. More than that, he knew that she was right. But since their days at school Nico had come to know just how truly alone David was, and because of that he took it upon himself to stand by his side. To protect him. He walked across the room and took a seat in the chair by the side of the bed.

"You're right," he conceded as the water in his eyes now spilled over. "I just needed to talk to you right now because if he doesn't wake up—"

"Nico?" David's groggy and inquisitive voice startled Nico, who now missed what comforting words that Sierra wished to impart. David's eyes were barely open, and though he attempted to speak a bit more, his words were barely audible. It wasn't long before he placed his hand on his aching head and writhed in the sheets of the bed. Nico couldn't help but flash a toothy grin as he wiped the tears away from his eyes.

"Baby, I'm gonna have to call you back," he said with a sigh of relief, and the sound of his voice seemed to make Sierra breathe easier as well.

"Alright, well take care of yourself," she cautioned. "I love you."

"I love you too," Nico responded. With the press of a button the phone call was over and his attention rested on the physically taxed author. "Hey, buddy. How are you feeling?"

"Like I was hit by a bus," David grumbled. He did his best to sit up, but the pain in his head forced him back down to his pillow. "You sound so cute when you're on the phone, by the way." Nico's eyes narrowed on his friend, but at the same time he struggled not to crack a smile.

"Shut up," he commanded. "And don't call me cute, you know how much I hate that."

"That, my dear friend is why I said it," David beamed, but the width to which his lips spread only exasperated his injury and so he groaned loudly.

"That's what you get, you jerk." David opened his eyes a little wider and noted the poorly disguised smirk on Nico's face, the kind that he'd always showcased in moments where he was forced to laugh against his will. It warmed his heart, but the shadow of worry in his eyes filled him with sorrow.

"I'm sorry to cause you trouble," he told his only friend. Nico instantly dismissed the comment.

"Don't say that. I'm just glad that you're okay," he responded in all seriousness. David never knew how to react when Nico got this way. It was rare that the jokes and teasing stopped. They were like brothers in that way. But in the serious moments that relationship dynamic became increasingly defined, and for David, shockingly so.

"Eva wasn't too worried was she," the author inquired wearily.

"Actually," Nico began as he stood up again and advanced for the window, "she's just down the hall." David was caught off guard, and quickly tossed his covers to the floor. As the bed linen dropped and the sound reached his ears, Nico instinctively moved to the side of the bed to force his friend to remain stationary. "Whoa, whoa, whoa, you can't move yet, David. We still don't know what happened out there tonight."

"Nico, I—"

"She's being taken care of. Actually, I wish you would learn to do the same," teased the manager. David's eyes met his, and the unusually stern look that Nico gave was enough for the rash writer to relax. "Thank you." Nico sighed and looked out the window from where he stood to see the shimmer of the morning light as it peaked over the sky-scrapers and chased the darkness away.

"Did you stay here all night," David asked after a couple moments of stark silence.

"Yeah," Nico responded, and bent down to grab the covers and put them back on his bed-ridden friend. "I couldn't leave you here alone. I mean after all, what kind of agent lets his best client run the risk of dropping dead?" David rolled his eyes, something that was sort of his signature move in terms of their relationship, and Nico laughed.

"You should go back to the hotel. Get some sleep," David suggested, but Nico shook his head and returned to his seat by the side of the bed to reinforce his conviction before David's eyes.

"Can't do that," he stated flatly. "I'm not going anywhere until I see you back on your feet and walking." David locked eyes with him, and the two stared for a solid minute before the author blinked first. He growled.

"Fine," he exclaimed, "do what you want. Did you at least bring my laptop?" Nico's expression distorted.

"Unbelievable," he started. "Near death experience and you just want to get back to work. Sorry, buddy, all of our stuff is still at the hotel. Like I said, I haven't left your side since you ended up in here."

"Oh…" David's head sank and his eyes fell to the edge of his bed. Flashes of the events in Alaedrea, of Aeridus and Raebon filtered into his mind. "Would you—"

"Let me stop you right there," Nico interrupted with his hand raised in protest. "Do you have any idea how worried I was? How worried I still am? I'm sorry, David but this is one of those times where I need you to take it easy—"

"But—"

"Whether you want to or not." There was no hint of a joke in his tone as the gravity of the situation finally began to resonate with the workaholic in the bed. His heart sank, because in their years of friendship David couldn't recall a time where Nico had ever been so serious. Or so scared, for that matter. The pain in his head returned, and he was quickly overwhelmed by it. He repositioned the covers to properly shroud his body and sank beneath them as he closed his eyes.

"It isn't that I want to get back to work," David told him in sickly tone as the image of Raebon's face, or rather his own, filtered into his mind. Nico's eyes softened upon his friend. "I just need answers." Nico donned an expression of utter confusion, and folded his arms as he tried to formulate a guess as to what his friend spoke of.

"Answers to what, exactly," he asked. The battle that took place in the valley beneath the incline, the names of the various figures and places, and the truth of the intimidating king all came to the forefront of his mind, not to mention the sounds and sights of war through the ages. David looked into Nico's eyes with an expression of sheer determination that the latter had only ever seen during the writing process.

“Tell me,” David spoke, “do you know anything about a kingdom called Alaedrea?” The name sent a chill down Nico’s spine, but he decided to give a faux chortle instead of a distressed expression.

“Only that Hollywood’s been trying to make movies about it for ages.” David’s eyes narrowed in frustration. “The only thing keeping them from doing that, though, is that there are so few records of the kingdom to go on. No real historical accounts, no definite geographic location or anything. All we know for sure, is that it was annexed to England at some point after 959 AD and since then all records of it have been destroyed.”

“I see…” David replied. He crossed his arms and cupped a hand beneath his chin. His brow furrowed, and in his pensiveness the adamant patient gave a slightly perplexed hum. “Have you ever heard the name Raebon?” Nico’s eyes narrowed, and his brain became frenzied as he tried to find a way to change the subject.

“Yeah, it was part of some legend I heard a long time ago. It was supposed to be related to the Alaedrean Kingdom but I have my reservations about it. Why?”

"I need you to see if you can find that legend," David informed him. "There's just… something about that place that seems familiar…"

"Familiar?" Nico's pulse beat rapidly now, and his eyes had yet to return to their usual friendly disposition. "What, are you saying that you've somehow *been* to Alaedrea before?" Upon hearing it from the mouth of another person, David realized just how impossible it sounded. Still though, he couldn't help but feel that the dream he'd had was far more than just some fantastic concoction of his mind. He'd felt the stone against his back, seen in stunning vividness the blood and blades, the palace and the people. He was *there*, and there was no mistaking it. He just needed to figure out how such a thing was possible.

"Yes," David said in all boldness which, understandably, caught his agent off guard. "I had a dream that I was there in the palace. Except…" Nico's eyebrows raised in intrigue as he folded his arms.

"Except…?"

"Except it didn't feel like a dream. What I saw… what I experienced, it felt more like a collection of memories," David described as his voice progressively became more puzzled.

“What, like from some past life,” Nico questioned as humor dripped from his tone. “Don’t be ridiculous David. You of all people should know fiction when you see it. I mean, there is a possibility that this dream is just an after effect of you working so hard on the *Death by Knight* story and ad campaign.”

“You’re right,” David conceded, “except it wasn’t an after effect. Even when my dreams are creative enough to be the basis for a book I’ve never seen anything register so clearly in my head.” Nico noted the absolute seriousness about his dear friend’s face, that determined gleam in his eye, the furrowed brow that convinced the agent that there was no way to turn back now.

“I’ll see what I can find,” Nico agreed. Upon his concession there came a knock at the door, or rather the doorframe. Both sets of eyes fell upon a middle-aged doctor with graying brown hair and a friendly look in his clear blue eyes.

“Mr. Masters,” he began with a friendly smile in place as he walked across the room with clipboard in hand. “I’m Dr. Thomas, I’ll be checking you out today to see if you’re ready for discharge. From what it says here you just collapsed on your way to dinner last night, but when your agent brought you here we didn’t see anything expressly wrong with you. Tell me, how are you feeling this morning?" David shifted his head to look at his best friend and then back at the doctor. His head still throbbed, but the splitting pain that he'd felt when he first returned to consciousness had lessened drastically.

"My head hurts a little, but besides that I feel fine," David answered calmly. Nico breathed a sigh of relief. "What about the woman that was with us, though? Her name is Eva Gallows; can you tell me if she's alright?"

"I'm sorry," the doctor responded as he checked the monitors. "Ms. Gallows isn't one of my patients, so I can't really give you any updates on her condition."

"Then I'll check on her myself," David asserted as he began to strip off the wires that connected him to the machine and placed his bare feet on the cold floor. Nico and the doctor, both alarmed, did their best to force him back into bed but to no avail. The author stood fully now, and walked for the door when the honey yellow eyes of the woman in question caught his attention. She stood there in the doorframe, a smile on her face and a folder in her hands. She was fully dressed in the same sweater and jeans combination that she had worn the day before, and casually leaned against the doorframe. "Eva... are you alright?"

“I’m fine, I just have this splitting headache,” she said through clenched teeth. “I have been cleared to leave, though, so I’m on my way out.” David momentarily cast his eyes to the floor.

“I see…” he managed. What else could he say? After all, it would be quite the imposition to try and keep her there, to pick her brain for any unusually vivid dreams or out of body experiences or the like. No, this was better for them both, as her relaxation period would provide him the perfect window to conduct the research he desired at the level he intended. With resolve, he looked at her once more and offered an apologetic smile.

“Listen, I’m in town for another couple of days,” she told him, and instantly his ears twitched with delight. “Maybe, I mean if you’d like, we could try to get dinner again before we have to head our separate ways?” David, completely in awe that she would maintain her interest after all that’d happened, slowly nodded in acquiescence of her suggestion. “Well,” she tore off a strip of paper from the inside of her folder and pulled out a pen. She scribbled for a moment and handed the slip to the still-groggy David. “Here’s my number. Call me later and we can work something out.” She gave him a wink, and Nico, who stood in the back of the room almost giddy with his back pressed against the wall, allowed a playfully serpentine smile to cross his lips.

“Stop,” David told him, his eyes still on the beautiful woman that stood in the doorway. She smirked as she held back a giggle and waved goodbye to the both of them upon her exit. David turned back to face the doctor, who stood with his clipboard down at his side and his pen back in his pocket. “Doctor,” he began, but Dr. Thomas held up his hand with a grin of his own in place.

“It seems like you’re perfectly capable of walking around and your vitals seemed perfectly stable. As far as I’m concerned you’re free to go. Just make sure you get something to eat from the hospital cafeteria before you leave, and try not to over exert yourself,” he advised. David felt as though he could breathe easier now as the doctor exited the room. He turned back to Nico, who now handed him the blazer, white t-shirt and camel chinos he’d previously worn.

“Good news,” Nico said with a smile, “you can get dressed. Don’t worry about the checkout paperwork. I’ve got that front covered.”

“You’re a saint,” David said in relief. Nico nodded as he filed out of the room and down the stairs. Though the topic had shifted to that of health, the mind of the cunning agent remained fixated upon the Kingdom of Alaedrea, and more importantly upon the name that for such a long time he’d forgotten. Raebon. He placed his hands in his pockets as he turned the corner, and followed the seemingly never-ending white-walled hallway toward the reception desk. He looked over his shoulder, and upon the realization that he wasn’t followed he took a deep breath.

“You seem nervous,” came a chilling voice from out of nowhere. Nico looked around, but amid all the patients, doctors and nurses that walked those halls, none seemed capable of such instantaneous intimidation.

“Who’s there,” the agent demanded, but all fell silent. The people around him gradually slowed in their strides and the color drained from their bodies. All stood still, and Nico allowed himself to slow all the same. He anxiously shifted his head in all directions and watched for any that might be as unaffected as was he. The deafening stillness of his surroundings made his skin crawl, and then the sound of a crash at the opposite end of the hall served to amplify his unrest. “Answer me, or I swear I’ll call the cops!" His phone, which was already in his hand, had already been situated with the numbers 9-1-1, but despite his lack of bluff the disembodied voice emitted a confident guffaw that chilled Nico to the bone.

"And what would your pathetic authorities be able to do to me," the voice answered back. Nico's eyes carefully assessed the hall for any signs of life. The air began to sting, and as the heat of it rose he began to sweat. What shadows that remained in contrast to the stark white of everything around him slithered into a singular point in the distance, and as the darkness piled upon itself a sinister figure began to take form. It stretched out a hand as it opened its pure white eyes. Nico stood petrified and mute, and his inability to act in the moment caused the being cloaked in the shadows to reveal the luster of a grin as white as its arctic orbs. "Tell me, boy, have you any idea who I am?" Nico's jaw dropped. *That voice…* he thought. *No, it's* him*!* "I see," hummed the Shade, "so you *are* aware." Nico clenched a fist at his side and narrowed his eyes fearlessly upon the *thing* that dared reveal itself.

"Why have you come here?" Nico demanded, which incited a laugh from the specter whose demeanor had immediately grown more sinister.

"I have come to deliver a message to your little friend," it growled. "This is where this little game of ours ends, and just as all the times before, he will die by my hand. Deliver it, or do not. It will do little to change the outcome." The creature snapped his fingers, and in an instant the world around the young agent returned to the way it was.

"You alright," David asked as he laid his hand on his best friend's shoulder. Nico jumped and subsequently scrambled to regain his composure. His breathing was heavier than usual and sweat poured from his head. His body trembled beneath David's hand, and as he turned to face the author he strained to mask the fear in his eyes. David's focus became more intent as he asked, "Hey did something happen?"

"No," Nico assured him as he grabbed his hand in an effort to stop the quakes. "No, it's nothing. Everything's fine." David sensed the obvious lie, but decided not to press the issue as he walked ahead of his friend down the hall. Nico lingered in the background for a moment, and as he watched his best friend pass the image of his blood on the ground penetrated his mind.

Chapter Five

"Okay, okay, enough about what's going on over here. How was the book signing?" The woman on the other end of the phone almost sounded like a teenage girl. "Did he ask you out? Did you say yes? Oh my goodness, are you *engaged*?" Eva removed the phone from her ear and stared at it for a moment before she put it back in place.

"Torrie, sweetie, don't you think you're getting just a little bit ahead of yourself?" The girl on the other end giggled in excitement, and Eva could only imagine the elated expression she wore. After all, Torrie Inglewood was only the best wedding planner in the country, so if it helped her business it was only natural for the redheaded bombshell to encourage love wherever she could… even if we weren't calling it that just yet.

"Well," she responded, "you know me. A girl's gotta make a living, you know." Eva gave an almost disapproving hum as she crossed the room to a chair and put her feet up.

"You *should* be putting more effort into your relationship with Jared while you're over there trying to fix me up," Eva shot back. She could feel Torrie roll her eyes as she grunted, and the combination of mental image and actual sound made her laugh.

"Enough, already! Tell me what happened at the signing! I've been dying to hear about it since last night but a certain *someone* didn't have her phone on so we couldn't dish," Torrie exclaimed. Eva rolled her eyes. "So, what was it like to be in the same space as one of the greatest authors of our generation?"

"Oh my goodness, he's so…" Eva spaced out for a moment as she thought about the complexity of his expression, the definition of his jawline, and above all else those deep brown eyes. It was such a common color, but there was a certain uniqueness in that commonality with him that just pulled her into the intricacy of his enigma.

"He's so…" Torrie prodded after a moment of stark silence. Eva jolted back to reality.

"Yes," she completed with a girlish giggle that reminded her of what it was like to be back in school. "I mean I wasn't a fan of his work before, but you know his recent story *Death by Knight*, right?"

"Yeah," Torrie said through the smacks of her gums, "but I haven't had the chance to read it yet." Eva raised an eyebrow as she got up from her seat and walked about the room.

"Torrie, are… are you eating," she asked.

“Girl, yes, I got hungry waiting for you to take me off hold!” Both of them fell into a minor fit of laughter before they automatically refocused on their main topic of discussion.

“Anyway,” Eva said in a drawn-out manner, “this new book of his is so incredible. It’s like he’s a completely different writer, like… like he put his soul on display.” Her tone shifted from humored to pensive in an instant. “Sir Alan is just so complex, torn between the love he knows and the hunger for adventure, and meeting David in person just made me feel like I’d met the character himself.”

“First name basis with the author,” Torrie cooed through the line, “not bad, kid. So, I take that to mean that he *did* ask you out.”

“Actually,” Eva sang with upward inflection to insinuate the opposite, “I may or may not have bought tickets to my concert for him, stashed them in my pocket and invited him as he was signing my copy of the book…” Torrie audibly spit out whatever it was that she ate and laughed uncontrollably.

“Oh, Eva,” she said as she did her best to restore some sense of seriousness. “You’re so gorgeous he probably would have asked you out, you know.” Eva cringed at those words. She *hated* that that’s all people took her for.

"Yeah, well, maybe I didn't want to rely on my looks just to talk to some guy. Besides," she added, "I wanted to afford him the chance to see me as more than just my looks anyway." Torrie hummed thoughtfully as she reflected on the statement.

"Well, if he went to your concert I don't know how he'd get a better picture of who you are. He did show up, didn't he?" Eva smiled from ear to ear at Torrie's question.

"He did, and this is after I basically ripped his work to shreds," she responded. Torrie spit again and Eva's face twisted in disgust.

"Oh no, you did that super weird analytical thing in front of him?" Eva's head slid to the side as she gazed aimlessly at the painting of a farmhouse that rested on her red- and yellow-striped wall.

"Well yeah, I mean he asked me questions about the books," Eva retorted.

"No" Torrie moaned as though she were in pain. "How did you not scare him off?"

"Oh my gosh, you're so rude," Eva groaned and placed a hand on her hip. "He likes me, weirdness and all! And get this, he was able to dissect *Appassionata*. On the spot." Eva recalled the moment as her best friend fell silent. The way he looked at her with those piercing orbs of his as he picked apart the piece and how it made her feel, how he saw into her, if only for a second and made her speechless with the strength of a whisper chilled her to the touch, and she thanked God above that there was no-one in the room to feel it.

"So what happens now," Torrie asked in all seriousness. Eva looked up at the ceiling and tossed herself on the bed. She gave a huff as she moved her hair away from her face and shrugged as if Torrie could see her.

"I really don't know. Well, I guess technically I might be seeing him again this week, but after that it's all a mystery," Eva contemplated.

"Just make sure to be careful, alright," Torrie begged. "You don't want a repeat of what happened with Brad." Her skin crawled at the mention of her incredibly handsy creep of an ex-boyfriend who groped her often and ridiculed her desire to wait until marriage before engaging in physical intimacy. That is, until she kicked him below the belt and punched him in the nose in front of all his sleazy friends. It was a shame, because the person she became interested in and the person he turned into once he "had" her were two completely different people. But then she thought about David and the feeling she had whenever they shared the same room. Even to her it was a conundrum. He just… didn't feel like other people.

"You know," Eva thought aloud, "I don't know if we'll have the same problems out of David as we did Brad. There's an air of sophistication about him that Brad never really had. Plus, I don't think his agent would let him get away with acting that stupid."

"Well neither will I," Torrie contested. "You just let me know if and when he slips up, and I promise you I'm coming with some razor blades and cayenne pepper." Eva burst into laughter. "Girl, you think I'm joking but I am absolutely serious."

"Trust me, Torrie, you won't be needing that even if he does screw up somehow," Eva assured her.

"I mean, if you say so," Torrie replied. Eva chuckled again as she stirred from the bed. "I gotta go. Don't worry, though, I'll be sure to tell the girls everything that's happening with Mr. Super Sexy Author."

"Oh come on," Eva giggled, "I haven't said anything like that this whole conversation and you know it."

"You didn't have to! I've seen pictures of that man and let's just say he could be the chocolate chip to my cookies any day," Torrie joked. Eva guffawed, and hated herself for it because she desperately wanted to scowl at the statement.

"Goodbye, Torrie," she responded, still thoroughly tickled by the antics of her friend. She ended the call and tossed her phone on the bed. *That girl,* she mused as she walked to the closet and pulled out a small purple suitcase with silver butterflies scattered along the surface. She pulled out a petite turtleneck shift dress. She admired the long sleeves, the violet color that matched her suitcase, the collar gently draped around the shoulders, and for a moment she thought about the look that David would sport when he saw her in it. She laid it out over the chair in which she previously sat, and with an exhausted breath she jumped back onto the bed.

What an unusual day, she thought as she stared up at the ceiling and listened to the quiet hum of the heater. The rising temperature soothed her senses. It calmed her, and that very sense of calm was exactly what she felt she needed. It came as a shock to her that morning that she'd awoken in a hospital room with hardly any recollection of the events that followed her concert. At first she thought that David or perhaps Nico could have drugged her at some point, but the fact that the former was admitted just as she was moved her to dismiss that hypothesis.

She yawned. *So what happened then?* She closed her eyes as she tried to imagine the possibilities, but as the warmth swept over her she instinctively curled into a ball and drifted off to sleep.

"Make way, for the crown prince returns!" The squall of the squire penetrated her eardrums, and the peaceful Eva jolted awake to behold a scene most unfamiliar to her. Horses paraded the road that ran between the pitiful gray and brown huts, and the knights that straddled them waved to the cheering citizens that gathered to either side of the passage. The people that tread upon the ground and watched the return of their prince were an amalgamation of rich and poor, but all cheered for him all the same.

"What *is* this…" Eva questioned aloud as she watched the central figure amid the group of knights raise his armor-clad fist. The crowd fell silent and watched him with adoration. Even from the distance Eva could see his penetrating white eyes, and something about them struck her as familiar, as though she'd seen them somewhere before.

"For the last ten years," spake the prince, "tensions have been on the rise with the neighboring Kingdom of Pragoria. They have cordoned off our borders, which in turn has driven our economy into the dirt and with it, the morale of the Alaedrean people. For ten years, you innocent people, victims of insufficient grabs for political gain and expansion, have suffered because of a conflict with which you had nothing to do." The crowd came alive with noise, but were instantly quieted by a slight wave of his hand. Eva moved forward, and made every effort to avoid contact with the people around her. As she closed the distance between herself and the prince, her heart beat at an accelerated rate. She watched his eyes through the grate of his helmet as she halted at the edge of the street. *Where do I know him from,* she pondered. "Now," he spoke again, "after ten long years of your pain and misfortunes, the Pragorian military has taken severe losses by our hands, and so the central government of their kingdom has agreed to withdraw from Alaedrea's borders. Our ability to trade with other nations has been restored, and now… Now we rebuild!" At his triumphant shout, the poor and suffering wept with joy and cried out in thanks to God above. Even Eva, a stranger to her present surroundings felt a sort of elation at the news.

She watched the people around her erupt with various modes of celebration. Singing and dancing abounded within the kingdom, and people of all ages and sizes ran throughout the capital to spread the news. As the prince, still atop the back of his steed, navigated the crowd for the palace, Eva noticed that a brooding figure in a brown burlap cloak stood opposite her. The figure's yellow eyes penetrated the shadow provided by the hood, and after a swift visual sweep of the people, all of whom seemed too preoccupied with their celebratory antics to pay attention, the figure proceeded to stalk the prince.

Eva followed, and shouted as she maneuvered through the crowd in the hopes that she would draw the attention of the young noble, but her shouts were lost in the sea of noise that permeated the atmosphere. Eva's attention reverted to the Cloak, who now ran atop the shakily-built rooftops of the huts about the village until it overlooked what was undoubtedly its target. Eva became all the more frantic in her efforts to reach his ear, but the prince simply could not perceive. The pianist, betrayed by sound which she fancied her ally, stood in the center of the road as the feeling of helplessness sank into the pit of her stomach. She took a step forward, but stumbled backwards as the head of a young girl no older than seven emerged from her navel. The girl, who had passed through Eva completely, escorted her little brother by the hand as they turned a corner and scurried out of sight.

Am I... she internalized, but before she could complete the thought, the hooded being pounced upon the prince from the roof of a nearby hut and knocked him from the back of his horse. The celebration came to an abrupt halt, and Eva watched in horror as the two struggled along the ground. The prince rolled atop the figure, and as the hood receded, the delicate face of a young woman was revealed to the horrified and irate onlookers.

Their former cries of joy and laughter had become darker in nature as many advocated her death. The prince, however, remained petrified as he pinned her to the ground. Eva moved closer, now indifferent in regards to evading those around her, and as she laid eyes upon the woman beneath the prince, she was stunned to see that it was… her.

The volatile young lady kicked the prince in the chest and rolled back to her feet as she withdrew a knife from her cloak.

"What is the meaning of this," demanded the young noble. "Who are you?" The amber yellow eyes of the young woman glowed with animosity. She paced the ground before him, ready to unleash her next assault. She dove for him, knife extended and hungry for royal blood. He deflected the hit and used her momentum to flip her into the air. The people in the crowd watched in awe, though, as she landed on her feet and followed up with a flurry of slashes.

The prince grabbed her arm and twisted it behind her back.

“Let me go,” she demanded as her sun-kissed skin dripped with sweat. The prince wrenched her arm until she was forced to release the weapon, and as soon as it hit the ground he kicked it into the growing mob of spectators.

“Not until you tell me who you are,” the king’s son shot back. She smirked as she drove the back of her head into his helmet. His vision was skewed, and out of compulsion he released her from the hold. She tumbled forward, and as her feet left the ground they successfully knocked the young man to his back. She, however, landed with elegance and grace.

“My name is Miria, daughter of Forsaeus, a merchant here in the capital,” she informed him in elevated tone as she prowled the ground like a jungle cat. Eva’s heart pulsed at the mention of the name, and instantly she fed on the same rage as her counterpart before her. The angry mob of spectators grew silent now as they listened to her speak. “My father was a kind man, a gentle man, a man well respected by his customers and colleagues and well beloved by his family… until three years ago he was drafted in the war effort.” Her voice shook as she explained herself, and with an exasperated growl she flipped into the air with every intention of driving her feet into his sternum.

He narrowly rolled out of the way and followed up with a leg sweep that only momentarily took her off balance.

As her back hit the ground she bounded back up to her feet and stared down the future monarch with intense hatred.

"Many great men were lost because of the war—" the prince offered, but a sharp spinning back kick to his midsection silenced him for the moment.

"Do not *dare* speak to me as though you understand the occurrences of *my* life, Raebon. He was not killed on the battlefield as you would expect," she told him with tears in her eyes. "No, this man, this *merchant* by trade who was forced into the army in order to provide for his family, was brought back alive but gravely injured." She wiped her eyes before the crowd, who now hardly knew what to say or think. The prince could only listen now, as even he was at a loss for words. "I fell before the king that night with my baby brother in my arms and pleaded with every ounce of humility that I could exhibit for him to do something to save my father. But our ruler, the beast that he is, had only just decided to move all medical personnel to stations near the borders *after* the fact."

"Nonsense," Prince Raebon challenged. Her eyes narrowed on him and she spat before his feet. "The royal physicians are never to leave the palace walls. My father would never be so foolish as to willingly send them to their deaths."

"I *know*," Miria yelled. "Later that night I snuck into the palace to witness his son in the care of the very same physicians of whom you speak. I watched my father die by the bedside of his only son while you sat in your chambers receiving care that should have been given to him!" She ran for him yet again and jumped into the air with her legs spread. Prince Raebon was taken aback by such an unorthodox method of combat, and by the time he'd formulated a counter, his head was already ensnared between her thighs.

In an exhibition of masterful control, she pulled her upper body downward with enough force to whip the fully armored prince into the air. He crashed to the ground a couple of feet away from her, and as she pulled a second blade from her cloak the Royal Guard saw fit to intervene. As he staggered back to his feet he held up his hand, and the guards at his command reluctantly stayed back. Eva could hear her heart as it pounded against her ribcage. Her palms began to sweat, and her entire being trembled as she peered upon the royal with disdain unfamiliar.

Miria launched another barrage of slashes with the dagger, but was just as easily caught as she was before. Raebon pressed down on her wrist which caused her to drop the knife, and subsequently pulled her close. He held her there, and for a moment she struggled to break free, but ultimately succumbed to the sincerity in the gesture.

"I am sorry," he whispered to her, and the honey yellow orbs of both Miria and Eva widened as the tears flowed more profusely. With her own ears she heard him say it, the words she needed to hear from the royals for all this time. She was relieved that he made no spectacle of it, that he issued no official apology that stood upon empty ceremony, and as he held her she wept all the more.

Together they fell to their knees, and the gentle prince stroked her long brown hair until the water ceased to fall. He motioned for the guards to come forward, and at his command they stopped mere feet away from the two. He took her by the shoulders and stared into her eyes.

"Miria, these men will follow you to your younger brother," he told her quietly. He gently released her as he stood back to his feet and looked around to the confused faces in the crowd. "Who among you is the wealthiest of the merchant class?"

"I am, Sire," shouted a rather round man with bald head and fine clothes. The prince smiled widely as he spread his arms to either side.

"Excellent, then you will be the one I elect to pay in return for the care of this young woman and her younger sibling." The merchant's face donned a look of uncertainty that was not lost on Prince Raebon. "Do you object to this?"

"Oh, no, my prince," the merchant responded.

"Then you shall start today," the prince informed him. He turned to face one of the guards at his side and laid his hand upon the man's shoulder. "Withdraw from my personal funds one thousand pounds of gold and pay it to this man. This woman's family has experienced far more than their share of hardship for one lifetime."

"As you wish, my prince," said the knight as he mounted a nearby horse and rushed for the palace. Prince Raebon knelt before the woman Miria once again, who now looked at him with sheer wonder in her eyes.

"You all bore witness to these things today. Miria, distraught over the loss of her father committed a crime against the crown prince of Alaedrea, one that I have chosen to overlook. Therefore, none of you is to take action against her regarding the matter. Any such act of vigilantism will result in the public execution of the perpetrators. You may disperse," commanded the prince, and the crowd around them scattered about the village to resume their day as was usual to them. Eva, who was the only one who remained within the area, watched as Prince Raebon gathered the daggers he'd forced from the hands of her historical counterpart and knelt before her. He took off his helm to reveal his face to her, a face that Eva knew to belong to David Masters. "I will never allow for your suffering again. This, I promise you."

Chapter Six

"So I think I might have found something you'd be interested in," Nico broke the silence as he scrolled down the screen of his phone. David looked up from his laptop with eyes as fatigued as they were interested. "So just as expected, when you run a search for Alaedrea you come up with only the basic information: how it became an independent kingdom after the Romans withdrew from the area, how it's believed to have been located in what is now the modern-day Netherlands region, and so on and so forth."

"You thought I'd be interested in *that*," David inquired with confusion firmly locked in his expression. Nico shook his head and refocused his eyes on his phone.

"Relax, I'm getting to it. Now as I was saying, you get nothing if you just search for Alaedrea, but if you search the name you gave me earlier, the results are filled with accounts from the surrounding territories of the time that at some point or another went to war with Alaedrea." David's eyes widened with intrigue. "Apparently, this Raebon guy was the crown prince, and he was the best fighter they had in their military. Or at least, that's what some notable historians have to say about him. Aside from that there aren't many records of what his life might have been like, but when you're a battle-tested prince one can only assume," Nico mused. David's eyes returned to his laptop screen as he input the name of the prince in the search engine.

"Seems like you're right," David admitted. "Search for Raebon and you find a decent number of articles and journals surrounding him. Now the question is, what exactly am I looking for?" Nico's eyes shot up from the screen of his phone and narrowed on his best friend.

"That sounds like the kind of question you ask *before* you spend a day in New York City locked away in a hotel room to conduct literal hours of research," he quipped, but David waved him off.

"I mean I know we're trying to dig up information on Alaedrea, particularly the fall of the kingdom. But how do we get there from the obscure details of Prince Raebon's life? Unless *you* know what to look for, I think we'll just have to try our luck with what articles we can find," David commented. Nico, whose mind was still discomforted by this sudden need for information and more so the appearance of the Shade, sighed as he quietly resigned to his research.

"I suppose you're right," he said in a mocking tone. David rolled his eyes.

"You'll be just fine," he comforted with a wry smirk. "Hey, didn't you say there was some legend related to Raebon or something?" Nico winced at the mere mention of the tale.

"Right," Nico uttered in a tone of faux recollection. He stared down at his phone, which already had the legend at its center. "Give me a second." He scrolled up and down the page in an effort to mislead his friend and buy himself time to think. *I'd really hoped you would have forgotten about this by now,* he thought. He scrolled back to the top of the page and toggled his thumb back and forth. With the image of the shadow-clad creature fresh in his head, he contemplated if he should simply deliver the message. It pained him to lie, as it was against his personal code of ethics. But if it protected David from ending up back in the hospital or worse, was it so wrong? *Yes,* he thought begrudgingly. He looked up for a moment and masked his discomfort with a friendly smirk before he handed the phone to the author. Surprise overtook David as he pored over the article.

"This is…" his voice trailed off as he continued to read the words on the webpage. His heart pounded with the ferocity of a sledgehammer against a cardboard box, and Nico took note of how his irises adopted glowing streams of white. “This poem at the center of the page, it… sounds familiar.”

“You must have heard the legend before,” Nico rationalized, but David shook his head.

“No, that’s not it. Until this morning I’d never even heard of the Kingdom or the prince. Listen,” he prompted. The sensation that overcame him was as if he’d lived the words upon the page as he traced line after line and began to read aloud:

“The blade has dulled and glory passed,
And times come frighteningly fast
Where children cease to sing his praise
And long forgotten are the days
Where Raebon walked upon this earth
And slayed the dignity of his birth.
As the Kingdom Alaedrea falls
So Raebon must, too, heed death’s call
As will that Temptress gone astray
Who made the King’s son Lechery’s slave.
The Lovers of dissociated class,
He a noble and she more crass
Are thrust henceforth through time and space

Forbidden to gaze upon the other's face
Unless the loving man should see
It is his writing that holds the key
To open doors shut in ages old
And reunite the Lovers' souls.
Forever more will they still rise,
As many times as they have died.
And when the earth blots out the sun
Will then this wretched game be done."

It started to click with him. The vision of World War II wasn't just some random image that cropped up in the middle of his vision, it was a glimpse at another of Raebon's lives. *Then that would mean…* he considered the sounds of bombs and of guns, clashing swords and chilling screams. In that moment he came to realize that those, too, were the echoes of a stranger's lives. David's head began to ache again, but this time his vision became as shaky as the rest of him. He placed his hand against his temple to bring about some semblance of stability, but the world around him continued to blur and clear. He hurt, physically, mentally, and emotionally as he recounted the words of that accursed poem over and over and over again in his mind.

He cried out, and Nico immediately rushed to his side to check on him. David's eyes were completely white now, and as the luster in them grew brighter by the second a shockwave pulsed through the building.

"David, are you alright," Nico asked at a slowed pace and moderate volume. David offered no answer as the temperature in the room began to fall. The air swirled, just as it had the night before at Carnegie Hall and the lights and electronics around the duo blinked erratically. Chills swept through Nico as the pain burrowed its way deeper into David's heart and body. His eyes widened as the ivory luster reached its peak, and as he called out in agony, a blast of sheer power emanated from his body and catapulted Nico into the wall across the room.

He stirred for a moment as he fought off unconsciousness and once the room stopped spinning, Nico braced himself against the wall as he climbed back to his feet. David's eyes slowly returned to normal, and much to his relief the excruciating pain that he'd experienced before lessened by the second. Nico, whose hand now pressed against his aching side, staggered to the chair in which David sat. He opened his mouth as if to speak, but the sudden sting in the now still air attracted his attention. The color drained from the room, and the feeling of uneasiness that persisted in Nico since the hospital intensified. He turned around, and just as he expected, the shadows congregated by the door.

"What's going on," David asked groggily. Nico was jolted as he looked to his friend, who sat in the chair as streams of sweat rolled down his face, fully aware of the events that transpired. *How are you awake right now? No, it couldn't have...*

"Well done," spoke the Shade as his cloak of darkness took form. "It has been a millennium since those words were uttered aloud." David's eyes trailed upward from the floor until he met the malevolent whites of the specter before him. A reptilian hum emerged from the Shade as he surveyed his prey. "The time is drawing nigh, and soon, this little game of ours will come to its end once and for all." Nico's fists tightened as his vision further fixed upon the Shade.

"What..." David groaned in confused exhaustion, and for an instant Nico could have sworn that the malicious eyes of the demon smiled at him.

"I won't let you hurt him," Nico warned as he pulled a gun from the breast pocket within his blazer. He aimed it at the monster with a defiant smile in place that soon transformed into an agonized grimace as the pistol grip began to overheat. Despite the desire to hold on, Nico was forced to release his weapon and pray that the shock of hitting the floor didn't cause a spontaneous discharge.

"His safety," taunted the ghost, "is far beyond your power." With the simplest wave of his hand, the shadows of the beast's cloak leaped for Nico's limbs and strapped him to the nearby wall. He was powerless to do anything as the abundant darkness slithered towards the barely conscious author. It stretched out its bony hand and wrapped its icy black fingers around David's throat. It hummed with sickening pleasure as it hoisted him into the air and raised its other jaggedly clawed hand. The atmosphere of the trashed hotel room became increasingly murderous, but as the Shade looked into David's eyes it released him.

David gasped for air as his consciousness slowly started to fade. The cloaked devil stooped over him, and as if they were old friends it put its clawed hand atop his head.

"Get away from him," Nico shouted as he lurched forward. The shadows that bound him tightened at his vociferation and the one to whom they belonged paid him no mind.

"Only when you remember who we are will I end you," spoke the Shade, "and not before I take from you the one you hold so dear. Only then will you know true despair." The creature disappeared into a whirlwind of black, and its departure marked color's return. As he fell, Nico landed on all fours and proceeded to crawl for his now unconscious friend.

"I'm sorry," Nico whispered as he picked David up and placed him on the bed. Drained, he lazily picked up his gun and tucked it away before he sat in the chair across from the subdued author. *It's just as I thought...* Nico contemplated as he fixated on David. *This is the end of the cycle.* He leaned against one of the arms of the chair and lifted up his shirt to survey the damage dealt to his side from the blast earlier. He pressed his finger against it and hissed from the pain, but thanked God that it wasn't as bad as it could have been. He rose again, and gingerly began to put the room back in order. He picked up his phone from the side of the chair where David had dropped it and surveyed its cracked screen.

We need to get out of here, he thought. He looked at David again as he straightened the light fixtures on the wall and hobbled over to the lamp that fell to the floor from the desk. He meditated on the Shade and the threat that it posed. He shook his head in disbelief of the raw power it possessed. He found

David's laptop in surprisingly good condition on the floor near the sink. *This will come in handy…*

"Nico…" David stirred awake and gently lifted himself from the bed. He rubbed his throat, and instinctively Nico grabbed a glass and filled it with water from the sink. David took it and drank, and within seconds the liquid had vanished. "Thank you."

"Don't mention it," Nico responded. "Hey, listen, I need to run out and replace my phone. Do you think you'll be good on your own for a bit?" He couldn't mask the worry in his tone. Even then his eyes shifted about the room to ensure that they were unaccompanied.

"Nico, you're not my babysitter. I'll be fine," David assured him as he continued to massage his neck. Nico smiled as he turned away, and was surprised by the weight of David's hand on his shoulder. "Hey, be careful, alright?" David's eyes, restored to brown, exhibited their typical gravity and confirmed that this brush with the shadow creature was not lost on him. Nico's heart sank, as he realized that it was only a matter of time before he had to reveal to him, no, to *them*, the truth he'd been hiding all along.

"I will," he assured the author as he resolved that that time had not yet come. "I'll try to be back before long. If you get tired of waiting, don't hesitate to go out and get something to eat. If anything, it'll give you a chance to catch up with Eva. You really shouldn't keep her waiting too long, you know. She might lose interest." Before David could provide a response, Nico walked out the door.

He sat back down in his chair and reflected on the words of the poem. Beautifully written though it was to him, he had to wonder what significance it had to that monster… but then he recalled the words of the Shade. *Only when you remember who we are will I end you…* the blood-chilling hiss of the Shade echoed into his mind as a scream through a canyon. Terrifying though that *thing* was, it struck him as unnaturally recognizable. But what did it mean? What was there to remember of the monster, or of himself for that matter? More importantly, why did it want to kill him? He was only interested in the research, after all.

David sighed, fully uncertain of what it was that he wished to do, and stood from the chair to pace nervously about the room as he watched for any movement in the shadows. He looked out the window, and much to his dismay the sun began to fall below the irregular line of rooftops. His stomach growled, and as he placed his hand over it he reasoned that it was time he showered and changed. When he emerged, he grabbed his coat from a hanger in the closet and with phone in hand he decidedly made for the exit of the hotel room.

The second his foot crossed the doorframe, he remembered the slip of paper with Eva's number on it and returned within the confines to retrieve it. He paused as he selected the phone icon and entered her number. He took a deep breath as he debated on whether or not he should dial it, and with a slip of the thumb he actually did. His eyes widened in shock, but before he could hang up he heard the inquisitive voice of a woman on the other end.

"Hello?" Eva asked. David froze, unsure what to say. "Is anyone there?"

"Hi," David almost shouted as he left the room. He slapped his forehead as he realized the volume of his voice and felt his embarrassment rise when he heard her giggle. "I mean, 'Hey, Eva…'" She laughed harder as his voice became slightly deeper in his best attempt at playing it cool.

"Hey," she responded when she recovered. "How are you feeling?" David rubbed his throat at the question as the image of the shadow beast crept back into his mind. He dared not speak of it, lest she believe him to be crazy.

"I'm feeling okay," he said calmly. It was, after all, partially true. "I was wondering if you'd like to meet up for dinner."

"Well that depends," she started in a voice that warmed the places that the shadow monster chilled. "Where would we be meeting?" David, who now walked casually into the elevator, chuckled as he rubbed the back of his neck.

"Well I take it from your tone that Papa's is out," he supposed. He pressed the button for the lobby, and without delay the suspended box began its descent.

"You would be correct," she confirmed, and though he had no way of knowing it for sure he could still feel her smile.

"Alright, well first let me ask you," he started, "would you like to take a trip?" His voice was deep and mysterious, and out of sheer excitement she momentarily froze.

"I suppose I might be. Where to?"

"Harlem. It just so happens that I know this great little place on Lenox Ave that's got the best chowder in the State of New York. You'd love it." She hummed with uncertainty, and just like that David started to sweat again.

"How are you so sure that I'd love it?" He grinned, because he knew now that she toyed with him.

"You mean aside from this being New York," he started blankly, "I'd have to say the live music that they have in the restaurant." Eva fell dead silent, and the grin on David's face grew wider as he contemplated her response to his trump card.

"What time shall we say," she inquired, and he laughed heartily. He'd won the game, and victory was as sweet as the scent of her perfume.

"I have reservations for 8:30," he informed her as he stepped out of the elevator and into the hotel's main lobby.

"Then it's a date," she said in that quieted tone that drove him mad with curiosity. "I'll see you there." She ended the phone call, and as David walked across the populated lobby his stride shifted from timid to powerful, and for a split second it felt as if he had become the Prince of Legend. He approached the front desk with a stern look about his face and patiently waited for the clerk to end her phone call. She held up one finger as she smiled politely, and within seconds the phone was back on the hook.

"May I help you," she inquired of the author.

"Yes, please," he began. "I'm in room 396 on the third floor, and earlier today my agent and I found that my room had a little bit of a…" he looked around as the young clerk, no older than 25 he assumed, widened her eyes, "rat problem. Anyway, he freaked out and made a little bit of a mess, and I was wondering if it would be possible for me to maybe relocate to a different one?"

"Oh, of course," the nervous clerk confirmed loudly as she typed away on her computer. David couldn't mask the humored expression he sported, but the young woman was far too preoccupied to notice. "The only room we have available for you is the loft suite on the top floor. Would that be alright?" David's eyes went wide with excitement, and the image of Nico's shocked and jealous face crept into his mind.

"Absolutely," he responded. "Thank you so much." The woman beamed at him as she completed the transfer of rooms.

"Really, it's no problem at all. Alright, that should take care of it. I'll alert the concierge and we'll have your bags moved into your new room shortly. In the meantime, here's your key in case you wanted to head up and look around," she said as she handed him a small white envelope with green stripes on it.

"No, I don't think I'll be going up just yet," he informed her as he briefly looked through the window of the lobby. "I'm actually on my way to meet someone for dinner. I'll trust the concierge to have me all moved in before I'm back."

"Absolutely," she replied. David gave her a nod of approval as he turned and walked for the door. "Enjoy your date!" He couldn't help but smile at her well-wishes as he pushed the door open and embraced the slight chill of the city. He walked the sidewalk, and admired the fading lights as he entered the subway station and patiently awaited his train. He looked at the time on his phone, and as the train drew audibly closer, his excitement could barely be contained.

Chapter Seven

David sat nervously at the table in the back of the dimly lit restaurant. The smooth jazz that the band played in the background did little to calm him down, but nevertheless he bounced his knee to the beat. He checked the screen of his phone for the time. She was half an hour late, but it did little to bother him. There was no question that she made him nervous in a number of ways, and the fact that the business dinner he'd planned with his agent had transformed into a date — his first, in fact, — only added to the pressure of the evening.

He carefully surveyed the door in the hope that it would spur her arrival, and all the while begged for more time to prepare himself. His heart beat to the rhythm of the music, and the azure hue of the lights created an almost enchanting atmosphere. He lowered his head as he smiled down at the glossy covering of the menu before him, and he realized that it was the kind of scene that he'd written about a number of times.

"Excuse me, sir?" He looked up to see the pleasant smile of his server. She had dark curly hair that rested neatly on her shoulders and smooth dark chocolate skin that beautifully complemented it. Her light-colored eyes, when hit by the rays of mellow blue that penetrated the otherwise dark room, emanated a pale glow that almost mirrored the demented orbs of the monstrous attacker that prompted a change of room. He froze, and the young lady gave him a look of concern and compassion as she asked, “Are you alright?”

“Yes,” he exhaled in response, “I’m sorry.” The woman twisted her lips in uncertainty, but pulled out her notepad and pen.

“Would you like to order a drink while you wait?” David glanced at the door, and reluctantly nodded as he turned his attention back to the waitress.

“Just water is fine,” he told her in a hushed tone. She quickly jotted it down.

“It’ll be right out.” As soon as the waitress walked away, the bell above the door chimed beneath the mellow vibes of the music and gently struck David’s eardrum. He turned his head, and through the many darkened faces of the café’s populace came the glow of the living melody as she spoke to the hostess. Her expression radiated tranquility and confidence, but her stunningly golden eyes shimmered with excitement. She tucked her sleek brown hair behind her ears as she made conversation with the hostess and smiled, and the way she did so filled him with soothing exhilaration.

The resident entertainer graciously guided her through the crowd, and with every stride towards David, the eyes of every man she passed fixated on her. She approached the table, and on instinct David pulled out her chair for her. His eyes met hers, and as she stepped in front of him to take her seat he admired her more expressly. Her hair bounced with every motion in a way that breathed life into him and the curves of her body were tastefully complemented by the violet dress that graced it. The vanilla peach of her perfume danced into his nostrils, and he began to wonder how much it would bother her if he had a taste.

"Thank you," she mouthed to the hostess, who gave a pleasant nod and returned to her post. "I'm sorry I'm late," said Eva, whose attention at last fell on David. She placed her black handbag on the tabletop and straightened her dress. "I made the mistake of hailing a cab in New York City." He flashed an unconscious crooked smile.

"It's okay," he exhaled. "I understand that the traffic here can be a little insane. You look wonderful tonight." The sincerity in his voice melted her as the flickering flames did the candles between them.

“Thank you,” she returned as she surveyed her surroundings and bobbed her head to the song in the air. “So is this the kind of place you have all of your business dinners or is Nico just special?” His eyebrows raised as his goofy smile grew ever larger. He leaned forward as his gaze fixed on her, and despite her calmed exterior a chill shot down her spine.

“Well believe it or not, he’s been my best friend longer than he’s been my manager. Sometimes it’s just nice to get out and explore the local culture a little,” he explained as she bit her lower lip. The song changed, and the waitress from before marched to the rhythm as she returned to the table.

“Good evening,” she greeted Eva, whose eyes remained locked with David’s as she smiled back in response. “My name is Tiffany and I’ll be your server this evening. Ma’am, can I start you off with something to drink?”

“Iced tea will be fine,” she said with an intrigued upward inflection.

“Great. Can I get you guys going with any appetizers?” Eva opened the menu and glanced at what options were presented, and found the decision nearly impossible to make.

“Sure,” he responded as his expression sobered. “We’ll go with the chicken and waffles.” Eva cocked her head to the side, puzzled that he'd suggest something that she'd always figured for comfort food. Tiffany scribbled on her notepad once again.

"Alright, then, I'll put this in and I'll be back to take your orders in a little." The young waitress tucked her pad and pen away as she turned, and stopped abruptly as an elderly couple slowly moved past her.

"Chicken and waffles," Eva asked as Tiffany scurried through the crowd and back toward the kitchen. David wiped his mouth as an unintentional simper took its place upon his countenance.

"Trust me," he told her, "that was the best choice." Eva leaned forward as she lightly tapped her finger to the beat.

"And why's that," she asked as her eyes lit with humor.

"So we could eat something with a little more weight before the soup," he explained. She raised an eyebrow and placed the back of her hand beneath her chin. "Again, trust me. The Du Bois Chowder is definitely the right choice for a first timer."

"Eh, the food's only half the reason I came," she admitted with a shrug. "The other half is that." She pointed to the band on the stage and watched them lose themselves in the music. "You don't hear a lot of passion in music nowadays. It's there, don't get me wrong, but there's just something about a classical piece that sweeps you into the melody."

"It's good that you bring that up because I wanted to ask you, what got you so interested in music?" Her eyes fell back on him, a little softer now, and as she tossed her head from side to side indecisively, she resolved to explain.

"When I was a little girl," she started and watched as his expression changed from playful to considerate, "my mother and I would practice our scales together on the piano. She was a wonderful pianist. Better than I am now, actually. And I used to tell her, 'Mommy, when I grow up I wanna be exactly like you,' and she'd smile and pat me on my head when she asked me, 'And why's that?' And I remember, each time I'd give her this big smile and tell her, 'You become the music, Mommy.'" Eva looked around the room again and chuckled sadly at the memory, but still she went on. "It's funny, she always looked at me strangely when I said that, but David if you could have seen the way she would get so wrapped up in the notes her fingers played you would understand. She was like—"

"An angel of music," David completed. Her eyes snapped back to him, and as he observed the inquisitive expression she sported he clarified, "The apple doesn't fall far from the tree, you know." She gave a wry smile and took a deep breath as she played those sweet memories repeatedly in the confines of her mind.

"She was amazing, David," she told him with a tinge of pain behind her voice.

"Was?" The question was superfluous, and once uttered compelled the author to kick himself out of sheer stupidity. Eva shadowed the performers with her eyes as they dipped into their repertoire for a slower number, and donned a grin of disbelief as her emotions were continually played with.

"When I was nine, my mother was shot in front of me outside of a bank in my hometown of Los Angeles. The shooter was caught almost immediately by the security guards and a few nearby policemen, but they…" her voice trailed off as tears began to fill her eyes. David reached his hand across the table and grabbed hers.

"It's okay," he whispered gently, "I wouldn't want to make you relive something that awful." She looked at him as a single tear strolled down the side of her face, and instantly his heart shattered. She took a tissue from her little handbag and wiped her eyes with it as she blushed.

"I'm sorry," she started with a wave of the hand. "I don't even know why I told you all of that." She observed the seriousness on his face, the intensity of his eyes that she'd become so accustomed to in only two short days, and for reasons unbeknownst to her she felt soothed by the mere strength of his presence. It reminded her of something. Of Prince Raebon, of how he comforted the woman Miria and provided for her… protected her.

"Well, I'm no stranger to losing a parent," he uttered as he massaged her hand with his thumb. "When I was sixteen, my parents died in a house fire. I was on the bus home from school when I saw the smoke, and police and firemen had the street blocked off so we just sat there." His thumb ceased movement at the image of a sixteen-year-old version of himself, alive with panic and desperate to get home. Despite his feelings he abstained from tears as he continued. "I got off and took a shortcut through some of the neighbors' yards, but when I got there my parents' bodies were already being excavated from the house's remains. Ever since then, the only person I've really bonded with on a personal level was Nico. He's the closest thing I've got to family." Eva trembled as the words struck her heart. She offered him a tearful smile as Tiffany filed back to their location with a circular tray loaded with the chicken and waffles as well as Eva's tea.

"Here you go, ma'am," said the waitress as she pulled the glass from the tray and set it down before her. "And your chicken and waffles… excellent. I'll be right back with your water, sir." She darted back towards the kitchen and quickly returned with a glass brimming with clear liquid. "Are we ready to order?"

"Yes," Eva said just as David opened his mouth. She caught his gaze, and the suddenly mystic gleam in her eyes made him smirk with anticipation. "We'll have the Du Bois Chowder that he keeps talking about."

"Ooh, excellent choice," exclaimed the waitress. "Now you know that's a meal for two, right?" Eva's jaw dropped as she turned her eyes toward David, whose intrigued smirk grew to a humored grin.

"I didn't," she said with audible surprise as her expression sobered. The amusement of his expression fell into terrified uncertainty, and just as a drop of sweat slid down the side of his head she curled her lips. "But that's fine. We'll go with that."

"I'll have it out as soon as it's ready," Tiffany said as her eyes excitedly switched between the two. David exhaled and allowed his back to collide with his chair. She giggled at him as she took a sip of her tea.

"You really like to mess with me, don't you," he asked with a chuckle, and wiped his forehead. She lowered the glass and locked eyes with him once again.

"I just wanted to lighten the mood a little bit… and it's really fun to make you sweat," she admitted. He rolled his eyes. *Great, another Nico.*

"You know," he said as he pulled his silverware from the napkin and dug into his waffle, "changing the subject works just as well."

"You'd like to think that, wouldn't you?" They both laughed. "I guess we can try it out. What did you and Nico do after the hospital?" His smile lessened as the image of the Shade crept back into his head.

"I had Nico help me with some research, actually." She leaned forward in fascination as he placed a fragment of the waffle in his mouth and savored the buttery taste.

"New book," she asked excitedly. His now stern eyes met hers, and for a moment the conversation ceased.

"Something like that," he responded modestly as he lifted another bite to his lips. "I've actually been doing a little digging into the Kingdom of Alaedrea." Eva's skin chilled to the touch, and as the words left him she saw Prince Raebon briefly take his place.

"Really," she questioned in an attempt to mask her uneasiness. "What got you interested in it?"

"Well, if you couldn't tell from *Death by Knight*, I'm fascinated by the Middle Ages. Knights, chivalry, monarchs with a touch of megalomania, all of it just sends a tingle down my spine and I feel like I can pull some really good stuff out of it," he explained with a crooked smirk. "On top of that, I've been looking for a way to break away from the overdone 'legend of Medieval England' model, and Alaedrea's history may give me a chance to do just that." She cocked her head to the side.

"But I thought that Alaedrea was *part* of England," she questioned with a mouth full of chicken. He chuckled, and as her sun-kissed cheeks donned a reddish hue he shook his head.

"It was, but it was annexed at some point after 959 AD. Geographically it was located in mainland Europe in what's now the Netherlands," he clarified. She gave an understanding nod. "And get this, it was under the control of a family of moors."

"That is peculiar," she said pensively as her eyes fell to her plate. She grabbed the syrup and generously drizzled it on her waffle. She cut and ate, and with the utmost euphoria she closed her eyes to truly savor it. “This is so good.”

“I told you it was the right choice,” David laughed. Eva waved her fork in the air as she finished off the food in her mouth.

“How did you find out that Alaedrea was under the control of moors, though? I mean there are no known records of anyone of a darker pigmentation heading an entire kingdom at any point in European history, and the records of that particular kingdom were lost a long time ago.” David opened his mouth, but Tiffany returned with the pot of chowder and a bowl for each of them. She placed the soup on the table with a smile, and both David and Eva offered one in return.

“Here you are,” she spoke cheerfully. “I hope you enjoy.”

“Thank you,” Eva said, and the young waitress walked away with as much haste as when she’d arrived. “So,” she redirected her attention back to the man with whom she sat, “you were just about to tell me how you found out about the Alaedrean royal family.” He smiled modestly as he filled his bowl with soup. The heavenly aroma filtered into his nostrils as well as hers, and while she fixed her own bowl he started to eat.

"Well," he started with his mouth full of mussels, shrimp and clams, "there aren't any concrete sources that verify their ethnicity. I guess it's more of a hunch when you get right down to it."

"Well that's the plus side of being a fiction writer, right? You get to write about whatever you want." Eva's tone had grown somewhat distant and she watched the author as she sampled the chowder. There was something strange about this conversation to her. It was almost as if, from her perspective, he'd experienced the same kind of dream that she had. More so, it felt like he was hiding something from her, and from previous experiences, that didn't bode well. She narrowed her eyes on him as she wondered if she could prompt his honesty.

"Yeah, I guess that's true. But even still, I wanted to do a little digging before I actually got started. But what about you? Have you done anything interesting today," he inquired, and she choked on a piece of lobster meat as she recalled the hilarious conversation with Torrie.

"Oh, nothing too major," she gasped, and quickly worked to regain her composure. "I just went back to my hotel and caught up with my best friend Torrie over the phone. She's so great, by the way. Other than that, I took a little nap." She took another sip of her tea as her cheeks became further discolored under the blue lighting of the room. David couldn't help but feel a sense of wonder, because before him wasn't the concert pianist or the literature enthusiast from the day before. She wasn't suave or sensual even in the least. She was simply Eva.

"Sounds like a relaxing day to me. I'm almost envious," he commented in a rather relaxed tone that suddenly eased Eva's tense mind.

"Yeah, it was." She paused for a moment as the song changed, and looked over toward the stage with joyous expression renewed. "You know, it's interesting that you've been looking into the Kingdom of Alaedrea."

"Oh? Why do you say," he asked as she bit into a juicy shrimp. She chewed and swallowed as her face twisted with false exasperation, but soon returned to normal when she went for her tea.

"Ugh, I hate it when that happens," she said, and again they shared a laugh. "To answer your question, though, I… Huh. I'm not sure if I should tell you this."

"Oh come on," David shouted jokingly. "Must you bait me like that? And here I thought we'd come to a good place in our relationship." Her ears perked up and her eyes narrowed as she took her iced tea in both hands.

"So we're putting labels on things now? You work fast, Mr. Masters," she teased, and he couldn't help but roll his eyes again. He looked to his left, and the white eyes of Tiffany the waitress remained fixed on the pair. His skin began to crawl, but despite his discomfort he looked back to Eva as his lips curled into a smile. She took a moment to analyze him, and as soon as her facial features shifted to reflect her thoughts, they returned to normal. She shrugged. "I'll tell you, but not here."

"Agreed," David commented as he surveyed the area once more. "I can't shake the feeling that we're being watched." He pulled out his wallet and withdrew a few bills that he slapped on the table. He stood from his seat and took his place at her side as he extended a hand to brace her. She stared at it uneasily as the blackout from before came to the forefront of her mind.

"I don't know," she started as she massaged her wrist. "The last time we came into direct contact we ended up in the hospital with no memories of what happened." He mulled it over for a moment.

"You have a point," he said, but took her hand regardless. "Still, I've held your hand tonight already and nothing happened, so I'm more than willing to take the chance." Tiffany began her eager stride towards them as they made their way through the crowd. They could feel her as she stalked them with a chillingly animalistic hunger, but left the establishment quickly and ran across the street towards Central Park. Tiffany's malevolent whites watched through the glass door as her prey scurried off into the night, and for just a second, her eyes flashed brighter still.

Chapter Eight

Nico's face maintained an eerie solemnity as he stared down at the screen of his new phone. The white eyes that seemed to transfer from face to face were not lost on him since he ignored the people around him and walked the sidewalk in silence. There was a certain comfort of being alone now, of knowing that David was with Eva and could ensure her safety while Nico ensured his. He looked up now and watched as the people passed him left and right, only to notice that no matter how far he seemed to walk he remained within the same stretch. He was frozen in a loop, another type of temporal paradox, just as he had been twice before. He pinched the bridge of his nose and briefly closed his eyes.

"This crap is getting old. What do you want," he demanded, fully aware that the Shade could hear him. Its snicker resounded over the clamor of the city, but none besides Nico took notice of the sickening sound.

"How bold of you," spoke the monster as it appeared before him on the sidewalk, "to speak to me as though I were some lowly pest. I trust you are aware that I could end you where you stand?"

"At the cost of your own existence, yeah, I know," Nico retorted. The Shade's eyes widened with vehement disgust as it released a reptilian growl, but the emboldened agent remained unshaken. "You were about to tell me what you wanted." The creature dispersed into a cloud of black mist, only to reform behind an unimpressed Nico. It wrapped its bony finger around his throat and pressed its razor-like talon into the side of Nico's neck and still, his face maintained its expressionlessness.

"What I want," whispered the twisted being, "is actually quite simple. It seems as if you know something, Moderator, and it is my wish that you give me the answers that I seek." Nico cringed at the name as the Shade slithered off to his side. Nico's hazel orbs fixated on the beast and emanated a glow of their own.

"I'll tell you this once," Nico snarled, "don't you ever call me that again. My name is Nicholas Dominic Alaimo and if you call me by any name it'll be my own." The Shade stood perfectly still, and for the first time since it appeared, it flashed a toothy yellow grin.

"Oh my, it would seem that someone has gotten overly attached to a life in which he does not belong," it sneered. "Regardless, you will tell me what I wish to know."

“Then for your sake I’d suggest you ask a question,” Nico fired back.

“Raebon has begun to recall who he is, has he not,” asked the shadow as it paced the concrete. Nico’s eyes remained trained on it as his hands twitched in anticipation of war.

“What business is that of yours,” demanded the agent as his eyes narrowed on the Shade. “Let me remind you that as the overseer of the game, my job isn’t to supply you with an advantage over your enemies. I’m supposed to be impartial and allow things to play out the way they’re meant to—”

“That is true,” interrupted the hooded abomination, “but from what I was able to glean from our earlier encounter, you seem to have grown rather fond of my enemy. That, of course, is something that I am willing to overlook… provided you tell me what it is I want to know.” The Shade’s luminescent white eyes became focused on Nico, whose fists opened and closed as he pondered his next move. “I will ask you again. Has Raebon begun to regain his memories or has he not?”

“He has,” Nico muttered, “to a degree. He knows of Raebon and Miria, but doesn’t remember that his memories are his. To him they’re nothing more than dreams.” The Shade’s eyes became wide with fascination and humor.

“And what of Miria?”

“I don’t know. To be honest, she just showed up at the book signing yesterday and I haven’t seen her since the hospital this morning. Whatever knowledge she has come to possess about who she really is, I am not privy to,” Nico stated icily. “There, I’ve answered your questions. Let me go, I have a lot of work to do.” The callous creature cackled into the night sky.

“Patience, dear… Nicholas, was it? My inquiry has yet to be concluded.”

“Well as much as I hate to disappoint you, the answers that I’m able to give you are very limited at the moment, so if you’ll excuse me,” Nico said as he pushed past the Shade and down the sidewalk, but with the simple wave of its hand the demon brought him back to where he’d previously stood.

“You really get on my nerves with that crap. Don’t you have something better to do? Scare small children? Freak out the elderly with your Grim Reaper impression,” Nico teased as the monster’s toothy grin reverted to pitch-black. The Shade appeared before him and aggressively grabbed him by the shirt.

“Do not mock me, lowly filth,” spat the malevolent darkness as he hoisted the manager into the air. “I am well aware that you spend your days by the prince’s side and that you know what sparks his abominable inspiration." Nico's expression became smug with realization.

"You want to know if these dreams of his will prompt him to write," gasped the agent. The glowing white eyes of the Shade became even more enraged as it pulled him closer in.

"Indeed," it spoke through obviously clenched teeth, "and you will be the one to report to me when it does." Images of his old life flashed about in Nico's mind, and in a burst of pure rage he slapped the arm of the Shade away from him and landed on his feet. He extended a hand, and as his hazel eyes glowed in contrast to the darkness the Shade was suspended in midair, gradually warped by a Paradox of Nico's own design.

"I'll only tell you this once, do you understand," Nico asked as the volume of his voice rose. "I am *not* your servant. You sacrificed your power over me when you damned me to the position of Moderator for this accursed game, and were it not against the rules then I'd rip off your head and parade it through the streets of New York with a smile on my face." The Shade unleashed a wild guffaw as Nico's severity heightened.

"Do you really think I would be so stupid as to bring you my demands without any sort of leverage?" Nico slowly began to close his extended hand, and the space around the Shade started to press violently against it.

"You're bluffing," the agent accused as he scowled at his adversary, "and I'm in no mood for your games." The shadows beneath the hood of the cloak bent around the yellow smile once again as the creature's colorless eyes filled with amusement.

"Take a look, dear boy," it said as it twirled its finger by its side. The space beside Nico's head ripped open, and through a darkened portal the agent could see into a room with crisp honey walls accented by a deep brown mold along its top. The matching brown curtains fell behind a golden couch upon which sat his wife. His heartbeat increased rapidly as he observed her painfully from afar. Her petite frame lay masked by the somewhat baggy fit of her pink silk pajamas, and her ruby-red lips that begged to meet his twisted with curiosity as her deep blue eyes fixated on the little white stick in her hand. She twirled a lock of her long, curly, raven-colored hair around her finger as she pulled her legs up from the floor. Nico, who would typically be overjoyed at the sight of her, grew livid.

"I wonder what you're going to be," Sierra whispered, and her eyes shifted from the stick to her belly. Nico ground his teeth now as a blade of shadows completely invisible to her appeared just centimeters from her throat. The infuriated manager's attention returned to the Shade within his grasp, who smiled audaciously at the chaos it had created.

"It seems as though my control over you remains intact. Now, let me go," demanded the despicable creature.

"How dare you? She's my wife," Nico shouted, and for a moment he considered ending the Shade right then and there, but he knew that he couldn't.

"Oh, I am well aware," taunted the monster. "I think it kind of you to go out of your way to provide me with just the leverage that I needed. So, you are aware of my demands. Should you agree to them, then *she* will live. However, if you do not, then I shall take her life as well as that of your unborn child." Nico, now powerless, trembled with fury as he struggled with his memories. He begrudgingly released his captive, and cursed beneath his breath. "A wise decision. You will serve me the information I have requested, and as the lights drain from your dear friend's eyes I shall inform him of your true part to play in all this." The darkness of which he was made began to swirl until there was nothing of him left. "Until next time…" The Paradox in which Nico was trapped dissipated along with the voice of the Shade, and the agonized Overseer fell to his knees. He screamed, which, despite the hundreds of people that passed by, attracted no attention.

He was alone, completely and utterly, and in a fit of rage he pounded his fists against the pavement. This was the second time he'd betrayed the prince, the second time he'd been forced to sell out the one friend he'd ever made in the kingdom, and as the seconds ticked by he grew increasingly disgusted with himself. He stood to his feet again with his phone in hand and opened the contacts. Since its replacement, only two names filled the list: Sierra and David. *But who do you call,* Nico wondered, *when you've lied to everyone you say you love in ways they can't forgive?*

His nose started to flare as tears fell from his eyes, and Nico swiftly paced the sidewalk until he'd returned to the limousine.

"To the hotel," he ordered, and the driver nodded in silent compliance. Nico closed his eyes as his mind began to wander back to that time. He hated to think about it, about the loneliness that he'd felt back then, the abuse that he'd suffered from the king's men, but every once in a while, his days in the Kingdom of Alaedrea would resurface.

"Move, vermin," shouted Eulic as he shoved Sorin out of the way as Prince Raebon walked in tow. "Have you no respect for your prince?" Sorin stumbled into the puddle of mud that lay beside the dirt road, and the muscular bully looked down at the peasant in his weakness with a superior flare. The crowd of people that walked the streets of the Alaedrean capital gathered to indulge in the conflict. Eulic's lush brown hair and sea-green eyes, when paired with his sharp features and bronze skin conveyed the image of an angel, which sharply contrasted the devil that Sorin knew him to be. Nico had been a philosopher in that age, well versed in expanded thinking and knowledgeable in the ways of time. In the warrior state of Alaedrea, however, his intelligence was of little value to those around them. That is, unless they could use it for the purpose of war.

"General Eulic," called the prince in a stern tone of voice. The general turned and bowed before the son of King Aradmus, and dared not lift his head to meet the gaze of the prince's fierce white eyes.

"My liege," he said earnestly. The Prince walked around his kneeling servant and extended his hand to the muddied thinker.

"You will apologize to this man," Raebon demanded as he gestured to Sorin. Eulic's eyes lifted from the ground now, but as his mouth opened to protest the prince raised his eyebrows. Eulic, not foolish enough to pick a quarrel with the future king, resigned to his task.

"Please," began the general, whose attention lay fixed upon the olive-skinned gentleman, "forgive me for my blatant lack of proper etiquette." Though his tone was sincere, Sorin could tell by the look in his eyes that he wished him dead for the humiliation that was brought upon him.

"There really is no need to apologize to the likes of me, my prince," Sorin insisted modestly, but Raebon waved it off as he took in the crowd that gathered to witness more of Eulic's foolish actions.

"General Eulic," Raebon spoke with a tinge of agitation in his voice, "the people of Alaedrea, particularly those of the philosophical variety are the lifeblood of the kingdom. Therefore, it is our responsibility as the nobles of this kingdom to treat each citizen as such. Our higher status is not given to us because we are superior, but because we have a duty to protect those who depend on our strength. Do you understand, General?" The general cut his eyes at Sorin but remained silent. The prince returned his attention to the young philosopher and smiled as he asked, "What is your name?"

"Sorin, sire," he said bashfully. Even now, Nico couldn't believe how different they were. Then again, a lot can change in the course of a thousand years.

"Well, Sorin, from this day forward under my authority you will live in the palace alongside the royal family of Alaedrea, in service to my father the King. There, you will do as he sees fit." Nico remembered how his eyes lit with joy at the sound of those words, and folded his arms across his chest as the driver made a turn towards the hotel. This, what should have been a happy memory, proved to be one of the most excruciating of his elongated existence. Despite Prince Raebon's kindness, despite the genuine concern he exhibited to his people, to *him,* both publicly and privately, it was Sorin who was ultimately to blame for the prince's downfall.

But things were different, now. Now it was his wife who fell to the mercy of the Shade, and after so long that sense of helplessness that he felt so long ago had returned. *You will pay for this,* he thought as his face writhed with animosity. He stared down at the name of his beloved as he thought about her. He couldn't protect her, at least not by his own strength like a good husband would, like he vowed to do as they stood upon the altar on their wedding day.

"I'd cross over eternity for you," he'd once whispered into her ear and moved to kiss her neck. It was truth, for indeed he had, but that truth had been ripped to shreds before his very eyes by the claws of a wretched wraith from his past. The more he thought about it, the more he hated himself for keeping this aspect of him a secret from her. *But would she have believed me?* His eyes stung with hate-filled tears. With the sword against her neck Nico resolved that that was of little importance. Because of him, she was in danger. Because he loved her, the Reaper stalked, and the only way to save her, to save their baby, was to betray for the second time the man who first showed him kindness.

He dialed her number, and wrestled with the thought of telling her what was going on, but decided against it. If the Shade even felt for a moment that it'd been crossed, her blood would color the carpet floor and Nico would have been made to watch helplessly from 2,000 miles away. He exhaled deeply as he listened to the ring of the line and desperately wished for the end of this game.

"Hello," came Sierra's sweet alto voice from the other end, "who is this?" He smiled briefly through the tears he sought to hide from her.

"It's me, honey," he told her as calmly as he could have.

"You got a new number?" He wiped his face of what water had already spilled and withdrew a tissue from the box in the cup holder in the back seat.

"Yeah, sorry," he said in a near perfect rendition of his usually jovial tone. "I slipped pretty hard on the sidewalk and my phone got launched into the street from my hand. By the time I looked up it'd already been run over by a passing car, so I went and got a new one." His gut churned with disgust. *Am I even capable of being honest with you?* She snickered, and the fake chuckle he responded with further served to ease her mind.

"It's not like you to be so clumsy. What were you up to that had you so preoccupied?" He cringed as he gripped his heart. *This was a mistake...*

"Just preparing for our next stop on the book tour. You know, same old thing, just a new destination," he lied, and with every new deception a little more of his heart chipped away.

"Sounds stressful," she replied. "You know, it almost sounds like you could use some good news."

“Good news,” he reiterated inquisitively. “Do tell.” He listened as she took a deep breath and repositioned herself on the sofa in their living room.

“Okay, here goes…” she paused, though Nico knew her well enough to know that it was purely for dramatic effect. “I’m pregnant!” The excitement behind the words dealt his soul a blow as devastating as the words themselves had, and though his mind produced a number of responses his lips uttered none. “You there?”

“Yeah, yeah,” he responded pensively, and subsequently bit his lower lip until it bled. “I don’t know what to say, I mean, I’m gonna be a dad!” He wrapped his fingers around the edge of the seat and squeezed with all his strength, because in that instance he realized that that day may never come. “Hey, babe, I’m gonna give David a call and tell him the good news. I’ll call you back soon, okay?” She giggled.

“Of course, I mean you have to let him know that he’s gonna be an uncle,” she responded almost playfully.

“Hey,” Nico said before she could hang up the phone. His voice was unusually cool, and instantly she felt a tinge of worry spike in the back of her mind. “I love you. So much.” Her heart jumped, and a goofy smile crept across her face.

"I love you too," she responded thoughtfully. "Goodnight, honey." She hung up, and as they pulled into the parking garage of the hotel he desperately hoped it wouldn't be the last conversation that they would share. He stepped out of the car and made his way through the parking structure. He arrived back at the sidewalk. The entrance to the hotel was a short walk away, but the gravity of Nico's life made it seem like it was so much farther.

He shook with every step, though the dire state of his life affected him far more than the chill of the New York air. No… that still wasn't it. What rattled him to his core was unrelated to the Shade's malevolent antics.

"Does he know," asked the General as Nico's mind wandered backwards through time. Sorin met the unsettling blue eyes of his superior, and as terror coursed through his veins amid the blood that Eulic longed to spill, he shook his head rapidly in response. "Excellent. Then the plan is to be carried out as scheduled. I trust you are aware of your part to play in all this?"

"Yes," Sorin responded remorsefully as he took a small roll of parchment from his cloak. "The Paradox Curse is ready for use." Eulic snatched it away from him, and a deeply unnerving look swept his face.

"Perfect," he hummed excitedly as his eyes widened. "In three days' time, Prince Raebon and Miria will meet their doom… and their damned child along with them."

Chapter Nine

"Nico," David called like an elated child from across the lobby. It shattered his concentration, but nevertheless the agent offered a smile to his adopted brother and the beautiful woman in his company.

"Hey," Nico started in a moderately shaken tone. "I was actually on my way up to your room. There's something I wanted to discuss with you." He gave an uneasy smile that naturally provoked David's concern.

"Everything alright," he asked as he laid his hand on Nico's shoulder.

"Yeah," Nico assured him. "Great, actually." His attention shifted to the lovely pianist. "Am I interrupting something?" David looked over his shoulder to see a pair of ghastly white eyes as they peered through the window of the hotel lobby. His skin began to crawl at the sight, and with a slight twitch he smiled back to his immediate circle.

"No," Eva spoke up before David had the opportunity. "Not at all. We were actually on the way up to his room to continue a discussion we started over dinner. I don't see why we can't include you." This was her chance to pick his brain about what happened at Carnegie Hall, and for the life of her she wouldn't dream of missing it.

"Then let's get moving," David said as he noted the sound of the opening door. He briefly looked behind him and met the distant gaze of the White-Eyes as it methodically approached their group. Its body was like that of an average man, though its face was as absent of color as the eyes that shifted about the red and brown room. David cut a look to Nico, who nodded, and the three of them slowly moved through the populated lobby. "Take it nice and slow," David cautioned. "If we start to run then the people around us will stop and watch, and it'll give away our position to the person following us." He glanced back at the person possessed and noticed how its nostrils flared like a bloodhound.

"There's someone following us?" Eva inquired, and as she began to look around David grabbed her hand. Her eyes met his, and sternly he shook his head. They kept moving at an even pace, and the creature with eyes of white surveyed the faces in the crowd as it guessed the direction in which they moved.

"You shouldn't look around too much," Nico informed her as they continued to tread as inaudibly as they could. "Just play it cool. Once we're in the elevator we should be in the clear for a while." Eva flashed him a puzzled look.

"But wait, why are we being followed in the first place," she asked as her voice started to carry. "I mean, we haven't done anything to draw unusual attention to ourselves, so we should be able to reason with whoever it is we're running from."

"Keep your voice down," David commanded, which prompted Eva to raise an eyebrow at him. "We'll explain everything once we get to the room. I promise."

"You didn't do anything illegal before dinner tonight, did you," she hesitantly inquired as they stopped before the elevator and rearranged their position.

"No," said David, who stood with his back to the elevator door and surveyed the movements of their pursuer. Nico pressed the button, and impatiently tapped his foot with a careful look over the shoulder. Eva stood between them, unsure what it was that she was supposed to do in this instant, and decidedly watched as the illuminated numbers above their heads descended. The door opened.

"Alright," Nico all but whispered to the others, "everyone get into the elevator." Eva entered first and Nico after her, but David stood petrified. "David, let's go." David offered no response to his best friend, and only watched as the White-Eyes hunted them through the crowd. It sniffed the air, this animal in human flesh, all too unnoticed by the droves of people that surrounded it. Like a dog its ears twitched at the sound of the elevator's bell, and instantly it locked eyes with the paralyzed author.

"David, get in here now," Eva urged with panic in her tone. She couldn't see it, the White-Eyes that pursued them all, but she could feel the sting in the air that it brought with it. David held his chest. His heart became pained, but just before he could drop to his knees Nico ran and grabbed him.

The beast picked up its pace, and even dropped to all fours as it slithered through the crowd. Nico, whose own movements slowed from the additional weight of his friend, did his best to make it back to the elevator. David's vacant eyes began to glow white once again, and Eva's heart raced as he took on the appearance of Prince Raebon right in front of her.

David's body pulsed with every step the demonic pawn took towards him, and with each of the inward tremors his eyes grew brighter still. *This feeling...* he thought as his hand drifted subconsciously towards his aching head, *this sting, it's...*

“Eva, hurry and press the button to close the door,” Nico instructed calmly. Eva, now frantic for air, stumbled forward and did as he asked. The doors slowly drifted closed, and the beast, whose eyes now shone with a hint of red, drove its hands and head through the door after them. It snarled as it snapped its teeth at them, and Eva fell backwards at the disgusting sounds as the monstrous hunter became known to her eyes. She looked at her companions for but a moment as fear shot through her, and eagerly pushed herself into the corner of the lift.

“Alright, that’s enough,” Nico said as he gingerly lowered his petrified friend to the elevator floor. He stood upright, and as the pale creature gripped the doors to force them back open, Nico began to utter what sounded like poetry to Eva:

“Unsightly beast from the depths of Hell,
With eyes as white and deep as wells,
Bear witness to a Paradox’s Might
And by compulsion now take flight
Without the chance to e’er return
Lest those white eyes smolder and burn.”

The outraged monster fought hard to cross the threshold of the door, but was pushed back by what seemed to be Nico's volition alone. It was catapulted from the elevator, and the doors slammed shut as the platform began to move.

"Top… floor," David managed through clenched teeth. Eva stood back up and for a moment quietly stared at Nico, who considered for a moment whether or not he would press the button for the top floor as prompted.

"What was that thing," she demanded with a shake in her voice. She looked at her date for the evening, who now sat motionless on the floor with eyes so glazed over that she thought he could be dead. "What did it do to David?" Nico turned around and looked at his uncomfortably seated friend, but calmly shifted his gaze to the young pianist. He observed her carefully as he paced the floor.

"Were you able to see it," he inquired sternly, and for a moment she caught a glimpse of his chilling hazel eyes. She shook her head as she placed her hand on the cold steel wall.

"I couldn't," she admitted, "at least not at first. Then it started to make its way into the elevator. And there was this stinging sensation in the air that just got worse as it got closer to us." Her eyes returned to David, and second by second her heart filled with desperation and fear.

"Good," Nico sighed, which only exasperated her sense of alarm.

"Good? What's so good about it? You still haven't told me what the hell that even was," she snapped as her amber eyes began to glow bright with emotion. Nico's expression intensified, and immediately Eva checked herself. "Sorry, it's just that that thing was freaky."

"Yeah," Nico responded, "they are. But don't worry, I'll explain everything once we're in David's room upstairs. Here," he said as he handed her the gun from within his jacket. The elevator pulled to a stop with a ding, but it wasn't on the top floor. Nevertheless, Eva quickly took the firearm from Nico and hummed with excitement. "Be careful with that. It's a—"

"A 9mm Smith & Wesson," Eva completed as she pulled back the slide and readily aimed it at the now opening door. Nico raised his eyebrows with a smile as he observed her stance.

"I'll admit, I didn't expect that at all," Nico joked, and Eva gave a cocky grin as she lowered the weapon that felt so good in the palm of her hand.

“To be fair, we did just meet yesterday. There’s bound to be a few things you don’t know about me, right?” He glanced at the doorway and noted the lack of light in the hallway. An ominous growl came from the darkness, but still Nico stood unfazed. He looked down at David, whose eyes had completely whited out.

“I need you to keep an eye on him while I go get something from my room,” Nico informed Eva as his eyes carefully watched the open door slowly drift closed again. “Hopefully it won’t take me too long.” He pressed the button to reopen it, and without another word he left. Eva exhaled a breath of solace and took a seat across from David as she gazed into his eyes. Amid her worry, she wondered whether or not it was the same man who had sat in the audience at her concert the night before. He groaned subconsciously.

The sound jolted her, and were he awake at that moment Eva would have cracked a joke, but seeing him this way, so lifeless and still, rattled her something awful. She looked back at the door and tightly held the pistol within her grip. *What is happening,* she asked herself as she patiently awaited Nico’s return. She understood the importance of her vigilance since the doors would open again at the press of a button, and should the wrong entity open those doors, then negligence would mean the end for the both of them. She chuckled to herself, because she never once believed that she would find herself in any situation even close to this one. After all, it's not as if monsters go on the hunt every day.

The doors reopened, and there stood the mysterious Nico with a small, metallic-looking quill pen in his hand. He pressed the button for the top floor, and as the elevator moved upward still he tossed it to Eva. She caught it, and awkwardly stood to return the gun.

"No," he told her, "not yet. If one of the White-Eyes has made it up to the top floor, then you're gonna need to shoot at it while I pull David into the safety of his room. Once we're safely inside, then I'll tell you everything. Both of you." He looked down at David, and with a mild scowl in place he picked him up. Eva stepped forward as the elevator stopped again. The doors drifted open and she cautiously surveyed either end of the hall before taking her exit. Nico reached into the breast pocket of David's blazer and pulled out the key card envelope.

"Any idea where we're supposed to go," Eva called back to Nico as he walked David along the lightless path.

"Yeah," he told her in more of a hushed tone, "this way." He walked more briskly, and the movement jarred David awake. His head throbbed for a moment, but when he realized that he was moving, his eyes quickly surveyed the surrounding corridor. *We got away,* he thought as he moved to stand of his own volition. "You're awake," Nico noticed, and with a jolt of worried excitement Eva turned around.

"Yeah," David responded with his hand still on his head. He braced himself momentarily against the wall and stared at the floor. His vision blurred, and the darkness around them did little to aid his sight. "What happened? One minute I was standing in front of the elevator with you and Eva, and the next…" He closed his eyes as he tried to think. Eva cautiously stepped backwards from her position in the hopes of rejoining the two of them, and all the while kept watch for anything out of the ordinary.

A grunt came from a minimal distance behind them, and just as in the lobby thirteen floors below, the air began to sting. The trio glanced over their shoulders, and as a pulse went through their bodies a pair of ghastly pale eyes appeared in the intensified darkness. Nico took his gun from Eva and tucked it back into the holster as he turned entirely to face the White-Eyes.

“Get out of here,” he demanded as he tossed the key at David. “I’ll handle this and I’ll be right there.” David’s eyes widened as his jaw dropped in protest. The pair of whites drew closer, and as they did so its lupine form became all the more visible.

“Absolutely not,” he shot back, “I’m not leaving you to deal with that thing on your own—”

“You’re no good to me the way you are now,” Nico assured him with authority. His eyes locked with the White-Eyed Wolf as it prowled before him. It released a snarl, and with a tinge of uncertainty David and Eva made a break for the room around the corner. David looked down at the small envelope, and with the aid of the brightened screen of his phone he noted the number. He refocused his attention to the path and darted ahead of Eva as they came to the door of room 1432. He scrambled for the key as a bead of sweat dripped from his forehead. The beast howled, though whether from pain or hunger they couldn’t distinguish, and sparing no hesitation David inserted the key into the door. It opened.

“Nico!” David screamed his agent’s name through the hall as Eva moved past him and seated herself on the couch on the other side of the loft suite. Nico, who continued to battle against the enraged creature in front of the elevator, extended his hand as his hazel eyes adopted a luminous glow. Without warning the wolf took flight in the direction from whence it came, which left the Moderator free to calmly trace the path of his friend.

"You don't have to sound so worried," Nico told David as he approached the open door of the suite. He crossed the threshold and closed the door, and as David stepped back Eva returned to her feet.

"Good," David asserted, "so then you can tell me what the hell is going on!" Eva's eyes fell on him, the man who had seemed so certain downstairs and even calmer back at the restaurant.

"Please, calm down," Nico begged as he walked further into the room.

"Calm down? How do you suppose we do that, Nico? Since this morning I've been strangled by a shadow, stalked by a waitress, attacked by some zombie-looking *thing* and — what was that — a wolf?" He came face to face with his friend now, eyes alight with uncertainty and just a hint of anger as he surveyed his agent. "You're the only one who knows what's going on, so talk." Nico stared into his eyes for a moment as he rubbed his hand across his mouth.

"You're right," he sighed as he moved to the sofa. He wracked his brain for the starting point. "I haven't been honest with you about all this, and I'm sorry about that."

"Who are you, Nico," Eva asked with rattled voice as she folded her arms together. David looked at her in desperate need of the calming effect that her eyes provided him, but all he could see was a woman nearly in tears from the stress of all that had happened.

"Answer her," David spoke through a sigh of defeat as he turned his head back to the enigma that was his friend. Nico gave pause as he sought the words to speak, but ultimately resigned to the task with which he had been charged.

"In this timeframe, you know me as Nicholas Dominic Alaimo," Nico began to explain, and as he did David's head throbbed as the image of Raebon and Sorin in the palace flashed before his eyes, "but you know me by another name…"

"Sorin," David interjected with a confused hiss. He squinted from the splitting pain in his skull and took his seat in the little black chair across from the couch. "But… I thought that was just a dream." Nico shook his head.

"Not a dream," he told them both in that uncharacteristically serious tone. Eva's gaze swiftly fell upon him as her heart pummeled her chest. “They’re memories.” The pianist donned an immediate look of disbelief.

“Memories of what, exactly,” she prodded as she tilted her head slightly to the side. “And from whom?” Nico sighed as he leaned forward to look at them.

“Do the names Raebon and Miria mean anything to you,” he asked and watched as their eyes narrowed on him. “I thought as much. It was only a matter of time before you started to remember who you really were, though I gotta say it was a little unexpected how that happened.”

“What are you—” David started, but as the memory of the night before swam to the forefront of his mind he cut himself off.

“When you came into physical contact with one another for the first time, it triggered your memories as Raebon and Miria from your first life, and in David’s case, memories from your other lives as well,” Nico explained. “Within the last thousand years or so, you’ve been reincarnated hundreds of times, seen countless conflicts, and witnessed history being made. The colonization of Brazil, the American Revolution, the French Civil War, both World Wars, all the way down to Iraqi Freedom and that’s just the tip of the iceberg. You’ve spawned in dozens of places the globe over. Every time you two have come into contact with each other you would release your memories, and the Shade along with them."

"The Shade," Eva inquired with a slight tremble of voice. Nico looked to her and noted the confusion and fear that mingled in her expression. "I don't think I understand..."

"The Shade is exactly what it sounds like. It's a creature born of the darkness within a man's heart. Typically, they don't last very long, especially after the person of origin dies. This particular Shade, though, was born of something else... anyway, he'll continue to live as long as we do, or at least until the curse is finally broken," he elaborated. David shook with terror as he recalled the icy chill of its all but dead fingers wrapped around his throat.

"The curse," David questioned. "You mean that poem from the legend I read earlier?"

"It isn't just a legend, I—" Nico froze.

"Well, go on," Eva invited as she unfolded her arms and paced back and forth in the space between the living and dining areas of the suite. He cut his eyes at her.

"I can't really say that much, actually," he admitted with a flare of attitude in his tone.

“And why can’t you,” David wondered aloud. Nico stood now, and paced the floor with mild unease as he ran his fingers through his slick black hair.

“This curse,” he stated, “comes in the form of a sick and twisted game, and I’m stuck playing the part of the Moderator. Because of that, I’m limited in ways that I can help you.”

“So in other words, you’re useless to us,” Eva fired. Immediately he turned around and stormed towards her.

“Maybe you didn’t notice but I’m the only reason you’re even *alive* right now. If you care to dispute that then by all means, walk out of this room with no protection and see what happens!” Nico’s nostrils flared like that of an angry bull, and David grabbed his shoulder to pull him away from the emboldened Eva.

“Watch it, Nico,” he demanded as his best friend slapped his hand away.

“Look,” Nico responded in a calmer tone of voice, “those things out there with the white eyes are not here to make friends. They’re pawns of the Shade, and they will kill you without hesitation if given the chance. My job is to make sure that order is maintained, so you’d be right to assume that I won’t be able to save you anymore. Your memories are coming back, slowly but surely, which means that this is a battle between you and the Shade alone." Eva and David exchanged looks as fear instantly took hold of them.

"So what then? We're just supposed to fend for ourselves? Fight and die in a conflict we know next to nothing about," Eva challenged with a scowl.

"No," Nico responded coolly as his eyes drifted to his client. "You're supposed to write."

Chapter Ten

David's nervous laugh filled the suite as he gripped his sides, but Nico only glared at him. Eva looked down at her clenched fist and wondered about the small golden quill that rested in her palm.

"I'm sorry," he started as his hysterics subsided. "I thought you were gonna say something that made a little more sense than we need to write." Nico shook his head.

"There's no 'we' involved in this. *You* need to write," he corrected. David became completely sober now as he sat forward in his chair.

"Come again," he begged as his brow furrowed and his tone became slightly more agitated than before. Nico shrugged with an audible sigh as he leaned on the arm of the couch and pulled out his phone. He pressed the lock button and restrained his tears as his eyes met the image of his beloved Sierra. Nico looked up, and with renewed ferocity glared at his best friend.

"Last I checked it was your job, right? I don't see why you'd have a problem doing what you've always done at this stage in the game," Nico stated flatly. David stood now, fists balled at either side and body atremble with frustration.

“It just doesn’t seem practical,” Eva interrupted before the author could speak, “to have him sit at a computer and write right now.”

“It’s not impractical at all, Eva. If anything, he has all the incentive needed to put pen to paper and produce. What’s more endearing for an author than adversity and adventure?” Nico responded.

“But what would writing even do to keep us safe from the Shade,” David inquired as he ran his fingers through his curly black hair. Eva’s amber eyes trained on the young man, completely unaware of the power of Nico’s poetry from before.

“I have a few ideas,” she uttered with uncertainty. Nico’s eyebrows raised as he fixed his attention upon her.

“Do you now,” Nico asked, and reluctantly the angered David turned his head.

“You mentioned something about ‘Paradox’s Might’ when you were trying to pull David into the elevator. I couldn’t see what happened, but that sting that came off of whatever that was that you spoke to disappeared almost instantly. Judging by what you’re telling us, David’s writing may be related to this Paradox thing and if I’m right, that may be the key to defeating this Shade character who’s trying to kill us,” she deduced. Nico smiled as he stood and walked past David to the refrigerator behind the bar.

"You're not far off," he began in a much lighter tone now, "but David's writing *is* a type of Paradox."

"How do you figure," David asked as Nico, who now had a bottle of water in his hand, turned around. He cracked it open and took a sip, and relished in the soothing sensation of cold as it slipped down his throat.

"Well, how do you feel when you write," asked the agent. The author, caught off guard by the question, staggered in his speech as his mind contemplated the answer.

"Writing," David began thoughtfully as his eyes shifted to the black and white Persian carpet that rested beneath their feet, "is everything and nothing at the same time. What I write is fictional, yeah, with only minimal research into the world around me but the thoughts of my characters, their emotions, their every hardship, it's all real, because whether we live their reality or not, those characters are us. Each one of them has enough reality to break free from fiction, to touch the lives of the reader and pull them into that world of fantasy, to teach us and transform us into mirrors of themselves but in an alternate reality than the one they've experienced. And what I feel when I write, that's adventure, because even though on the outside it seems like I'm sitting in one spot and staring at a screen I'm exploring every crack and crevasse of this new plane of existence as it unfolds before my eyes." Eva watched him carefully as he spoke, saw how his now piercing white eyes came alive with familiar intensity, how he struggled to restrain the smile that crept across his lips, how his hands shook and fingers twitched at the mere idea of it, and the more she saw of him, the more she heard that soothing whisper that he sported, the more she got lost in the passion of his words.

"You see it, don't you," Nico asked with an eyebrow raised. David looked up, his face just as pensive as before. "When you write, it's real despite being fiction, true and false, fact and fantasy and that, David, is a paradox." David groaned and rolled his eyes before he lazily fell back into his seat. Eva's brow furrowed as she paced by.

"It's a contradiction, or at least it appears to be a contradiction at first glance," Eva chimed in in thoughtful tone, "but when you explore it, it happens to make total sense. But what does a definition have to do with anything?"

"I'm glad you asked," Nico said as he gestured to Eva. "The world is thought of by most people in terms of absolutes and congruencies, but it's so much wider than that. The Paradoxes are the evidence of this, as each one creates an infinite array of enigmas that contradict common perception. Storytelling, poetry, music, painting, sculpting, dancing, acting, all of these serve as a Paradox in and of itself, because each can complement and contradict what we know to be real."

"Spoken like a true philosopher," David joked, and as his lips curled to smile a sharp pain shot through his skull. *So*... he heard the voice of the prince, *you are a philosopher*...

"What are you seeing," Nico asked as David moved to place his hand upon his temple. David shook his head with a pained expression in place, and Eva, who clenched the quill in her hand to the point of pain, gradually grew in discomfort.

"I'm not seeing anything," the author spoke through clenched teeth. "I'm hearing my own voice, it's just... it hurts for some reason." Nico gave a barely audible hum as his eyes narrowed.

"That's to be expected," said the agent. "As your memories return to you, your soul will begin to stitch itself back together."

"How do I stop it," David asked, but Nico chuckled at the futility of the question.

"Unfortunately for you, you don't. And you shouldn't want to. Your combat skills, how to properly use your Paradox, even your love for one another is embedded in the memory you've lost over a millennium, and in order to break the curse and defeat the Shade you'll have to expedite the process you're so quick to try to avoid."

"And what if we don't want to?" Eva spoke up now in vocal discomfort. "I mean, my life was just fine before all this weirdness started happening, and the Shade is only trying to kill us because it thinks that we're trying to—"

"The Shade is trying to kill you on principle. There isn't any reason as to why it should spare you now when you've complicated things for it in the past. Whatever plans it had before have faded into the shadow of its ambition to kill the two of you," Nico told her. Eva huffed in agitation as she turned away from the others and paced the room again. Her nerves took hold, and David could understand that, empathize with it, but for a second it sounded as if she wished they'd never met. The pain in his head steadily diminished, and with downcast eyes he looked at her as the pain in his heart rapidly grew.

"So then what do I have to write?" David asked in his best attempt to mask the sudden anguish that pressed to control him.

She turned around to look at him, and immediately his eyes met the floor as a bead of sweat trickled down the side of his face. It had been made apparent to him just how little he wished for adventure, how full and joyous his life seemed to be even in the face of ravenous monsters that sought his end, and he knew, though at this point he would never admit it, that it was *her* that made him feel so complete. Nico took note of his expression, one that radiated concern and announced the planting of the seeds of reborn love, and the agent smiled.

"Sadly it's not that simple. Your Paradox has to be unlocked first in order for you to regain the memories that you once had," he informed. He stood up and approached Eva, who watched with caution as he drew nearer. "If you don't mind," he said with outstretched hand. She looked down at it, and though she knew he desired the quill, she wondered whether or not she should hand it over to him. Reluctantly she dropped it in his palm, and with a wink and a smile he returned to the side of his best friend. "Under normal circumstances, it would take months, possibly even years to reeducate you on how to use your Paradox, but from the looks of things you have a couple of days at best. The Shade already has eyes on you, which means without your abilities in place you'll probably be killed."

“You don’t have to say that so casually, you know,” Eva chimed in. Nico couldn’t help but smile, but quickly returned to severity at the realization that the cycle was broken.

“That wouldn’t be a problem, though, would it,” David inquired, and Eva gave him an icy glare. “I mean, if we die then we’ll just be reborn in some other time, right?” Nico sighed as he pinched the bridge of his nose.

“Typically that would be the case,” he started as he refocused on the pair before him, “but when you read the curse aloud in your old room, you ended the reincarnation cycle.”

“So in other words if we die, we stay dead now,” David whispered. “Great.” Eva’s eyes went wide as she tapped her foot anxiously against the hardwood floor of the dining area.

“But you won’t die. Not with this,” Nico assured the two of them as he handed the small golden quill to David. The author looked down at it, puzzled but intrigued.

“What exactly is it,” he asked as his eyes met Nico’s.

“That, my friend is the key to your Paradox. As soon as you write your former names with that quill, you both will relive the memories from your time in Alaedrea,” Nico informed them, and did his best to maintain his cool as the guilt with which he’d battled for years crept back to the surface of his psyche.

“What do you mean by ‘relive,’” Eva questioned with eyebrow raised and arms folded as she approached him. He analyzed her face, and as the image of his pregnant wife resurfaced before his eyes, Nico could only feel the utmost anguish at her skeptical expression. *How much more severe will it get,* he pondered, *when you finally learn the truth?* “Will we start having more of the dreams from before or are we time-traveling or what?” Eva’s voice was all business, which worried the agent deeply. Whereas David was trusting of his best friend, even in the wake of secrets exposed, the witty pianist knew in the very pit of her soul that something was wrong, and as her finger tapped against her elbow she resolved to discover what.

“You won’t be doing either. The moment that quill writes your names down, you’ll both be rendered unconscious. You’ll see, feel and experience everything that happened to you in the life you used to have. Meanwhile, your bodies with the exception of David’s hands will be completely immobilized. Now, I’ve gotta warn you that doing this will most likely alert the Shade to our location if his little friends haven’t already. That said, we should probably go someplace that’s a little less… conspicuous,” Nico suggested.

"Hold on," Eva demanded as her hands dropped. "If the Shade has eyes on us, then what good would it do to leave this room to find a different hiding spot? Wait, wait, better question: How are we going to survive if the Shade finds us?"

"It won't kill us until we remember who we are," David replied before Nico had the chance. "Or at least, that's what it told me when it had its hand wrapped around my throat."

"Yeah," Nico responded, "but you have to take into consideration the beasts that showed up at your front door this time. The Shade isn't afraid to play dirty." He knew that all too well, and as he reflected on the pitch-black sword that previously rested against the neck of his beloved, Nico failed to suppress his enraged tears. "Now, wait here. I have some extra clothes in my bag downstairs. Once I bring them to you, put them on and we'll relocate, understand?"

"Yeah," David and Eva responded simultaneously.

"Good," Nico confirmed, and without another word he moved for the door. "Keep this door locked until I'm back. No doubt that there'll be some White-Eyes prowling about and as it stands right now, you're not equipped to deal with that sort of thing."

“Got it,” Eva agreed right away. With a shaky smile, Nico passed through the door as though it wasn’t even there and the room momentarily grew still. Eva paused for a second longer and turned to David, who sank back into the chair in the suite’s living area. “Do you have paper?” He tilted his head in confusion.

“Yeah,” David confirmed as he left his seat and marched across the room, to the bags the staff had failed to stow in the closet. He rifled through his suitcase and found a small, black, leather-bound notebook that he kept close in the event that inspiration struck. “Why do you ask?”

“Start writing,” she demanded in utmost severity.

“I don’t think that’s such a good idea. I mean you heard Nico. The minute I start we’re stuck in here, unable to move and totally defenseless against the things that might try to break down that door,” he conveyed. She knew that he spoke nothing but reason, and given the circumstances she shouldn’t be so hasty to subject herself to a lack of motion, but something wasn’t right about Nico’s information, or rather the lack thereof. However, if what he said was even remotely credible then it was her prerogative to find out for herself and judge him accurately.

“You’re probably right,” Eva said, “but the sooner we find out what’s going on, the better. There’s something I don’t trust about Nico. Maybe you can't see it because you've been friends for so long, but—"

"I do," David interjected with a dose of seriousness in his tone that all but paralyzed her, "but if what he says *is* true, even slightly, then we can't take the chance of falling into the hands of a supernatural enemy like the Shade. One thing I can verify is that that *thing* is out there, and there's no doubt in my mind that it wants us dead. Believe me, Eva, it's nothing to take lightly and we shouldn't do anything reckless right now. Once we've relocated, we'll—"

"Be at the mercy of a total wildcard," Eva pressed. She drew closer to him, and David's heart practically stopped and restarted as she placed her hand gently against his shoulder. "We need to find out what's going on, David."

"You're right," he conceded, "and I get that. But at the same time, it seems as though the risks involved in gaining that knowledge outweigh the benefits." She looked at him earnestly, and under the power of those amber orbs he felt all power drain from him at once.

"David," she whispered, "please." He wrestled with himself for a moment and contemplated the frustration his actions — no — their actions would cause Nico, but ultimately he returned to the chair with notebook and quill in hand. Eva rested on the couch across from him and observed the seriousness of his face as his hands trembled. He stared at the page, and against his will his grip tightened on the utensil between his fingers.

He pressed it against the page, and as his wrist flicked the pen, which despite being clean wrote, he could feel an unfamiliar power surge within him. It was neither chilled nor burning, neither soothing nor stinging, but rather ineffable altogether. It pulsed within him, and before long created in the very depths of the man a longing for its swell.

Eva watched as his eyes flickered between the deep pools of chocolate that made her weak, and the lustrous white that suddenly discomforted her. The first name appeared on the page: Raebon, and at its completion she, too, felt the overwhelming euphoria brought on by the mysterious burst of power. She lay there upon the couch as her body twitched with delight, and it took every sensible bone in her body to repress squeals of delight that longed for escape. Neither author nor musician had ever felt such strength pass through them, and as David's quill slowly danced across the page in revelation of the second name, that strength grew. Sweat beaded down the faces of the two, smiles crossed their lips, bodies atremble with the excitement of what was to come, and Eva's stunning ambers transformed into the bright yellows of the past. As her eyes solidified in color, so did David's, and then it was done. Miria's name appeared upon the page, and as a wave of otherworldly energy overtook their senses the city itself began to rattle.

They rested where they were, unfazed by the commotion of the quake, and as their consciousness began to fade and their eyes started to close, David's hands moved across the paper in unimaginable speed as he penned the story of the life that started it all.

They plunged into the past as their bodies remained in the present, and as they spiraled downward through a plane of utter darkness, they saw in the distance below them the faintest glimmer of white light. Their speed increased, and as it did the light grew larger, brighter. They closed their eyes as they continued their descent until suddenly all movement ceased.

Crickets chirped in the distance, and the cool gentle breeze brushed against the blades of grass that skimmed the surface of David's exposed skin. The air smelled of an odd mix of livestock and freshly baked bread, and the clamor of a nearby village filled his ears. He jolted awake, and after brief surveillance found himself on the hill where he'd previously met Miria, and with a sinking feeling in his heart noticed her poignant absence. He stood now, and as he momentarily took in the dark and star-scattered sky, he made his way towards the sounds of life. In the distance he could see the tall golden spires of the palace, and immediately recognized it as his home. He walked through the rather lively village and eyed the massive stone wall that surrounded the capital.

So it worked, David thought as he looked through the eyes of Prince Raebon, *I'm in Alaedrea... but where's Eva?* As the thought crossed his mind he felt the head of a child collide with his knee. The restored prince quickly bent down and gripped the shoulders of the little one, who staggered a bit and nearly fell. The boy was rather thin, and the brown leather tunic that draped over his baggy white shirt proved to be a bit too big. His trousers fit him well, though he twitched about from discomfort. Raebon studied his face, and noted the same golden eyes as the woman he sought. He was taken aback, but despite this he offered a thoughtful look to the boy, no older than five, who did his best to avoid eye contact.

"Are you alright, little one?" came the voice of the prince. He smiled at the boy, who now slowly lifted his head in fear and nodded. Raebon placed a hand upon the boy's head and tussled his hair. "Excellent. You have a surprising amount of strength for one so small. Have you ever considered becoming a warrior in the Alaedrean Army? A knight, perhaps?" The boy's eyes grew bright with excitement as he shook with vigor before the prince. Raebon's grin grew all the wider, but before he could speak again, he heard footsteps approach him through the elevated noise of the lively village. His head lifted from the boy, and there, only mere feet away, stood the breathtaking Miria.

Chapter Eleven

He stood paralyzed under her gaze, and watched her as she drifted as if on air in his direction. She wore a brown dress that complemented her every curve, and a line of beads woven into a lock of her flowing brown hair. Her skin, sun-kissed as it was in the present, gave off a warmth that contrasted her expression sharply. Nevertheless, Miria looked well since the last he saw her, though admittedly the image of her tears in the streets lay overshadowed by that of her near inhuman assault.

"So, you recruit them this young, do you," came the woman's sarcastic tone as she stooped down to pull her little brother closer. The David in him was disappointed. She was still apprehensive of him, and he was certain that the faux promise of knighthood did little to appeal to her better temperaments. "You have to be more careful, Orasus. It isn't nice to run into people. Especially not the prince." Orasus smiled as he kissed his sister's cheek. "Come, we'll make our way back home. It's almost time for bed."

"But I don't want to go to bed," whined the boy as his face shifted to a mildly rebellious pout, and Raebon stood with a smile on his face. "I want to be a knight like the prince said!"

Miria glared at him, and despite his position he felt unusually intimidated. He knelt before the boy again and took him by the shoulders.

"You know," he began with a lighthearted smirk, "if you really wish to become a knight one day, then you will need all the sleep that you can get. It helps you to grow big and strong, and that is what we look for in our future warriors." Miria visibly resisted the urge to smirk at him as she laid her hand on Orasus' shoulder. The boy looked at her with hesitation and groaned.

"Fine," he exhaled as he rubbed his eyes, "take me home." Miria's stony face cracked a smile as she playfully scooped the boy into her arms.

"Then let's be off," she told him, and pecked him on the cheek. Raebon could hardly believe his eyes, as the woman who once sought his death exhibited naught but loving tenderness in his sights. Her laxity and otherwise playful disposition were completely alien to him at this point, despite the fact that he knew the tender creature that was Eva within her. But he ultimately had to accept the fact that she was not Eva, nor he David, but much more amplified versions of the selves that they'd grown to know. He gave pause, and considered this a valuable opportunity to truly learn her as well as himself. “Are you coming?”

“What,” he muttered in confusion, and as he resurfaced from the pool of his contemplation he noticed that she’d carried the boy a few yards ahead.

“Well do you expect to simply watch as a young lady and a child traverse Coraena with no more light than the moon and stars allow,” she called back to him as her pace slowed and she rocked her little brother in her arms. “What sort of man would even think to allow such a thing?”

“I am a *prince*, you know,” he chuckled as he advanced after her, to which the corner of her mouth lifted in amusement.

“Oh, trust me, I am aware,” she responded. “I hesitate to think that you’ve forgotten that I recently tried to kill you because of that very fact.”

“How could I forget? The speed, ferocity and fluidity of your movements made you quite an adversary. Fiercer than any I’ve faced in battle, actually,” he complimented. She looked down at Orasus, whose eyes slowly drifted shut, and brushed her hand against his silky dark brown hair. “Where did you learn to fight like that?” Miria’s eyes fixed on the path and narrowed.

“There is much to learn from life on the cobbled streets of Coraena. The capital city of Alaedrea is dangerous for anyone not fortunate enough for the higher class, and death is almost a certainty,” she explained solemnly, and the gravity of her voice made the hairs on his neck stand on end. He was horrified, utterly disgusted by the events that led her to that point, and though he’d already done something about it he wished that he could do even more.

“And yet here you are,” Raebon responded contemplatively. Miria, who now stared at the boy in her arms, continued to play in his hair as he nestled into his beloved sister.

“Because of *him*,” she informed him with a downward nod as they turned down a narrow road that led to the house of the merchant in whose care they’d been placed. It was rather large and made almost entirely of stone. Its size mirrored that of a small castle, and even served to impress the prince. Raebon’s eyes fell upon his new little friend, though, and as the child slept sweetly he felt affection grow as Miria continued. “I had to survive, Prince, because if I failed to do so my precious little brother would have been left on the streets to die.” She came to a halt in the middle of the path and clutched the sleeping Orasus tightly to her chest. She trembled a bit, and when he noticed her sudden lack of movement Raebon turned to face her.

"Is there something wrong," he inquired of her with softest worry in his tone that contrasted the fierceness of his burnished white eyes.

"Nothing," she assured him as she continued toward him. "I merely wished to thank you for ensuring that what remains of my family is cared for. I am in your debt, Prince Raebon." Neither her face nor tone matched the gratitude she expressed. She remained steeled to the bone, but now that he knew that there was something under that hardened exterior he longed to explore her. A smile slithered onto his face as he crossed his arms behind his back and walked alongside her toward their new home.

"Very well," he started after a moment's reflection. "Then I will collect on the debt you say you owe." Miria raised an eyebrow to her companion as they moved, and noted the smirk he sported and pitifully tried to mask.

"How do you intend," she questioned cautiously as they gradually approached the door.

"Simple," he started. "I would like to come here on occasion to spend time with Orasus." She pulled to a stop again, and had it not been in her nature to cling to him then surely she would have dropped the boy out of shock.

"I…" Miria paused both physically and verbally, as she was momentarily unable to form a decisive response. "Forgive me, I thought I heard you say that you would like to spend time with my little brother…"

"I did," he assured her with a casual smile. She carefully studied his eyes and saw no malice or deceit, but nevertheless she was reluctant to grant him, then still a stranger to her, time with her little one.

"I suppose that it would be alright, provided this time is spent under my supervision," she affirmed, to which he chuckled.

"Of course," conceded the prince. "If you would allow, I would like to come and see him in the morning. Aeridus, advisor to the King, is said to have something of a revolutionary discovery that he would like to share with the royal family and citizens of Coraena. I can think of nothing better for a future knight to do than to attend a royal address from the standpoint of nobility."

"As generous an offer as that is, I have to decline," she said flatly as they came to the door of the estate. Raebon gave her a puzzled look, and for a moment lost himself in the amber orbs that even the David within him fell prey to. "I work in the tavern near the palace until this time every night, and as per our agreement you are not permitted time with Orasus without my being there."

"I have not forgotten the conditions of our agreement, though I fail to see how your work schedule would pose a problem," answered the son of the king, and for a moment Miria's expression twisted as she contemplated what it was that he meant. "You forget that I am a prince. Every soul from within the walls of Coraena to the outer borders of Alaedrea adheres to my command with the exception of the King himself. You may find over the course of time that there is very little that I cannot work in your favor, Miria." She flashed a confident grin as he opened the door for her.

"Well then, it would appear that we will be in attendance," she stated as she coolly masked her excitement. "I trust you will not be late."

"I would never…" Raebon's voice trailed off as Miria carried the boy inside and stared intensely into the prince's eyes. She closed the door, and for a moment he stood without the estate in awe of her. He turned back to the path, and with one final glance at the merchant's domicile he made his way towards the palace.

He calmly walked the streets of Coraena the capital and relished in the gentle breeze that again brushed against his skin. He shivered, though the reason proved to be a mystery, and with each step he realized more and more that there was something about this Miria that pulled him back to her. It was as if the hands of Fate pushed them together, as if they were but characters in a story of cosmic imagination. And what would it be, this tale that unraveled before their very eyes? Would it be one of love? Of war? Though the premise was apparent, Raebon and the David inside of him were left to ponder over the contents. What events led to the curse? And for that matter, who was responsible?

The people who passed him by smiled and bowed their heads to him, and child and parent alike rushed to meet him. Some even hugged him, and as he willingly accepted their every embrace he was relieved to find that he was a benevolent prince rather than some entitled brat that required protection. But then, who besides Miria would dare stand against him in battle in this kingdom? He desperately searched his memories for any sort of revelation, an answer so long overdue to the question of who gave rise to the affliction of the prince and his love, but the stinging sensation in his skull forced him to the nearest wall. He lingered there, one hand pressed against the stone façade and the other against his temple, and though he sought some semblance of recollection it all proved hazy.

“Is something wrong, my prince?” Raebon turned around, and through blurred vision saw the familiar face of Sorin at a few feet’s distance. “Shall I take you to the royal physicians?” Raebon cringed at the sight of him, shuddered at the anger he felt for secrets kept for apparent eons, but waved him off with a friendly expression nonetheless.

“No,” said the prince as he found stability in his previously shaky legs. “We will return to the palace courtyard. Our lesson will continue as planned.”

“Understood,” Sorin replied as the pair continued through Coraena. The prince took the lead, and the philosopher followed closely at his left as they marched onward to the distant palace gates.

“Will my father and General Eulic be joining us?” Raebon’s eyes narrowed on the path, and as his pace quickened his companion struggled to keep up. It took him a moment, but when Sorin realized what the prince was doing, he exhibited a smirk as he came to a light jog.

"Your father the king is meeting with the High Counselor Aeridus regarding the address tomorrow. The general should be in attendance, however, though I would prefer it if he found some alternative means of temporal occupation…" he was audibly agitated, and in a burst of mild anger pushed past his prince as he took to a nearby wall and landed atop it in a single bound.

"From your tone I would assume that the two of you still have difficulty getting along," Raebon projected as he shot past his friend and ran up the side of the wall. He darted ahead, and as he caught a glimpse of Sorin with the turn of his head, he kicked off from the brick partition and onto the roof of a nearby house. "Nevertheless, it is his brutish nature that made me pair you with him. I cannot very well have the general of my armies show such hostility to the people he is charged to protect." The palace drew ever nearer, and in a matter of moments the two of them would land before its gate and make their way to the inner courtyard. Sorin bit his lower lip.

"While I greatly appreciate your kindness to me, my prince," he called as he dismounted the wall and sprinted for the slowly opening palace gate, "my service to that man proves to be more of a punishment. Is it not enough that I provide my philosophical instruction to King Aradmus and his son? Must I continue to fester in the pool of torment in which he has me submerged?" Raebon kicked off hard from a rooftop and launched himself a few feet ahead of his philosophical friend. Sorin was caught off guard, but nevertheless he sped after the prince.

"Your service to the general is meant to soften his heart, not to harden yours," Raebon said as the two of them slowed to a stop before the gate. "Strive to know him as I have, Sorin, and show him who you are. Bridging the gap between the nobles, the officials and the commoners is the only way to ensure Alaedrea's inner peace for ages yet to come. Father says that Eulic may pose a threat to that ideal, and that it would be wise to snuff out whatever embers that might burn within him in an inconspicuous manner. It seems that as he fights on the front lines for our country, his memory grows hazy in regards to what it is to be a citizen." The two of them advanced, and Raebon casually greeted the guards with a smile on his face. Sorin stood in admiration of his prince, whose heart was, almost frighteningly so, on display for the entire kingdom to see.

“You seem to care a great deal for this man, Prince Raebon,” Sorin spoke after a moment of silence as they continued toward the courtyard. Raebon looked at his friend and almost laughed.

“You may call me by my name if you so wish.” Sorin’s eyes widened as they rapidly fixed upon the prince, whose warrior’s glare rested on the path. “You are my friend, after all. Let us not stand so much on formality that we fail to see each other for what we are. I am a man, as are you, neither of us greater than the other.”

“You are…” Sorin struggled to find the word, and as he cupped his hand under his chin to ponder, the prince spoke.

“Unconventional in many regards,” he answered. “The Kingdom of Alaedrea has structure, yes, a hierarchy that is observed rather closely by her citizens, nobles and officials, however it has always been customary for the royal family to regard all who dwell within the Alaedrean domain as citizens. No frigid caste system serves to divide us by the classes that have existed in our society since the Romans once occupied this land. We do not see ourselves as any better or worse off than any other, nor do we see those of arguably lower status as possessions as some monarchs do. We are all family, and family exists to serve and care for one another if only in the most basic sense. While we, the royals, head the nation and manage the difficulties that arise beyond the view of the general public, it is for the individuals that constitute that public that we do what we do." Sorin silently refocused on their surroundings as Raebon's words seeped into his mind, but to his greatest displeasure Eulic sat cross-legged in the center of the courtyard. The general's eyes fixed on the philosopher with intensity that rattled the man's soul, but a sharp glare from the Prince served to stay Eulic's obviously impending offense.

"So," spoke the brutish soldier, "you have arrived. I was beginning to wonder if you would not show, and whether or not I would be forced to practice my Paradox by my lonesome."

"Perish the thought," Raebon said coolly as he stopped and sat with his back to a nearby bed of purple orchids. "I merely took it upon myself to check on the woman Miria." Eulic grunted.

"If I may be so bold, sir," he began in a low but thunderous growl, "perhaps it is not too wise to engage with a woman who once had mind to kill you." Sorin rubbed his black goatee as he considered his prince.

“I would agree with the general, Raebon,” Sorin spoke. Before any clarity was given, Eulic launched himself upward from the ground and in seconds wrapped his hands around Sorin’s throat. Eulic’s sea-green eyes lit in much the same way that Nico’s did when he fought the White-Eyes, and with a surge of power he thrust the philosopher into the ground. He held his prey still by his throat, and watched with delight as the thin man squirmed.

“Eulic,” shouted the prince, whose white eyes glimmered along with the luster of the moonlight overhead. The general, snapped back to his senses, instantly released his victim and knelt before his master. “Please, your hostility is unappreciated in such a tranquil setting. It was my choice to allow him the luxury of informality with my name. Do respect it, would you?”

“Yes, my lord,” spake the seasoned combatant as Sorin sat up and gingerly rubbed the back of his head.

“In any case, with whom I choose to spend my time is none of your business. I merely wish to see the girl and her younger brother well taken care of. Now, unless I am mistaken we are here to explore the world of Paradoxes, yes?” Raebon looked to Sorin, who nodded and took a deep breath.

"Right, well it would seem that you both have gained a substantial understanding of the foundations of the Paradox. Now, the both of you will choose one of these," Sorin told the two of them as he waved his hand over the ground between them. His hazel orbs shimmered in the moonlight, and as the air before him crystalized, a series of objects manifested in the space between the three. Raebon and Eulic leaned in to peer upon the list of items. "Before you rest the Seven Keys of Paradox: The Melody," he said as he gestured to the golden lute at the front of the line, "maker of music. It creates depictions of what it is the wielder feels and enables them to manipulate the hearts of all that hear their playing. And then you have The Play." His hand hovered over a silver mask with cerulean designs along the forehead and cheek. Its lips curled upward and smiled to one side but downward in a frown at the other. "This gives the wearer the ability to adopt any form their minds are capable of conceiving, and grant them any ability along with them. Next," his hand drifted further down the line and lingered over the next object, a ball of clay with hypnotic swirls of both gold and silver on its otherwise ivory surface, "you have the Earth. From it you can create a series of beasts to walk the grounds of mortal men, each one unique to their master's design. Following that, there is the

Sight," Sorin continued as the prince and his general gazed upon the articles of wonder, fully captivated by their luminescent glow. The philosopher smiled as his hand stopped just above an ivory paintbrush with pitch-black bristles. "With this, the user paints an ever-adapting portrait of the subject's soul."

"What do you mean," asked General Eulic, who glared defensively at the brush. Sorin's smile lessened as he pondered the best explanation.

"The image of the person in the portrait will change depending on their moral alignment. That would be the easiest way to explain it. For instance, if a person were to kill their beloved friend or lover, perhaps a parent or sibling after the Sight has captured their image on the canvass, that reflection of their soul would grow gradually more twisted. Conversely, if they were to act in strictest kindness and compassion, then the painting would emanate an almost saintly luster," the philosopher clarified, but then his expression grew severe almost instantly. "In either case, the subject of the painting would die should anything happen to the painting." Raebon glared at the brush now, reluctant to even have such a dangerous tool in the kingdom at all. "Now then," Sorin picked back up as he hovered his hand over a pair of onyx turnshoes that glowed in the light of the moon and stars, "here is the Motion. These shoes give the wearer the ability to place any and all who witness their dance under a petrifying spell that can only be broken at the whim—or the death—of the user." Raebon and Eulic sat in awe of the tremendous powers granted by the Seven Keys of Paradox, and both shook with the fear of having to choose one of their own. "The last two Keys are by far the most powerful… and the most dangerous. The Poem," he said as he gestured to a small leather-bound notebook, outwardly crimson but inwardly fawn, "which bestows upon the wielder knowledge of the things most cherished in the hearts of those around him and modifies the world in which he lives. The final Key, that dwarfs the powers of the others, is the Tale."

"What makes the Tale so much stronger than the others you have shown us, Sorin," asked the prince, who now struggled against the frosty winds that billowed through his soul as he gazed upon the final object, a miniature golden quill, the likes of which he'd never seen before that point. Sorin met his gaze, and the sheer intensity reminded him of the increasingly grave Nico, who patiently awaited his return to the present.

"The Tale is derived from Word itself, that which creates and destroys entire worlds, that establishes the foundations of a myriad of universes and directs the paths of so many lives. Now comes the time where you must choose. But know this: the Key that calls for you is the one to which you are best suited. It would behoove you to heed that call." Sorin extended his hand over the Poem, and instantly it levitated into his grasp. "Now, then, General…" General Eulic slowly stretched his hand out and paused as the Tale caught his eye. He slowly lowered it upon the quill, but before his fingers could even brush against its length a shockwave blustered through his entire body that compelled him towards the Earth. Eulic took the sphere of clay into his hands, and with a smile on his face the sea-green hue of his irises flashed like the light of day.

"The Earth," whispered Prince Raebon, and instantly Sorin the Poet locked eyes with him once more.

"It is your turn, my lord," charged the philosopher. Raebon, too, outstretched his hand, and with conflicted heart considered which of the Keys would tempt him the least. The gentle breeze that stalked them through the night grew savage instantly, and as the dark clouds in the heavens above blotted out the light of the moon the Tale lifted itself off the ground and into his hands. A staggering bullet of air dropped between the three that sent all but Raebon into flight. Power surged through him, and lightning flashed in the darkened clouds overhead as the general and philosopher landed harshly at opposite ends of the courtyard. A now aching Sorin turned his gaze on his friend and Eulic followed suit as they moved to sit up. Whereas the Poet saw wonder at the brilliantly chalky aura, the General was visibly disgusted that it was the prince that the Tale had chosen, and tightened his fist as he picked up his clay.

Chapter Twelve

Miria sat on the floor beside her little brother's bed, and gently ran her fingers through Orasus' hair. The dim light of a single candle flickered as a strong gust of air shot through the open window, and though it drew her attention for but a moment, her attention returned to the young boy that she loved with all her heart. He would want her to rest, and would tell her that night time is for sleeping like she used to tell him when he was even smaller. *But how could I sleep,* she asked herself as she reflected on the prince that she so desperately wished she could despise. Her face wrinkled into a scowl at the complexity of the situation. She hated everything about his father the king, how the royal family prioritized themselves over the people, and how they made speech after speech about how it was the public's wellbeing that took center stage.

She never did trust the political type, not since she was a little girl, and the royal family's selfishness and hypocrisy were so rampant that it only served to prove her right. *But then...* the image of Raebon with his arms wrapped around her crashed against the forefront of her mind, and though the air within the room chilled she instantly filled with warmth. She shook her head. *No, absolutely not. I will not be swayed to the side of the prince so easily,* she told herself. Miria hated the way he made her feel, as though she had been part of the family all along despite the cold glare of the king from so long ago that provided a daily reminder that she never would be. It was almost as if he was innocent, totally unaware of the political moves of his father that would ultimately leave the people, the commoners of the kingdom like herself and her little brother Orasus, stagnated in their misfortune. It was because of that feeling of innocence, that image of clean hands in a kingdom riddled with the filth of the king and his people, that Miria found it so easy to get lost in the delusion that they could be something… more.

She kissed her baby brother's forehead. It was dangerous for her to think such things while she tended to the young Orasus. He was her world, and she had to do whatever she could to protect him. There was no point in even considering the prince's rather obvious advances. Why would she jeopardize the safety of her little prince for a prince she knew not to trust? One so dedicated to his country that he rarely graced the city he called home? Had she desired a warrior as companion, she would have likely already responded to the feelings of General Eulic that, despite her previous assault on the son of Aradmus only seemed to intensify.

Miria smirked at the desperation of the General, and considered that such a frequent visitor of the tavern would only amount to be a poor choice. And what of this arrangement with Raebon? She rose from the bedside and moved to the door. With one final glance at the sweetly sleeping child, she took her leave and headed down the hall towards her own bedroom. *What will tomorrow bring,* she questioned as she gracefully strode along the hardwood path and entered her chambers. She gave the prince credit. He expertly capitalized on the desires of her little brother to stand on the side of a noble at a royal address and by doing so attain a taste of the knighthood he aspired to reach. Of course, she knew this was all just an elaborate excuse to see her again.

She closed her door, and sat on the edge of her rather meager bed as she looked up at the dark stone ceiling. Her heart was aflutter with an odd mix of uneasiness and excitement, despite the fact that she so easily saw through him. She fell backwards on the mattress, wildly uncomfortable with the idea of spending a day in the world of the class of people she detested most, but simultaneously comforted by the prospect of the prince's presence.

She ran her fingers through her dark brown hair in frustration. *Ugh, what is it about you, Raebon, that I simply cannot ignore?*

I will never allow for your suffering again… she heard him whisper gently, as though he were nearby. Her skin tingled from his touch despite his absence. She turned over in bed and stared through the window at the full moon that slowly emerged from the dark clouds of the night sky. She wondered if it was true what he said. No, she knew it to be true as she reflected on the sincerity that melted her hardened heart. There was no falsehood in him, at least not with her.

Her eyes slowly closed as she fell under the spell of the moon. A peace emerged in the midst of her turmoil that she knew to be Eva's assurance of him, of David, and with a slight smirk she fell asleep.

"So, you ended up here too," came David's voice from behind her. Eva opened her eyes and took in the black of their surroundings. She turned around, and there before her was the present-day form of the prince, garbed in black slacks, a plain white tee and a dark blue blazer. He looked rather dashing with that grin on his face, and captivated her with his strong brown eyes.

"Where exactly is 'here,'" she asked as they moved towards each other.

"I'm not exactly sure," he admitted, "but I'm actually really glad to see you. You know, assuming you're not some incredibly gorgeous figment of my imagination." She rolled her eyes as they drew near each other and stopped only a foot away.

"Trust me," she told him as she reached out a hand. "I'm real." The author reciprocated the gesture, but the progress of their contact was halted by a wall imperceptible and as cold and solid as steel. "What's happening," Eva asked, startled and somewhat dismayed that she couldn't experience the warmth of his touch as Miria had Raebon.

"I'm not entirely sure," he told her with furrowed brow. "But I gotta say, it does dampen the mood just a little bit." Eva raised her eyebrows as a sultry but smug smirk slithered across her lips.

"You act like you missed me," she teased, and in surprise David stumbled slightly. He searched his brain for some casual explanation, but the penetrating glare from Eva's sharp amber orbs all but forced his honesty.

"To be honest, I did," he stated, and chose to ignore the feelings of embarrassment that swelled within him. "And I'm not sure if that's me, or the Raebon I once was, but I can't shake that feeling." Eva's eyes widened a bit as her cheeks adopted a slightly rosy hue.

"Seems like we came back to a time period where we were just figuring things out. Miria's less than thrilled about being surrounded by the aristocrats of Alaedrean society, but she can't help but feel giddy about seeing Raebon again," she shared, and David smiled.

"Well at least we know that the excitement aspect is mutual. I won't lie, I'm a little intimidated by Miria," he chuckled, which coaxed a face from the humored pianist.

"Is that so," she prodded, and David's smile grew larger.

"Oh, most definitely," he blurted out. They both laughed, but the author quickly mellowed. "You're funny and brilliant, and your musical ability makes you a marvel to behold without question, and I never thought you'd be the spark I'd been missing in my life. When I met you, I became enraptured by the fire of your soul. Miria, though, this person you used to be, she's just… I don't know. It's as if that fire of yours fans into an inferno when I see her through Raebon's eyes. Like she's constantly seeking the truth of who he is."

"She is," Eva interjected. She turned around and sank to the dismally black ground upon which they stood with her back against the invisible wall that divided them. "She wants to make sure he's as good as he makes himself look to the public. But can you blame her when you've seen the light in Orasus' eyes?" David remained silent, and sat against the invisible wall with his back to hers.

"I really can't. I've only just seen him and I'm already attached. But I know that I—" he paused, because for the first time since this madness had begun he truly accepted that he and the prince were one and the same, "I would never do anything to hurt him." Eva turned her head, as did David, and in that moment he could see her, not as the woman he'd met at a book signing in New York, but as the incredible blaze that commanded his attention a millennium ago. He turned his head and stared into the endless black before him. "I've come in contact with Nico. Well, Sorin, anyway."

"How did that go," she asked softly as she wondered what monsters warred against him in the present.

"Well as it turns out, he's been training me and one of my generals to use Paradoxes. Tonight, he had us both choose one of the Keys that unlocks one," David reflected on the surge of power that, even now, made his every hair stand on end.

"And you chose that quill," Eva questioned as the golden gleam of the aforementioned object shined in her memory. He chuckled again.

"Actually, it's more like it chose me. But I don't mind having it at this point. If this royal address tomorrow is conducted by Aeridus then it'd be better to have some form of protection," he told her. Her brow furrowed, and in a slight panic she turned to face him. He still sat with his back to her, but he knew the look of uncertainty that rested on her face. "In one of my later memories, Aeridus is leading a rebel army against the Alaedrean forces. Even though there's no telling how long it'll be between this address and that battle, I just can't bring myself to trust that this will go smoothly."

"Would he really try something with every person in Coraena watching him," she asked as she turned her back to him once again.

"Well, you did," he reminded her. "You tried to kill me in broad daylight." Her eyebrow raised as Eva stared straight ahead and clasped her hands together.

"I don't recall ever telling you that."

"I know. But I remember," he said thoughtfully, with a hint of happiness in his voice that for some reason relaxed her. "I remember that we first met in battle. That you almost killed me, and that for some reason it compelled me to take care of you."

"I think that reason is fear," Eva said with a giggle. David rolled his eyes and, unbeknownst to her, attempted to take her hand in his through the wall.

"No," he whispered as he felt desperation rise. "I was captivated by you, even then—"

"David," she interrupted as her heart beat rapidly within her chest, and the swell of emotions that twisted and raged in him like a hurricane grew fiercer. "I'm sorry, it just seems a little soon to be talking like this. There are still so many things we don't know, and past or present I'm a little reluctant to get too close to you without understanding you from all sides." Her words stabbed at him with the force of a thousand knives, and for a brief instance he merely sat in quiet consideration of her expressed thought. He watched in the distance as the darkness began to fade with the light of a new morning, and as the rays of the sun caressed his skin he stirred to his feet and turned to the woman who upset and soothed everything in him.

She already faced him, watched him carefully with his every motion, and though what she said was true, the emergence of an already triumphant smile on his face made it clear to her that falling for this man, present and past, was inevitable.

"Then we'll just have to understand each other," David said in almost princely confidence, and without another word he turned towards the light and vanished into it as Eva watched on. She lingered for a moment, caught between the darkness and the light as a grin forced its way through her lips.

"That we will," she muttered as she walked in the opposite direction.

Miria awoke to the joyous shouts of her younger brother, who ran through the house in excitement as per his morning routine. It had been this way since Yural the merchant took them in, and Miria was ever grateful that her little one had perked up so much in the two weeks since they'd moved in. Of course, Yural and his wife Sayera were never able to conceive, and so the noise that he produced was more than welcome.

She adored them, because they loved her little brother almost as much as she did. Almost. She quickly rose from her bed and donned her finest blue dress before the excited Orasus could barge in like he typically did, and ran through how she was going to tell him that they had been invited by the prince to spend the day in the palace. She paced the floor, fully aware that the already exhilarated child would only grow more enthused at the news, and it was all that she could do not to crack a smile at the thought of his overjoyed face. There came a knock at her door, and like a falcon on prey her attention fastened upon it.

"Come in," she called as she patted down the front of her dress and clasped her hands together. The frizzy red hair of the merchant's wife entered the room, and the rest of her rather stout body followed.

"Good morning," Sayera spoke cheerfully as she gawked at the dress. "My, my, what on earth is the occasion?" Miria twiddled her thumbs as she forced a grin that more closely resembled a dog bearing its teeth.

"The prince has invited Orasus and I to the palace for the day. I thought it would be better if I wore something a bit more formal than my usual attire," Miria explained. Sayera adopted an almost smug expression that coaxed a genuine smile from the blue-clad woman. “What? What is it?”

“It would seem that *someone* has acquired somewhat of an admirer. And of the royal variety as well… not bad,” Sayera teased with a wink. Miria cupped her hand around her mouth as she giggled. “You have nothing to worry about, dearie. Orasus will be in his finest vestments before your breakfast grows cold. It is on the table, love. Go on and have a bite.”

“Yes, ma’am,” she said as she hurried from the room in the direction of the stairs. Sayera followed behind, albeit at a slower pace, and headed down the hall as she watched for the wired youth.

“Orasus,” she called through the estate, and the pitter-patter of little feet halted instantly. “To your room, young man. Now. Your sister has a bit of a surprise for you, but you can only find out what it is if you get dressed in your best clothes.”

“Coming up now,” Orasus yelled from the lower floor and sped through the house once again. Before Miria had the chance to pat him on his head he breezed past her on the stairs and into his room. Sayera stopped and turned toward Miria, and with an exchange of looks they took to their respective paths. Miria reached the bottom floor and almost instantly ran into Yural’s big round belly. He chuckled as she stumbled back and grabbed her by the arm before she fell.

"A surprise, eh," he started with a twinkle in his eye that warmed her heart. "This is good. Orasus is a wonderful boy. He deserves it. So… what have you prepared for him?" Miria glanced back up the stairs to check and see if he was near, and due to her restricted sights she pulled him into the kitchen. "Why so secretive, my dear? Will you not have the boy know of what is in store for him?"

"Yes, but not quite yet. If I tell him now, he may not be ready in time," she explained as her heart beat wildly. She walked around the wooden island at the center of the room and headed for the tray of sweet rolls that rested atop the stone counter next to the brick oven. They produced a cinnamon-spiced aroma that both tickled her nose and pleased it, and as she took one in her hand and bit into it she noticed the more or less confused expression that an eager Yural sported.

"Ready for what," he begged as his voice escalated a bit. "What in the world is happening, dear Miria?" She quickly swallowed her food and opened her mouth as if to speak, but the sound of small feet echoed through the house as Orasus made his presence known.

"Miria! Good morning," he shouted as he entered the kitchen and tackled her for a hug. She returned his embrace and calmly stroked his hair as Sayera strode in behind him.

"Orasus," she scolded between gasps of air, "you know very well that you are not to run through the kitchen! You could easily get burned or cut in here should you fail to tread with caution."

"Yes, ma'am," responded the little boy, who looked up at her with somewhat tearful eye and melted her heart instantly. Sayera approached the siblings and took one of the sweet rolls in her hand. She offered it to the boy, whose eyes went wide in a combination of hunger and joy.

"Just make sure to take greater care in the future, little one. After all, if you are to become one of the king's knights one day then you would be wise to take care of yourself while still young," explained the merchant's wife. Sayera looked over the two siblings, who matched in blue attire, and tears started to flow. They were hers, precious children that came to her by way of God and word of a prince, and it brought her so much joy to see them together in the home she worked so hard to maintain over the years.

“Is something wrong,” Miria asked softly, but with a shake of her head the older woman gently placed a warm hand against the maiden’s cheek.

“No, child,” she whimpered. “I just… Look, you match.” Miria took Orasus by his shoulders as she stooped down and looked him over carefully. His shirt and trousers were a royal blue that acted as perfect complement to the sky color of her own dress. His shoes were black, as were hers, and with a look of pride in her eye at her little man she couldn’t help but kiss his cheek and tussle his dark brown hair.

“You look very handsome,” she told him, and Sayera cupped her hand around her mouth as she sobbed hysterically.

“You do,” Sayera howled as she pressed her tear-soaked face into her husband’s shoulder. He kissed her lovingly on the forehead and rolled his eyes at her humorous display as he turned his attention back to the children.

“So why did I have to get dressed up like this, sister?” Orasus asked thoughtfully. “Is it because of the surprise?”

“It absolutely is,” she told him, and as his mouth opened to yell she cupped her hand around it. He licked her palm, to which she made a face and immediately wiped her hand in his hair as payback.

"Hey!" he shouted, which only made her giggle. He brushed his fingers through his hair in frustration as he asked, "What is this surprise anyway?"

"Oh I have something for you that I know you would love, but we have a bit of a problem, you see," explained the older sibling. His head tilted to the side in adorable confusion as he twisted from side to side.

"What problem," he begged as he took a bite out of his sweet roll.

"Well you see, we have to go into the city to get it for you." His eyes went wide and he hopped excitedly before her.

"Then why are we still here," he squeaked happily as he ran for the door. Sayera rolled her eyes as she slammed her hand onto the counter.

"Orasus! We just talked about this!" Miria laughed as she strolled after him through the house.

"Not to worry," she assured the couple, "I will make sure no harm comes to him." She left the kitchen and turned down the hall that led to the foyer of the estate. "Orasus," she called as she approached the boy whose hand had wrapped around the door handle. Slowly he pulled it open as his sister scolded him again. "How many times must we tell you to control—" she cut off, as the figure that stood in the doorway trained his stern white eyes on her and smirked.

“Good morning,” he spoke, and with the force of a thousand knights a clearly startled Miria crushed the pastry in her hands. “Are we ready to go?”

Chapter Thirteen

"Those idiots," Nico muttered as the lights in his room faded in the aftermath of the shockwave that quaked through the city. *They haven't been this impatient since the Civil War.* He pulled out his phone and pressed the lock button to check the time, but the absence of light provoked further discomfort and irritation. He glanced downward at the bag he'd opened, at the outfits he'd pulled out for their disguises, and with a sigh he turned for the door without them. He wrapped his hand around the cold steel doorknob and listened carefully to the outer sounds of commotion in the hall. He exhaled calmly as he slowly lifted his eye to the peephole, and with greatest caution did he look out at the blackness that filled the area. He sighed in relief, and to his surprise a large white eye opened on the other side.

In an instant, the battle-ready Moderator fell to his back as the door was blasted off its hinges and lodged itself sideways in the wall behind him. Before he could rise of his own accord, a massive reptilian tail wrapped around his ankle and pulled him into the hallway. Like a ragdoll he was tossed against a distant wall, and found himself incapable of making out more than the beast's sinister white eyes. He stirred to his feet and stretched out a hand as he braced against the partition with the other. He took a deep breath, and as the sound of his heartbeat grew ever quieter he noted the sound of slithering against the carpet.

The air shifted at his left side, and with a sudden burst of energy that sent unbridled pain through his upper back, Nico lunged forward and evaded the strike of the enshrouded monster.

"That all you got," he taunted as he spit out a little blood and shakily stretched his hand forward. His eyes glowed with the same hazel intensity they'd exhibited moments before, and with total confidence he began to speak:

"Monsters cloaked in shadows of Night,
That eagerly flaunt their Master's Might,
Obey the power of Paradox Poem,
Erase the evil you've always known
And wear the Poem's luminous glow
As you help take down my foe."

Little by little the darkness that surrounded him began to dissipate under the light that slowly swept the giant scaly body of the serpent before him. It hissed at him as he paced around the creature and looked over its brown and yellow pattern. He tapped a finger against his chin as he met its eyes, now as black as the shadows in which it previously hid and devoid of any signs of white. He pointed down the path that led to the staircase, and the great snake slithered ahead of him. He paced behind it, scowl firmly in place, and considered the monumental stupidity of his rebellious friends. *Yeah, we're gonna have to sit down and have a long chat about this later...*

The snake's movements ceased, and Nico froze behind it as they both surveyed the darkness ahead. He knew them to be near the stairwell door now, and the sound of heavy thumps confirmed it.

"Go," he ordered as second by second the pounding noises from the other side of the door grew louder. With visible hesitation, the serpent moved forward and its new master followed. With each step it was as if the air that surrounded him grew to suffocating heat. Nico's vision blurred as the sweat poured profusely from his forehead, and though he thought the liquid should cool him, it further accented the already present burning sensation in his flesh.

"What a fool you are, Sorin," echoed the smug voice of that abomination of a Shade. "Did you really think that you would be able to take control of one of my pets without suffering consequences for it? You are in too deep, Moderator, and the time has come for you to answer for your numerous violations of the rules of this game." Nico's eyes narrowed on the path, and for a moment his vision cleared.

"Break it down," the agent commanded the serpent as they stopped at the door. The snake obeyed, but as it drove its massive head into the steel obstacle a sharp pain swept over Nico. He stumbled and caught himself on the nearby wall before he fell, and as he surveyed his hands he heard a monstrous cry ring from just before them. The serpent cried to its destined opponent, and with a nod from Nico slithered down the stairs to meet it. Nico lifted his hand towards the now open pathway, and with his eyes closed he spoke again:

"Luminescent Evening glow,
Gaze upon the Earth below
And rest on me power anew
As on plants rest the morning dew.
On the path before me shine
And reveal all before my eyes."

The stairs themselves began to glow, and a series of White-Eyes creatures filtered into his mind. The modern age Sorin stepped into the stairwell, and as he began his ascent the light of the stairs pulsed and swirled about his aching body. He could feel it, the slow mending of his bones and muscles, the restoration of his strength both physical and metaphysical, and with every step towards the top floor his vision was restored.

A massive thud shook the foundations of the winding staircase, and the pained hiss of the snake reverberated upward. Nico moved on, visibly disquieted by the sound of his servant's defeat. The sinister snicker of the Shade filled his ears as he approached a White-Eyed monkey with contrasted kettle-black fur that beat its chest and bared its fangs. The Philosopher stood upon the landing, totally unfazed by the gleam of animosity in the beast's eyes. It lunged for him, and without any shred of hesitation Nico lifted his hand and constricted the creature with the beams of light that encircled him so.

"How long can you keep this up, my deeply philosophical friend," asked the snide voice of the Shade. Nico's hand trembled with a mix of rage and power, and with a flick of his wrist the beams of light snapped the neck of their prisoner. Nico looked upward with an expression of unmitigated disdain and climbed up flight after flight of stairs. The intensity of the air escalated as he did, and the closer he got to the top floor the more eyes he could feel lock onto him. The beasts' locations had changed.

"Well, I gotta say that I'm not really one for surprise parties," Nico quipped as he bent down and braced himself with his hands spread across the floor. His eyes began to glow intensely, and as the power surged through his body and the light of the illuminated stairwell began to shimmer, the walls of the building itself began to warp. The agent smiled, and with a solid kickoff he darted up the remaining flights of stairs. The glass windows that overlooked the city on each platform shattered from the sheer force of the wind left in his wake. He grinned with excitement as previously darkened portions of the stairwell gave way to new light, but ultimately his expression would revert to its former sobriety at the sight of the group of White-Eyed zombies and snakes that greeted him outside the door to the top floor. Nico pushed his hands forward, and with the agility of his master the prince, he lunged through an opening in the hoard of monsters.

The impact of his palms against the surface of the door proved too much, and it rocketed from its hinges to the opposite end of the hall with a deafening clang. Nico rolled a few feet away from the doorway and stood again as the carpeted hall of the top floor became alive with shimmering moonlight. He turned to see the mob of aggressors, mutilated by the power of the gust that followed him, and in a moment of victory he smiled and balled his fist. He turned back to face the empty hall and moved for the suite, but as he took his first step his body all but collapsed from fatigue.

“This isn’t good,” Nico muttered as he slowly pulled himself from the ground. “I’ve used up too much power. What’s more, I’ve interfered too much in this game. If I don’t do something about it now, then…”

“They will all die,” cooed the sinister Shade. The entirety of Nico’s surroundings drained of color as the heat of the atmosphere reached its peak. The light beneath him gave way to a threatening darkness the likes of which he’d never seen, and as a bead of sweat trickled down the side of his face, that darkness pulled to a single spot in the air. “Even your precious Sierra will not escape the consequences of your death. One by one, everything you love will be stripped before your very eyes and I, my roguish pet, am left with little more to do than watch the sparks as they fly.”

"If that was really the case, then why'd you go through the trouble of sic'ing your White-Eyed dogs on me," Nico fired back smugly. The Shade grew closer to him and wrapped its icy fingers around the back of the Overseer's neck.

"I had my suspicions that your powers had been rapidly depleting, and knew that despite your present weakness you would come running if you thought I was to make a move. My slaves served to fan the flames of your own desperation, a ploy that worked quite well, if I must say. Now then," asserted the Shade as it floated in circular fashion around the pained and exhausted manager, "what is it that you will do, Sorin? How will you prevent this reality, crafted solely by Paradoxes multiplied, from crumbling before your very eyes?" Nico had to admit the validity of the question. He looked down at his shaking hand, and with every moment that passed he felt more of his power slip away. He looked back up to the Shade, who reveled in the anguished expression on Nico's face. "Perhaps I should leave you to it," it continued. "It has always amused me to watch you squirm."

"I thought you'd be a little more reluctant to let me die," Nico spoke as the Shade slowly filtered out of reality. "After all, what fun would it be for you to watch your sworn enemies keel over with me?" The monster cackled wildly as its disappearance stopped and it slithered through the air back towards the downed Sorin.

"You and I both know that you of all people will find a way to survive, Moderator," it whispered to him, "if not for the sake of your friend the prince, then for your beloved — What was her name? — Sierra." The reptilian hum of his voice on her name drove him mad.

"You keep her name out of your mouth," Nico barked, and the Shade flashed an eerie grin before it slowly faded before his very eyes. The air lost its sting and Nico, far more broken than he cared to admit, staggered back to his feet and gripped the nearby wall with what force remained in his limbs. He grunted with every step and grew fiercer in rage as he imagined the lifeless eyes of his beloved wife, still pregnant with his unborn child. He willed his way through the silent hallway with the loft suite in his blurring sights. He felt defeated, as if the laughing demon that grew in power as Nico himself weakened had finally won. Nevertheless, he couldn't allow that monster the satisfaction. As much as it bothered him to think about it, pained him to even contemplate leaving his beloved Sierra at the mercy of that wretched abomination, he knew he had no other choice.

He reached the room and waved his hand before the keycard slot. The light flashed green and the door flung open. The room was just as dark as the other areas of the hotel, but the light of the moon shone through the window and enlightened him to the scattered mess of the furniture and décor. David and Eva remained in their positions, completely unperturbed by the city-wide quake that no doubt they'd caused.

Nico sighed as he stumbled toward them, and did his best to avoid the debris strewn all about. He stopped just a couple of feet away from his best friend and the spirited pianist, and as he wiped the drying tears from his face he gathered his strength in infinitesimal increments. He did what he could to ease his mind and focus on what he needed to do. He closed his eyes as he stepped upon the shattered remains of the coffee table between the chair and the sofa, and as the air in the room shifted under the weight of his fading Paradox, he lifted both hands and spoke softly:

"Realm beyond the Shadow's reach,
Impregnable to outsider's breech,
I beg of you open your gate
And shield us from the hellish fate

Of withering like fallen leaves
And then my wife I'll not bereave."

The room itself twisted together and stirred like cream poured into a broth, and in moments an entirely new plane of existence emerged that glimmered like pure silver in the light of the summer sun. An exhausted Nico fell to one knee and gripped his aching side. He breathed a sigh of relief, as he knew that there in that dimension the three of them would be safe. He eased into a cross-legged position and lifted both hands once again. His entire body trembled from the discomfort of using his Paradox so heavily, and he could feel the Shade on the outside of the shimmering plane grow in power. Still, though, he needed to use his Poem once more to do something that he swore he'd never again attempt. He grunted in dissatisfaction at the mere thought, but with his eyes focused straight ahead and his brow drenched in sweat he parted his lips once more:

"Body, mind and spirit, One,
Before the present day is gone,
Swim backwards through the sea of time
And take the reins of former life.

Replenish power running low
By living again the Noble's woe.
The time has come and evil nigh,
Together fight… or all shall die."

A chill ran down his spine as the final phrase of the poem left his lips, but nevertheless he moved away from his friends and towards a portal that manifested opposite him. He glanced back at them with sorrow all but burned into his every fiber, because though he would be reunited with the two whose material forms rested on the floor of this impenetrable plane it was his wife, his beloved Sierra that would remain a thousand years beyond his reach. His heart sank, and though it tortured him to abandon his new life and the only woman in a millennium to truly love him, he knew that it was far better than the alternative.

Nico slowly moved through the brilliance of the plane, and one leg at a time stepped through the doorway to his past. A cool sensation washed over him as he spiraled downward through what closely resembled the night sky. There was no sound, no conflict, only him. He couldn't help but chuckle, as an ethereal calm washed over him. There was no worry here, as much as he had reason to, as much as he wanted to, but after another moment of tranquility in descent he accepted this reality. He resolved that he would worry when he arrived in his old body, and that he would fight with every fiber of his being to preserve not just the present in which he indulged, but the future for his expected child.

He closed his eyes, somehow sure that she was safer this way, completely aware of the horrors of the age to which he traveled. The swirling lights that surrounded him faded into nothing, and all around the spiraling philosopher went dark. His skin tingled with a mellow warmth that deeply contrasted the heated sting of the demon that no doubt waited for his return. He allowed this gentleness to sweep over him and surrendered to the stillness it brought to his mind. *It won't be long now…*

His body accelerated, and though he felt the sudden increase in pressure he found it impossible to care. After all, in mere moments his time in the present would end, and he would be forced to live through the horrors of that accursed day until Raebon and Miria met their gruesome end. More than that, he would once again be forced to engage with the Shade in its previous human form, which only served as further deterrent. There was hardly anything to go back to.

Glass shattered upon the marble and onyx floor of the palace halls, and the sound that blasted through the air shocked him awake.

"You really have no knack for this sort of work, do you Sorin?" The strong voice of Aradmus, Warrior King of Alaedrea filtered into his ears, and though his tone was kind it made the flesh of the Philosopher tingle with trepidation. He turned instantly and bowed before the king, and though he could not see it, he could feel the steel gray eyes of the monarch watch him carefully. "I feel it rather strange that even though your master Eulic knows this, he demands such things from you."

"I would be inclined to agree with you, Sire," an incredibly nervous Sorin replied with his eyes firmly trained upon the floor of precious stones. The king placed his stony hand upon the philosopher's shoulder.

"Come," he commanded with a smile. "I wish to speak with you. Never mind about the mess. One of the servants will surely clean it."

"As you wish," Sorin hesitantly responded, and the two began to walk. There was silence at first, and the lack of noise filled him with an unbelievable terror. He glanced over at King Aradmus, and found himself awe-stricken by the sheer power of his presence. This was the first time they had been alone together, and so the intensity that radiated from the intimidating monarch had escaped him before this moment.

"I hear tell that you have allowed my son and your master to choose one of the so-called Seven Keys of Paradox," Aradmus finally spoke. He glanced in the way of Sorin, who silently nodded as a bead of sweat dripped down the side of his face.

"Your own Key still awaits you, my king," he assured him nervously. "It would only stand to reason that I allow you the same opportunity for selection since you have attended and participated in all of my lessons on the subject." An unsettling smile crept across the face of the king.

"Very well," he told him. "My guards are quite astute, and because of this they are able to act as informants to the King on all matters. I have been made aware of each of these 'Keys,' and what it is they do." Sorin's eyes narrowed now, as there was something that he didn't trust about the delighted tone of the Warrior King.

"And so which of them do you choose, King Aradmus," Sorin inquired, and did his best to keep the distrust from filtering into his tone.

“One whose call I have heard from a very young age, my boy,” spoke the king as they continued to stride through the monumental and lustrous halls of the palace. “I choose the Play.” Sorin’s eyes fell on him, not out of fear, but out of expectation of what was to come. He waved his hand through the air, and in a flash of light the silver mask with cerulean accents manifested before them. The king took hold of it, and as a devilish flare radiated from his steeled eyes, Sorin was able to see the first glimpse of what would eventually become the Shade.

Chapter Fourteen

Orasus ran along the shaded path with childlike wonder in his eyes as his sister and the prince watched him from the background. Raebon's eyes periodically fell on the beautiful Miria as they steadily moved towards the palace on the back road beneath the overhanging trees of the forest. She glanced at him, and in utter embarrassment he turned his attention back to the boy. Orasus froze, and the slightly concerned Miria tilted her head to the side.

"Orasus," she called, but the boy placed a finger against his lips to signal for quiet.

"There is a bunny over there," he whispered rather loudly as he watched the brown rabbit hop about and shift its stunning blue eyes. "I want to catch him." Raebon smiled, as did Miria, and the two approached the spot upon which the little boy stood. Orasus pointed as a giddy expression washed over him, and as if the small rabbit had been aware of the boys disposition it scurried away in the direction of the nearest trees and shrubbery. The small boy's eyes fell in disappointment, and Raebon placed his hand gently on Orasus' head as he stooped down to meet him on eye level. Miria watched him carefully through eyes of steel, and crossed her arms as she assessed his face.

"Do not worry, my young friend," he told him with a grin. "The rabbit may have escaped, but there might be a chance that you would find one in the gardens of the palace."

"Really?" The boy's eyes lit with excitement as he practically screamed in the prince's face, and Raebon nodded with a chuckle.

"They typically appear a bit later in the day, though," explained the prince, "so in the meantime you shall sit at the table of the king as my honored guest." Orasus rapidly nodded his head, and in a sudden burst of energy ran ahead of them once again. Raebon chuckled at how happy the boy was and felt a slight tinge of affection grow within him.

"I am impressed," Miria commented with mild but genuine surprise in her tone. "The war-hardened prince still has a soft spot for children." He looked in her direction and met her stunning amber eyes that sparkled in the morning sun.

"Women, too," he responded in modest tone, and by the twist in her expression he knew he'd caught her off guard. They both returned their attentions to the path and the boy who strolled farther along it.

“Yes, well…” she paused for a moment as they walked onward. “I wanted to thank you again, Raebon,” she started up again, and her outright disregard of titles caught his attention. “Orasus truly admires you, and to spend his day with you in such a way is more than I could ever give him.” Raebon’s heart sank a bit, as the tone in which she spoke reflected the sting his invitation made her feel.

“But you did give it to him,” he reminded her. “What, do you think me some spoiled brat that would have your brother summoned to the palace with or without your consent? You wished for his happiness, and you saw to it that it be granted him. I am merely an accessory to your whim.” She all but quivered at the utterance of those words, and as her cheeks adopted a rosy hue she cleared her throat and clasped her hands behind her back. The two of them silently observed the tranquility of the scene.

The rays of sunlight seeped through the openings of the leaves and branches overhead, and the sound of the birds that fluttered about breathed new life into an already beautiful day. The yellow and purple flowers that lined the trail danced with the gentle breeze, and as the delighted squeals of young Orasus filtered into his ears the prince wondered if this was what he would feel when he had a family. It struck him as odd how he'd never considered that possibility before. He was always so engulfed in his duty to his people, so invested in the on-goings of the battlefield that he ignored anything beyond the realm of public relations and bloody war, but something about this moment, walking alongside the good-hearted Miria and comforting the little brother she cherished so, seemed so alluring.

They drew near to the palace gate, and with a stern call Miria beckoned for her brother. The boy rushed back to her and grabbed her hand as the gatekeeper pulled open the door. The prince smiled at the two, and happily escorted them through the grounds and into the massive construct itself. Raebon held the door for them and watched with a smile as they entered. Orasus' head turned in all directions as he took in the white and gold walls, the marble and onyx floors, the massive marble staircase just ahead of them and the golden chandelier alight with burning candles.

Orasus gripped his sister's hand as the prince leaned against the doorframe silently. Miria looked back him, and inaudibly gasped when he winked at her. Raebon left his post at the door to beside and converse with the little one.

"What is it that you would like to do, Orasus," he asked, but before the young boy could offer a reply the sound of hurried footsteps echoed from around the corner.

"There you are," Sorin called from a few feet away and rushed the prince on sight. "The royal address to the public was set to begin an hour ago." Miria cut her eyes at Raebon, who shrugged and issued a wry smile that his friend the philosopher brushed off.

"What do you mean, 'supposed to?'" Miria questioned as her grip on her brother's hand grew a little tighter. Sorin turned his head to her, and after a moment's recollection realized that this was the very person who sought his death only two weeks prior.

"Who are you to inquire anything of *me*," Sorin barked, and the prince's eyes narrowed. "You have a lot of nerve, walking into the palace after what you tried to do."

"Sorin," Raebon spoke sternly, and the philosopher instantly found his silence. "These are my guests, Miria and Orasus. Now, the lady has asked you a question and it would be a terrible representation of the family you serve to leave it unanswered." Sorin opened his mouth, wholeheartedly prepared to rebut his prince, but Raebon stared so many daggers into his soul that he found it better to simply oblige the lady's request.

"The High Counselor refused to speak to the public until both the prince and his father were present. The aristocratic families from across the country have all gathered and await the Counselor's recent revelation as eagerly as the public without the palace walls. It seems that in his… *dealings* with you, however, Prince Raebon has managed to keep an entire kingdom waiting needlessly." Miria grabbed the collar of his shirt and pulled Sorin closer to her before Raebon even had the chance to chastise his servant. Her amber eyes grew more intense as the seconds passed, and Sorin shook in fear.

"Now," she whispered to him, and Orasus rushed to the side of the prince, who extended his hand for the boy to take, "what makes you think you can talk to me that way without consequence? Is that any way to treat a guest of the crown prince? Let us come to the point of understanding, philosopher. The only reason why these lovely walls are not painted with your poor man's blood right now is that I do not wish to ruin what has proven to be such a happy day for my younger brother," she pulled him closer, so as not to be misheard in the slightest. "That is not to say that I will not reconsider if you dare push again. Are we clear?" Sorin nervously nodded his head, and with a smug look she released him.

"Lead the way and we will follow, Sorin," spoke the prince. The future Overseer straightened his clothes and, in terror-induced silence, turned toward the stairs to begin his ascent. Miria approached the prince and her brother, and as she held out her hand the boy reluctantly took it. She turned away from Raebon, but the unsettled prince placed a hand upon her shoulder.

"There was no need for that sort of display," he told her quietly.

"And what was I supposed to do, Raebon," she demanded as she released Orasus' hand and folded her arms. "What, was I to let him openly treat me with disdain? To sit in silence like a fool and be berated by a man no higher up on the social ladder than I am? What next; am I to invite physical abuse as well?"

"You are to let me handle it," he told her flatly. "Have you already forgotten my promise to you?" He looked down, and her eyes followed his gaze to the space between them where Orasus shakily paced. "To him? I told you that I will never allow for your suffering again and I meant that. Trust me, Miria." His voice was sincere, and though she knew that he would do just as he said he would, it proved too difficult a task to place her trust in a man with whom she was barely acquainted.

"Prove yourself worthy of my trust and I will without hesitation," she barked in response. "Let us not delay the people any longer." She moved to grab her brother's hand, and as they continued to make their way up the stairs the prince gave a disheartened sigh. He followed after them nonetheless, and in moments they walked through a pair of massive wooden doors to stand amid a large body of people dressed in various vibrant colors. At the other end of the platform, the High Counselor Aeridus looked over the balcony and into the palace yard at the people who had come from far and wide to hear what it was he'd wished to say. One of the aristocrats took notice of him, and as he called out his name the heads of the royal staff and, of course, the king shifted to behold him.

Sorin stood next to the throne upon which King Aradmus sat and watched with uncertainty as the prince made his way onto the patio with his would-be assassin. General Eulic stood against the wall opposite them, and through the crowd bitterly surveyed the man who was supposed to be his servant as he attended to the king instead. The king himself took interest in the young lady, whose attire and demeanor both seemed a bit less…

refined as that of the others in attendance. He ran his thick fingers through his long, white beard as he tried to remember where he had first seen her. He waved for Sorin to move closer, much to the displeasure of his general, and as he adjusted himself in his seat his eyes remained locked on the mysterious and yet familiar woman.

"How may I be of service, Sire," spoke the philosopher as the general pushed his way through the high society congregation to stand at the other side of the king. Aradmus pointed over to the girl, and as both Sorin and Eulic turned their attentions to her the former grew increasingly concerned.

"Tell me," Aradmus began, "who is this young woman that my son has brought into the palace?" Sorin, whose palms sweat and body trembled at the ferocity in her eyes, opened his mouth to speak, only to find himself cut off by the man who served as his master.

"Ah, Miria," Eulic spoke as a smile crept across his face. "I believe she works in the local tavern not very far from the palace gate, my king."

"You speak of her as if you are rather fond of her," the king assessed with eyebrow raised. Eulic's fair skin glowed red with embarrassment, but as he cleared his throat he nodded in the affirmative.

"I very much am," he spoke proudly. "I have proposed to her on a number of occasions, and it is my fullest intent to make her my wife."

"Then one might hope she gives positive response to one of your future attempts, General," uttered the philosopher, to which the General flashed a menacing glare that silenced his servant instantly.

"Agreed," said the king. "It is still a rather curious matter that a bar maiden should find herself in the palace alongside the aristocrats and the royal family. General Eulic," the monarch asserted with power. The general snapped to attention and his flustered face immediately became steel.

"Sir," he shouted, and the power and depth of his voice caused those within immediate earshot to jump.

"It is my sincerest request that our guest be properly attended to," Aradmus continued as his eyes shifted to his commanding officer. "Do relieve my son of the burden of entertaining."

"Sir," Eulic exclaimed a second time, and with no hesitation at all, he braved the crowd again as he moved towards the object of his affection. Sorin breathed a sigh of relief and attempted to return to his post when the weighted hand of the king fell upon his shoulder. He turned and faced Aradmus, whose soul-shattering steel eyes stared into him.

“What do you know of this woman, Sorin,” he demanded, and the philosopher gulped as his body shook nervously at the man’s tone alone.

“Only two weeks ago she made an attempt on the prince’s life, justified in her mind by a claim that the royal family’s idleness and covert self-preservation led to her father’s death,” he informed him as calmly as he could, and as the words crossed his lips the king’s heart raced with a ferocity the likes of which he hadn’t experienced in the years since he’d left the battlefield behind. His expression intensified as he again looked over the girl who now did her best to push past General Eulic. Sorin could feel a sudden sting in the air, one that he knew was tied to King Aradmus’ emotions.

“That is interesting,” he said coldly, and released the grip he had on Sorin’s shoulder. He fell silent for a moment and watched the interaction of the general and the bar maiden, and the intellectual by his side grew increasingly discomforted.

“What will you do, Sire,” asked the keeper of the Keys of Paradox. The king hummed as he pondered his next step and relished in the intricacy of the situation.

“I will merely watch,” was all he said in reply, and as the beautiful Miria did her best to distance herself from the adamant Eulic, he sat back in his throne to enjoy the show.

“Will you not do me the honor of talking to me, Miria,” Eulic practically begged as the woman moved away from him, but a thought occurred to her that forced her to quickly close the distance that she had created.

“Do you even understand the reason I refuse you,” she asked him, eyes alight with irritation. He crossed his arms and raised his eyebrows as if to signal her answer rather than offer any of his own. “You see me as a prize to be won, a masterpiece crafted by the hand of God, and flattering though that may be, you reduce me to an object all the same. Our future would consist of you risking your life for this country and rushing to the battlefield at the beckoning of the king, and me managing the household, perpetually undermined by the people around us and longing for a return that may not even happen, and I have too much self-respect to be stripped of my humanity to become the trophy of a stubborn, irritating, unappreciative brute what only cares about himself and how others can make him look." His temper flared as she turned from him, and in the heat of the moment the general grabbed her by the arm. Raebon turned at the gasping sound that came from their direction and saw the meaty claw of the general wrapped around the woman's flesh.

"Miria," he all but growled as he tightened his grip. Instantly her attention refocused on him, and with an effortless jerk of her hand she broke free of his hold. Raebon noted the bloodlust in her eyes as he quickly moved back through the crowd of people.

"Is something the matter, General?" The sound of the prince's voice filled Eulic with seething hatred, and with flustered expression he shook his head. "That answer was the correct one. Understand that Miria is here with me, and that any offense against her will be treated as an attack on the Crown Prince of Alaedrea. If you feel the need to assert your dominance I would caution you to save your bravado for the battlefield and remember your place within the palace. If that proves too difficult, then you may consider falling on your blade now, because the next time you forget it will result in the direst of consequences. Are we clear?" Eulic slowly moved his hand for the Earth that rested within his pocket, but abstained upon the realization that he was severely outmatched by the Prince.

"Sir," was all he said in response, and with anger-induced haste he made his way for the door. Raebon, who in Miria's eyes stood stronger than she'd ever seen him, turned to meet her gaze with his best attempt at a comforting smile.

"I do apologize for the behavior of my general, and take full responsibility for his actions," he said earnestly.

"Never mind that," she told him outright. "I need to find Orasus. That boy has already made himself at home here, and there are few people within these walls that I trust around him."

"Very well," Raebon answered as his face grew more serious. "I will—"

"If I might have your attention, please," came the thunderous yet comfortable voice of Aeridus from the balcony. All eyes turned to him, those of the commoners on the ground below as well as the partygoers on the patio above, and to Miria's utter shock Orasus stood next to the High Counselor, still in complete wonder of the majesty of the day's events. "It is my wish that you not be delayed any longer than you already have been. Prince Raebon," he continued as he turned around to face the prince, "how nice of you to join us. Great people of Alaedrea, you have long suffered the consequences of battles waged in your name of which you wanted no part. You have long been subject to the principles of a warrior state when you wish for peace. For what seemed like an eternity, your once thriving economy became naught more than a decrepit shell of its former self at the hands of the Kingdom of Pragoria. Thank God that this is no more. Our valiant prince, Raebon the son of Aradmus, led the Alaedrean army to crush our foreign enemies." The people cheered below, and even on the patio the aristocrats and the king himself offered the prince their applause. "Yes, yes, it is truly a blessed thing to be liberated from the burden of conflict. But, it has recently come to my attention that such conflict will not end for our people." Raebon's eyes narrowed at the words, and his father Aradmus balled his hand into a fist while the aristocrats and commoners began to whisper among themselves. Aeridus took notice of their collective discomfort and relished in it like a pig in its own filth.

"Aeridus," spoke the king, whose tone radiated total gravity, "what is the meaning of this?" The dark green eyes of his High Counselor glowed with excitement as the clamor of the people dulled down. Aeridus pulled from his cloak a thick stack of envelopes and tossed them on the patio floor before the people.

“Here I have the letters exchanged over the last decade between King Aradmus and Homarus, King of Pragoria that detail an agreement made in which Pragoria would blockade our borders, along with the plans for the creation and subsequent expansion of—oh, please hear this, ladies and gentlemen—the Glorious Alaedrean Empire! Aradmus has manipulated us, the people who have pledged loyalty to the crown and to this country, into a state of total dependence on him, and at our expense he intends to steadily grow his power! And for those who dare not comply, as with the Pragorians who had outlived their usefulness to him, he shall turn on you and have his own son clean up the mess that he himself has made!” The entire congregation of Alaedrean citizens gasped and shouted all the same. From the patio to the city streets, the citizens were divided. Some, the gullible, stood in favor of blindly following a leader that had done them no “real” harm and that sought a better quality of life for his citizens, while others stood outraged that he would see them deceived and nearly destroyed without hesitation. Their chattering became more than he could bear, and the king rose from the throne.

"How dare you," spoke King Aradmus as his typically sturdy hands shook in a combination of anger and fear. "How dare you bring such slanderous accusations against the king who protects you from all danger?"

"Ah, from all dangers without the kingdom, yes, but what about the danger of the monarchy itself," Aeridus shot back as his grip tightened on Orasus' hand. The boy winced from the pain, and the discomfort he displayed sent both Raebon and Miria over the edge. The prince found one of the royal guards and quickly unsheathed the man's sword as he made his way before the High Counselor, but at the sight of the son of the king Aeridus pulled the boy closer, and in a rather sadistic display, pressed the edge of a rugged green dagger against the young Orasus' throat. "Stay your blade, Prince," demanded the villainous advisor, "lest the boy meet his end by mine." Raebon roared as a hungry lion at his father's former confidant, but the worried eyes of the little one he had grown quite fond of prompted him to drop the sword immediately. "Tell me, my dear Prince," continued the Counsellor, "how much time did you actually spend with your father outside of a war room? How much attention did he impart to your wants and needs as a human, or have you always been destined to be his soldier?" A few of the aristocrats and knights in service to the king surrounded the royals and the sister of the boy. Sorin retreated behind the throne and merely watched the events that unfolded before his eyes. A distressed Raebon desperately searched mind for a way to rescue the boy, but he was forced to square with the words of the present insurgent. He couldn't remember the last time his father was more than just the king to him, and for a moment he questioned the meaning of his very existence. But that didn't matter now. Orasus was in trouble, and he desperately needed a savior. It was then that the prince remembered the Key he'd received the night prior, and thought to exercise its power.

Raebon reached into his pocket and pulled out the small golden quill, and with a smile on his face he held it at his side. The room stood in confusion as the tensions rose, and Miria trembled with animalistic indignation as none around her dared lift a finger to rescue her little one. The prince looked back to her, and as he caught sight of the tears that streamed from her captivating golden eyes his own temper flared.

"Aeridus, I would caution you not to further anger the boy," spoke the prince. A humored grin slithered across Aeridus' face as he issued a minor cut to the boy's flesh. "If you do, then do not be surprised when your men run in terror and your blade turns to dust. There is a power within that boy that only I have been able to detect, and should you provoke him you will find yourself instantly overpowered." Sorin's ears perked up at the words spoken, and Miria's sobs turned to grunts of fury.

"Raebon," she exclaimed in disbelief. "How dare you wager my brother's life on such a poorly spoken tale?"

"Miria," he spoke in an unnerving calm that halted her before she could lunge for the prince herself, "no harm will come to the boy. Do you remember the promise that I made to you?" The bar maiden cried, and indeed it was the first time that Orasus had ever witnessed it. His breath became shorter by the second, and as the air began to cool around them the blade in Aeridus' grip disintegrated much to everyone's surprise.

"You made my sister cry!" The boy shouted, and as his voice reached the upper spires of the palace, the foundations of the building rattled with such ferocity that the traitorous knights and aristocrats fled the presence of the royals. Only Aeridus remained, but with a sudden elbow strike from the young Orasus he was sent over the balcony's banister and narrowly managed to grab hold. He dangled there for but a moment as the boy, watched by all present, ran to his sister and hugged her tightly. Prince Raebon lifted his chin and inspected the bleeding wound on his neck. The little one's face was wet with tears, and with the bottom of his now untucked shirt the prince cleaned him up.

"You will be just fine, my valiant little knight," Raebon assured him. His attention turned to Miria, who stood stunned by his open display of care for her little brother. His stern white eyes radiated power as he stood back to his feet and advanced for the balcony's rail. He looked over the side, but the traitor that previously drooped had vanished, as though he were naught but an imagination escaped in the wind.

Chapter Fifteen

Raebon paced the floor of his chambers as he stared upon the Tale in his hand and marveled at its power. It saved the boy, who now lay in the prince's bed submerged within a world of dreams with his sister at his side, but the prince remained rattled from the demonic eyes of the former High Counselor. To think that the man who had taught him in the ways of books and blade and served as Raebon's only friend since the days of the prince's youth served would threaten a child… and yet there was something about what Aeridus said that resonated with him. He glanced at Miria, who sat beside the bed and quietly watched her brother as his chest slowly lifted and fell. She had been silent since the incident, not to his surprise. What had started as such a wonderful day ended in chaos, and amid that insanity she was reminded that despite all the strength she had amassed, there could still come a time where she failed to protect her little brother.

Raebon gripped the quill tightly and stowed it in his pocket as he advanced for the bedside. Instantly his eyes fell upon Orasus' lightly bandaged throat, and for a moment he felt disappointed that he didn't act sooner. But this was hardly the time to consider such things. He was safe, albeit a bit hurt and scared, and that should have been enough.

"Are you alright," he asked the uncharacteristically silent Miria. She looked up at him for a moment, and with a pained expression she nodded. "If you need anything at all, I will do everything in my power to procure it for you. You need only let me know." Her tearful eyes grew softer yet as she returned her attention to the little one, and a new sort of pain shot through Raebon's heart. He couldn't bear to see her in such a condition, devoid of all the spirit and fire that made her so incredible to him. He thought to embrace her, to comfort her in this moment of weakness, but decided that the best thing he could do was to leave for now.

He turned away from the sun-kissed siblings and headed for the door when he heard the chair move behind him.

"Wait," Miria finally spoke, and prompted the young prince to turn back to her. His white eyes adopted a hint of yellow from the lamps that glowed about the room, and in them she could finally see the warmth that his personality had always conveyed. "I meant to thank you for what you did."

"I… do not understand," he responded in all seriousness, but his feigned ignorance did little to fool her.

“Orasus could not have broken free of his own accord. He is five, after all,” she responded, and her voice exhibited a docile humor that proved foreign to the prince. “Never in all his life have I witnessed that sort of power in him. Never in mine did I imagine such things possible. But, that does little to change the fact that the words you spoke somehow saved my brother, and so I am indebted to you.” Raebon stood stunned by the sincere gratitude with which she spoke, and moved back across the floor to stand face to face with her. Her heart beat rapidly and her skin grew warmer with every step he took, and though she wished to look away her eyes remained locked with his.

“You owe me nothing,” he told her, and smiled as he crossed his hands behind his back. “I merely sought to keep my promise to you. It was nothing more than that.” He turned away from her again, but before he could take a step towards the door she grabbed his hand and held it tightly. He could feel the way she shook, and more, how desperately she wanted his company in that moment. He froze as his heartbeat quickened in a way with which even his fiercest enemies could never compete. “You should rest, Miria. Mulling over the problems of the day would only exhaust you further.”

"How could I," she asked softly with another glance back at her brother. "How could I possibly think to rest right now?" Raebon looked at her as the tears welled up in her eyes, and from the bottom of his aching heart resolved to destroy the insurgent responsible for her strife. A knock came at the door that warranted their joint attention. Miria reluctantly released their protector and allowed him to open the door to reveal the aged and gentle face of Ramea, the royal physician. The old woman smiled at her master's son and the object of his affections, and in total silence moved to the chair previously vacated by Miria. Raebon looked at her as she attended to the boy.

"Come with me," he told Miria with a tinge of hushed excitement as he grabbed her hand and pulled her from the room. The door closed behind them, and the two traced the marble and onyx floors of the palace halls in silence. Miria did wonder, however, just what he was up to. He looked back at her and grinned at the startled look that had taken its place upon her face. It seemed that at long last she was able to look beyond the myopia of her expectations and into the reality of who he was.

He led her out into the terrace behind the palace and took a left toward the stables. Miria donned a look of confusion now as Raebon walked up to a jet-black Friesian horse. The beast neighed at the sight of him, as if even animals were aware of the kind nature of Alaedrea's hero, and with a gentle caress of the snout, the animal lowered itself for him. Raebon mounted the horse and guided it from its pen while Miria watched. Without a word, he extended his hand to her, and without a word she accepted. He pulled her up, and with a crack of the reins they were off.

Miria's face lit with wonder as she wrapped her arms around Raebon's waist, and as the dimly lit houses of the village sped by before her eyes she became lost in the winds that ran around and through her. The powerful sounds of the horse's hooves against the cobbled roads of Coraena were as sweet a melody as the lullabies she used to play for Orasus, and the warmth of Raebon's body against her own only accented the rapid pound of her raging heart. But she loved it, the cold night air, the stars and moon that shined down from the heavens above, the touch of a man who so clearly cared for her and wanted to go to such lengths just to cheer her up, and then the thought crossed her mind of what it would be like to build a life of moments like these.

She blushed, though he could not see, and with a mighty turn the beast made its way for the village's edge. The horse's movements slowed and the sounds of hooves against stone ceased as it ascended a grassy hill with a single tree at its top. Raebon recognized it as his haven, the place that he came to think when things were emotionally taxing or otherwise beyond his control. He dismounted and helped her down as well, and while the horse took the time to graze the grass and the flowers that decorated the ground, the prince led the girl by the hand to the base of the tree.

"What is this place," she asked. A peace washed over her as she surveyed the quiet hill. Her heart swelled with euphoria as Raebon gently squeezed her hand, and in a rush of nerves she squeezed back. He looked at her with a tender smile and sat before the tree's trunk. As she brushed her hair off to the side of her face she took her place beside him.

"This," Raebon began as his moon-like eyes trained upon the glimmering lights of the distant town, "is the hill my mother used to take me to when I was about Orasus' age."

"Your mother," she inquired as she massaged the back of his hand with her thumb. He nodded, and quickly rubbed his eyes with his free hand.

"She was a dazzling sort of woman," he told her as he reclined in the grass and stared into the shimmering, star-scattered heaven. "Vibrant, powerful, pugnacious, yet delicate and sophisticated, full of grace and intellect. And she would bring me to this place, every day she would, and ask me questions about life like what I thought about the common folk of the capital or the kind of ruler I thought my father was… the kind of life I would like to lead when I had grown. I would always answer that I would like to emulate my father, to wander the battlefield and conquer what remained of the former Roman provinces, and lead the kingdom with benevolence." It made him chuckle, since he had no idea if he wanted to emulate any aspect of his father's rule.

"You must have been quite the brilliant lad to use such vocabulary at the age of five," she quipped, and lied down next to him. He cracked a smile despite his best efforts to refrain, and slightly repositioned himself to create a comfortable distance between them.

"It was less the words and more the sentiment," he admitted with a chuckle, but as he continued the smile vanished. "In any case, she never accepted my answer. She always told me to imagine greater for myself than the mundanities of my father's past. She never wanted me to be a mirror of anyone, and more than anything she wanted me to be able to think for myself."

"Is that why you seem to have taken a liking to me," Miria questioned as she shifted to behold him. He reciprocated, and though his lips curled once more his eyes told of his sorrow.

"Yes," he said in all seriousness, "but there is more. You are stronger than any woman who serves as your peer. You have a sense of justice that you dare anyone to ignore, and from personal experience, you are as sharp with your tongue as you are with your blade." She quivered as the savory sound of his deep voice moved soothingly through her ears. "In many ways you remind me of the kind of woman my mother was. But there is something in you that even my mother never had." She raised an eyebrow as she shifted to her side, and again drew closer to Raebon in the process.

"Really," she prodded, "and what is this mysterious quality that deserves the attention of a royal?" He turned to his side as she had before, and gazed into her mesmerizing amber eyes.

"Miria," he began as he took her hand again. Their hearts beat faster, stronger, together, and as the woman's cheeks flushed red and Raebon's eyes softened, he moved closer to her. A gentle breeze danced about the terrain, and he tenderly brushed her wind-blown hair out of her face as he continued in a whisper, “You once tried to kill me.” The pair of them erupted in laughter, but as the humor gave way to sobriety, Miria sat up again. She looked around at the stark beauty of the silent mound and basked in the tranquility that seeped into the core of her being.

“Why did you bring me here,” she asked in whispered tone. Raebon fixed his attention on the twinkling heavens as he pondered the question.

“My mother once said that there was a particular mystique about this hill,” he explained, “that it was a place where the complexities of life could be unraveled and the imaginations of man could run rampant. It was the place to which she came when burdened by the world around her, and since she died it has been the place I have escaped to as well. I thought that with all that has happened in the palace today, you would need a place to clear your mind.” He returned to a supine position.

“You truly care for us,” she realized, shocked that such affection from a royal was even possible.

“Of course,” Raebon conceded as his heart pounded against his ribs. “More than I thought I would for such a short time, but cannot deny that I harbor affections all the same.” He cringed, embarrassed that he had given in to his emotions, but even so he knew that she needed to be told. Miria rolled on top of him and paused for a moment as she took in the startled and confused expression that he wore.

She leaned in, and instinctively he braced his hand lightly against her hip as she teased a kiss. Her eyes burned with an intensity that rivaled the sun, and he knew full well that his did the very same. The swirling wind did little to sooth the heat that shot through their bodies as she dangled her lips centimeters above his, and as the sensuality of the moment coursed within his veins he reversed their positions in one smooth motion.

She briefly giggled as she placed her arms around his neck and pulled him closer. He savored the delicacy with which she traced the surface of his body, and she noted the way his muscles tightened under her touch. He felt her power, and with satisfaction on his face he gave in to its pull. He kissed her, and passionately massaged his lips against hers as she ran her fingers through his curly hair.

Raebon felt it, the irresponsibility of entangling himself with a commoner, serving as a willful distraction from her duties to Orasus, but he was powerless to resist. She dug into his back, and the euphoria it caused provoked him to take to her collarbone. She gasped with delight as he teased her, and lost herself in the way he held her tight. She drew away a bit and looked at him, the royal, the target that she once wished dead, and marveled at how she steadily fell for him. Those eyes, those magnificent moon-adjacent orbs that filled with concern for her, enchanted her as much as they did frighten her.

Raebon shifted off to the side of Miria and merely stared at her, this angel beautifully melded with frail humanity that struck him so viciously with the celestial sting of her being, and though he knew his father would disapprove he wanted her. Just her.

"What is it," she asked as he adopted a thoughtful expression. The sound of her own voice alarmed her, as she suspected it would be impossible to speak so suddenly. He pressed his lips against hers once more, and subsequently returned his back to the dirt.

"Nothing," he whispered to her with a smile. Miria instinctively thought to question the validity of his answer, but decidedly placed her head against his chest and listened to the drum of his heart instead. She grew more and more relaxed with every beat, and as his chest rose and sank with every breath he drew, she drifted off to sleep. Raebon placed his arms around her shoulders, and in but a few short moments later, his eyes closed just the same.

“So, you’ve arrived,” Nico’s voice echoed through the familiar black. David and Eva opened their eyes and found that they faced one another, but quickly looked away as embarrassment crept in. “By the looks of things, you’ve reconnected as well.”

“How are you even here, Nico,” David asked as he stood straight and folded his arms. Nico cocked his head to the side and smirked.

“Long story short, I’m dying,” he stated flatly. David’s expression grew grave, but when he noted the tinge of fear and worry in Nico’s eyes he knew that there was no deceit behind his words. “I don’t know if I mentioned that, but if I kick the bucket then you all bite the dust right along with me. So, to avoid that I came to this plane to sort of recharge my batteries.”

“I don’t understand. You’re the Moderator, right? Shouldn’t that mean that you’re a bit beyond the whole ‘death’ thing,” Eva asked as she stepped closer to the invisible barrier that divided them. Nico chuckled.

“Wouldn’t that be nice? No. Despite having lived in this world for more than a thousand years, four things could cause my death. The first thing, is if the cycle is broken and one or both of you die, then I'd be free to live a normal life and die of (hopefully) natural causes," he explained, which incited wry looks from both the writer and musician. "Oh, relax. The only thing that would convince me to let that happen is if you did something to hurt my wife and neither of you are that cruel. The second thing, though, is if you or the Shade killed me."

"Immortality's just not what it used to be, eh," David supposed, and Nico offered a humored wink.

"It most certainly isn't. The third thing that could bring me down is if the game is over. It wouldn't kill me outright, but I'd lose the perk of my semi-limited immortality and would eventually keel over," Nico continued. He scratched his head as regret settled in, but then steeled his resolve so as to convince himself that they would win. "The final thing, something that I'd say I'm pretty guilty of, is interfering in the natural flow of the game."

"What do you mean by that," Eva wondered aloud as she placed her hand on her hip.

"Saving you, pushing you together, having a wife… a child… all of that is against the rules, and the more I interfere, the more I neglect my duties as a Moderator for the sake of becoming a player, the weaker I become until eventually—"

"You die," David interrupted as a sinking feeling overtook him.

"Exactly. And so because of that, my consciousness has been somewhat linked with your subconscious, and like you I'm reliving the memories of my history in Alaedrea," Nico confirmed.

"Well, I suppose that's a good thing," Eva voiced as she paced the black platform upon which they stood. "Since you're here, you can probably help us make sense of what's going on in this time period."

"Alright," Nico accepted, "what do you need help with understanding?" Eva opened her mouth to speak, but the only thing on her mind was the mess of feelings she'd garnered for David. He saw her hesitation, and decidedly jumped in.

"Let's start with the obvious. What is this place?" Nico's hazel eyes trained upon his friend.

"You remember how just a second ago I told you that my consciousness was somewhat linked your subconscious," the Overseer prodded, and his friend nodded his head. "Yeah, this is that. Your historical selves are sleeping, and that creates a temporary divide between your past counterparts and your present-day versions. The thing is, the purpose of you being here isn't for you to relive your entire past life. It's for you to understand how you felt about one another and, perhaps more than anything else, exactly what events led to this curse in the first place. That said, there's a possibility that the experiences you have next won't align with what you've just seen, so be ready, because if you were excited to relive you two getting… 'acquainted' for the first time, you might have to miss it."

"Wait, what?" David and Eva's eyes went wide, and though they wanted to glance at each other, they felt it would only make things more awkward. David waved the question off. "I had another concern, if you don't mind." Nico leaned slightly forward with eyebrows raised as if to inquire of him inaudibly. "That night when Sorin went over the Seven Keys of Paradox with Raebon and Eulic, he chose one for himself." Nico's hands began to sweat and his brow instantly furrowed as intense fear steadily weighed him down.

"The Poem, yes," Nico admitted. "What of it?" He knew that to ask the question was to insinuate stupidity on the part of his long-time friend, and more so spoke to his deepest wish that he hadn't reached the conclusion that Nico knew he had.

"The curse that's created all this, the Paradox behind it…" David paused, as he wished with everything he had that what he was about to say wasn't true.

"What," Eva questioned as she attempted to move closer to him. He donned a downcast expression as he looked into the eyes that suddenly filled him with adoration, but that feeling gave under the weight of the despair of what proved to be a shocking betrayal.

"The curse comes in the form of a poem," David finished, and the couple watched as the Moderator, their protector and friend cringed.

"Yes," he begrudgingly admitted, "that it is." The sorrow on David's face shifted to indignant rage as he slammed his fists against the barrier between them and yelled. The memory of that night with Miria and the wave of powerful emotions that surrounded it resonated with him, as did the reality that it was the hand of his best friend that had damned them to their fate.

"You did this," David snarled, and as he beat against the transparent barrier of their minds Miria grew increasingly terrified.

"No, I—" Nico began, but cut himself off. It was a difficult decision for him to make, but he knew that should he relay that truth now, his existence and those tied to him would cease. “Yes,” he lied as his body shook and his eyes filled with tears. “I did this.”

Chapter Sixteen

Eulic slammed Sorin's back against the outer wall of the palace, and cuffed his hand over the philosopher's mouth before he had the chance to scream. The bloodlust in his hardened blue eyes stayed his servant's tongue, as did the master's other hand upon the hilt of his blade. Nico knew this moment, just as he'd known that it was because of David's anger that the three of them were subject to relive it. His heart pounded as the cold air swirled.

"Does he know," asked the General. Sorin met the unsettling blue eyes of his superior, and as terror coursed through his veins amid the blood that Eulic longed to spill, he shook his head rapidly in response. "Excellent. Then the plan is to be carried out as scheduled. I trust you are aware of your part to play in all this?"

"Yes," Sorin responded remorsefully as he took a small roll of parchment from his cloak. "The Paradox Curse is ready for use." Eulic snatched it away from him, and a deeply unnerving look swept his face.

"Perfect," he hummed excitedly as his eyes widened. "In three days' time, Prince Raebon and Miria will meet their doom… and their damned child along with them." The general released his servant and made his way back toward the innards of the capital as Sorin watched. With every step the mighty warrior took the philosopher felt his heart rip to pieces. He'd attended their wedding three months prior as the only witness before God that their love was true. More than that, he watched it blossom into what it was since the prince saved the young Orasus a year before. It terrified him at first, but as the days went by he found his fears replaced with envy that transcended time itself. And now, because of Poetic Paradox, it was all sure to end.

"What have I done…?" he questioned aloud as the air around him slowly began to sting.

"Only what was necessary by the order of the King," spoke King Aradmus as he emerged from the shadows with the Play seated firmly upon his head and a black hooded cloak draped around his body. "You were right to bring this to my attention, Sorin, and using General Eulic's jealousy as the front of our plan only ensures that you will not be blamed for your role in all this. After all, if there is something that I know well about a devious plan is the necessity of a scapegoat."

"Do not act as if I had a choice in betraying my friend," he snapped, and though he expected death and even hoped for it for his lack of decorum in addressing the Warrior King, Aradmus merely raised his eyebrows behind the mask and smiled as his feet touched the ground. "How could you do this to your only son, to your unborn *grandchild*?" The king lowered the mask from his face, and as he smiled the steel-gray eyes penetrated the soul of the philosopher who slowly backed away from him.

"Have you ever questioned why it is taboo for a royal to wed a commoner as my prodigal son has?" The king paused for a moment to allow comment from the philosopher, but Sorin merely watched as the monarch's eyes became narrow with hatred. "The common folk of every country have their own presuppositions about what it means to be a ruler without the education and experience to which the royals have been privy for generations. They speak without understanding and make demands based on their feelings rather than any sort of political expertise, and have become so skilled at deceiving themselves that they run the risk of fooling the very rulers that endeavor to protect them."

"Protect them from what, exactly," Sorin questioned, but the Nico within him already knew.

"Why, from themselves, of course. The opinions of the commoners are far too varied to allow for any sort of civil self-governance, and representation within the established system would only go as far as the death of integrity and subsequent birth of corruption. No, what the people need is a bridge, so to speak, a figure who unites these differing whims and ideologies but still serves crown and country to maximum efficiency. My son Raebon has proven to be that unifying force, the perfect tool to sustain the power of our rule. And then, there is the matter of this Miria girl, the freethinker that jeopardizes everything I've built my son to be, who embodies the mixed and misguided presumptions and ideas of a society of sheep and, through love's grip, bears influence over my little prince's mind and heart," explained the twisted Aradmus. Sorin hated hearing these words, that his friend and beloved future ruler would be cursed and then killed for following his heart's command over that of his father, and yet in this age he proved powerless to stop the king and his general.

"Monster," was all the philosopher could utter, and the king chuckled in indifference.

"I suppose I am," he conceded with a disturbingly sinister grin, "but in my monstrosity, I have created a relationship between the people and their ruler the likes of which no nation of our day has ever seen, that poises our people to take the entire world by storm… one that cannot be put at risk under any circumstances." Sorin grew increasingly angered as what he assumed was Aradmus' plan came into full view.

"That is why you chose the Play. You had suspected that something like this would happen and so you have resolved to kill the prince and take his place using the Theatrical Paradox," Sorin said at moderate tone, and the king clapped.

"Well done," he commended. "Yes, I had my suspicions ever since the day Aeridus revealed himself a traitor. The way he tended to the girl and her brother served as the perfect image of the kind and compassionate ruler that we all have pretended to be over the ages, but the boy's eyes were too sincere. Her life mattered to him in a manner most inappropriate for the future king of Alaedrea. Love, you will find, is not something so easily broken by the word of man, nor is it swiftly undone by the steady flow of time. It becomes necessary for me, then, to accept that my son is ruined, and that the process of rectification must begin." Sorin's heart ached, as he never imagined a father capable of such thoughts. He pushed past the king, unable to take any more of the conversation. "Three days," the king reminded him, "and the rebirth of our kingdom as 'empire' can truly begin." The philosopher paused for a moment, but then quickly started back upon his course.

Sorin took to the streets of Coraena, frantic in the search for the prince. It taunted him, or at least the Nico inside of him, as he knew that past or present he was powerless to stop what was to happen. Raebon would be cursed, their unborn child would be lost, and for what reason? Nothing more than to save the life of a coward. He should have spoken up earlier when the prince had returned from the battlefield, or as he watched just hours before as the prince rushed out of the palace. His eyes stung with tears of self-loathing. After all that Raebon had done for him, how could he repay such kindness with a curse? How could he gift the very tools that would be the lovers' undoing to the ones who would so eagerly rob them of their happiness? How could he deprive their unborn child of a full life?

He needed to make it right somehow, but as the light of the sun grew dimmer still he knew that the time in which he could make a difference rapidly dissipated. He left the cobbled roads of Coraena in favor of the grasses that surrounded the capital, and there upon a hill stood the lovers Raebon and Miria.

"I've missed you," he heard her tell him shakily. "To see you here, unharmed—"

"I know," the prince responded as he pressed his forehead against hers. The remnants of Sorin's heart crumbled into dust at the sight of their sorrowful embrace, and though he knew it would only be right for him to climb the hill and speak with them about the coming events he stood paralyzed. Raebon took the lovely Miria by her shoulders and with sober expression gazed into her softening eyes. "There is something I wish to tell you, my love. Aeridus has been made to pay for his treason against the crown and his sins against your family." The woman came alive with life, but then sobered as she realized her rejoicing at his death was far more despicable than anything he'd done in his life.

"I see," she said, her voice fully stable, and clasped her hands together behind her back. "It seems as if you have more to tell, Raebon." He bit his lower lip, and nervously he sat down in the grass as he motioned for her to join him. She did, and for a moment they gazed into the sky as the stars began to flicker up above.

"Aeridus seems to have entered into an alliance with Odelia. It will not be long before they mount up an offense against the kingdom," he told her. Sorin's face distorted in anguish as he stepped forward, but the residual fear he had for the king cemented his position at the foot of the hill.

"No," Miria huffed as she placed a hand on her belly. "You have only just returned from battle, Beloved. How long should we go without you?" Raebon offered his best comforting smile, bent over and tenderly kissed her stomach. He withdrew his lips, but lingered over her as he stared into the possibilities that would never be realized.

"You have nothing to worry about," uttered the prince in an emotionally mixed tone that spoke more to his dissatisfaction than against it. "My father has ordered me into hiding in preparation for the coming conflict. Because of that, it may very well be difficult for us to spend time together." Miria paused and stared at him for a moment before she adjusted her sights to the town in the distance.

"Is it bad that I prefer you go to war," she asked, and he smiled lovingly as he sat back up. He shook his head and kissed her on her cheek.

"Not to worry, I share in your sentiment. It would be so much easier to protect you were I actively defending the capital, but my father wishes to protect the kingdom's future, and in order to do that he must ensure I live," he explained further, but the mother of his unborn child shook her head.

"We should tell him," she suggested, and his eyes went wide with shock. "The future of Alaedrea extends beyond just you now. Our son or daughter, the king's grandchild will—"

"You overestimate the level of my father's understanding, Miria," the prince cut her off. "If he should discover the imminence of our child's birth, it could very well spell the end for the both of you. That is why you and Orasus will go with General Eulic to a safe house in the morning." *It won't work,* Nico thought as he watched the scene again through the eyes of his former self. He was disgusted with himself, dejected that despite his desire to warn them of the things to come he stood petrified only a few feet away.

"You choose Eulic to carry out such an endeavor," Miria questioned with a worried look in her eye. Raebon took her by the hands and kissed her cheek.

"Despite his past affections for you, he remains one of my trusted officers. There is no finer man in all the Kingdom of Alaedrea to see to your safety," he assured her mistakenly. She gripped her husband's hands tightly in a sign of trust, and as a tear streaked from Sorin's eye he departed from the scene.

He walked the path back to the town in silence, and though his home was now the palace he refused to return there. His face twisted in pain as he marched the cobbled roads. He thought to die, to end his life before his friends could discover what it was he had done, but steeled himself against it. He would not run away as his instincts directed him, but would push beyond the allure of a quick death and commit to a futile attempt to save his prince from the horrible fate to which he was destined to fall.

He came upon the hut that had been his home before the prince had moved him to the palace, and with a simple wave of his hand he undid the lock. He entered, and as soon as his foot crossed the threshold the lamps upon his desk, dresser and nightstand came alive with fire and light. He advanced for the nightstand and opened its drawer to find the small crimson-colored notebook that was the Poem, along with a jet-black quill. He again crossed the room to sit at his desk, and after he took a moment to collect his thoughts, he began to write:

"The General hunts and growls, a savage,
That eyes the prince in hopes to ravage
The dreams the King's Son seeks to obtain

And cause him naught but suffering and pain,
But in the face of his former flame,
Mercy he will show at the sound of her name
That foils the plan of the ravenous King,
And frees the lovers of irreparable sting."

He watched with hope renewed as the words upon the page came alight with a mystique all their own, and as they dulled before him, Sorin closed the small book. He made his way for the poor excuse of a bed that rested in the center of the room and reclined upon it. He watched the shadows dance upon the ceiling as his mind swirled like the flickering flames of the lamps. Three days was all he had to make a difference, and though he wished he could do more, the poetic curse he'd written proved all he could manage.

He closed his eyes, certain that the era of Alaedrea would quickly come to an end.

"So, you failed to warn him after all," came the delighted voice of King Aradmus. He jolted from the bed in fear and gripped the Poem tightly in his hands as he stared into the enchanting mask that was the Play. "It would seem that you do not quite have the stomach to break the spirit of the ones you hold so dear."

"You know me," said the terrified philosopher. "I am naught but a coward." The king lowered his mask as a twisted smirk slithered across his face. He reached into the shadows from whence he came and to Sorin's alarm snatched the Poem out of his hands.

"Apparently not," spoke King Aradmus as he leafed through the pages and found the freshly penned curse. "My, my, what fortitude you have grown that you dare stand in the way of the plans of your king."

"You are *not* my king, Aradmus," Sorin spoke with boldness previously unseen, and the force behind his assertion caused the king to raise an eyebrow. "Aeridus was right to abhor you, to see you as the manipulative and controlling tyrant you really are."

"And how did that work out for him, my dear boy," Aradmus quickly retorted. His temper flared, and as his bloodlust became more pronounced so, too, did the near unbearable sting in the air. "Was it not my very son that you love as your own flesh and blood that slew him on the battlefield?" Sorin paused and clenched his fists. He was right, and had the philosopher pledged loyalty to the insurgents then he would likely have been killed along with them.

"What will you do, then," he questioned as he folded his arms across his chest and stared into the hollow gray eyes of this monster of a king. "Will you kill me and, in doing so, raise the suspicions first spread by the word of the High Counselor?" The king shook his head in response as he placed the mask back upon his face.

"Oh no," he hummed, and the burning air in the room began to swirl. "You are far too valuable to simply kill, Moderator. However, the actions that you have taken against the Crown must be met with some form of punishment. Luckily, I have just the idea of how I should repay you for this egregious disservice." The king waved his hand, and instantly the shadows warped around them. Sorin blinked, and when he reopened his eyes he found himself surrounded by darkness with only a small window before him. His heart pounded against his chest as sweat poured down his face, and time itself seemed to stand still. *Traitor...* called an amalgamation of voices through the dark. *Traitor...* his mind became heavy as they repeated the word over and over again. Frantically he waved his hands around in an effort to strike whatever demons chanted in his hearing, but his many strikes failed to land.

Fear set in, and the strong hand of the malevolent monarch fell upon his shoulder.

"Where have you taken me," Sorin demanded as he watched through the window. Raebon appeared before him, surrounded by guards and on the move. It was day, and he looked sorrowful.

"Consider this 'the Audience,'" spoke the king. "In this realm, you will be able to see the events of the world without, but like a spectator at a play you will be silenced, completely incapable of influencing the performance to which you will bear witness. I hope you enjoy it. Now, if you will excuse me, I have to teach my son a valuable lesson about life." The stinging air swirled once again, and as Sorin drew closer to the window into his former life the presence of the king vanished without a trace.

Watch... Traitor, watch... the voices taunted him even louder at the absence of their ruler, and Sorin began to panic ever the more as the seconds passed. His ears ached from their frequent call, and though he knew it had no effect he flailed his fists in an attempt to silence the things that beckoned to him. *Weak... slime...* the chanting continued, and new vocabulary that struck the many cords of Sorin's heart mingled with the insults hurled before. *Disgrace... slimy traitor... watch!*

Sorin lifted his hand and prepared to dispel the full force of his Poetic Paradox, but though his lips moved to the rhythm in his heart they produced no sound. No, only the voices of the Audience could be heard, only they had power here. His legs felt weak, and he collapsed unceremoniously to his knees. His head throbbed and the sweat of his brow dripped profusely, and as the many voices that drilled their way into his ears grew louder and louder still, he determined that it wasn't worth it.

"I'm sorry," he whispered to himself between the hate-filled screams that pounced upon him from all directions, and like termites in wood ate away at his mind. His eyes lifted to the portal that showed him Prince Raebon, and as he gazed upon the heartbroken face of his prince, no, his friend, a numbness overtook him. Darkness rested on Raebon's shoulders, and it was as if the very shadow of Death himself wrapped around the warrior prince. The waters that welled up in Sorin's eyes began to spill over as his hands trembled with renewed vigor. "I'm sorry," he sobbed over the voices in the background, "I'm so sorry!" He realized that he was no longer Sorin, but Nico reliving his most nightmarish moment, and even after a millennium he was powerless to break free of that realm.

Break... chanted the voices in the darkness, but the despondent Moderator shook his head in denial.

"No," he murmured shakily as he pressed his hands against his ears like a terrified child in a crowd of strangers.

Break, slimy traitor... the voices barked their demand now, determined to savor the taste of his tears and bask in the glory of his misery and madness.

"No!" His rage overflowed, but it did little to silence the demented voices that sought to cripple him. His head dropped as he bent over and pounded his fists against the shadowy floor. Sorin the philosopher and Nico along with him, resigned himself to blackest Hell.

Chapter Seventeen

Raebon paced back and forth within the disturbingly quiet chamber of the palace's covert sanctuary. It had been three days since he returned from battle, and the dark cloud of conflict loomed over the heads of all within the kingdom. He longed to join his troops on the front line, but more than anything he wished for an update on Miria's condition. That was his priority now, even more so than was the defense of his country. She, along with the baby within her, had to be safe. Even now he could remember the moment she told him with utmost clarity. He was shocked, so much so that he stumbled backwards and fell to the ground. But he was happy, and he eagerly looked towards the moment he would hold his child in his arms.

He did his best to put his mind at ease with the knowledge that Eulic could form an entire army out of a mystic ball of clay. They didn't need him, or at least that's what he told himself as he sat at the foot of the bed with his hands clasped together. Footsteps came from down the hallway, and the rhythm of the stride proved more familiar than any guard could possibly manage. It was his father. The knights that kept watch over the hardwood door adjusted to greet their king, and following a series of unintelligible murmurs Aradmus entered.

The prince was less than enthusiastic to see the king, and promptly crossed his arms as he rose from the bed. Aradmus took note of his son's hostility, but just as in the throne room he donned the kingly façade that masked the evil that swelled within.

"Is that any way to greet your king," questioned the malicious Alaedrean ruler as his eyes softened upon his son. Raebon gave a sarcastic chuckle.

"What will you be king of after today? You lock away your best warrior without hesitation as the enemy advances and have the audacity to believe that the kingdom will prevail!" Raebon's indignation overshadowed any attempt to stave it off, and the sight of his father only served to stir his fury. Aradmus, though a cold and calculating man, adopted an almost apologetic expression as he moved to the bed and took a seat.

"I understand the animosity you feel, my son. For so long you have opted to be the protector of the people and now, as per my order, you are subject to being protected. You must feel like a helpless child," mused the king, and the prince's eyes narrowed on him as they began to glow bright in the shade of the chamber.

Aradmus' face expressed a new severity that had never been shown to his son, but then instantly relaxed as his hands clasped before him. "You must consider, Raebon, that you are my son before you are a warrior or even a prince, for that matter, and as your father it is my duty to ensure that you have a future if all others should perish." Raebon shook his head as he brought his arms down to his sides.

"Selfish, Father, that is the nature of your reasoning," the Prince spat, and though he expected the reprimands of his kingly father, Aradmus merely smiled. "How dare you speak of the future when the children of the country are at risk outside these walls? Had that mattered, had you any consideration of this nation beyond your own concerns then you would do what you could to preserve the futures of the others!"

"You speak of the peasant boy who was held hostage by Aeridus at the address," guessed the king, and though Raebon thought to speak of the child he had yet to see with his own eyes, he hesitated a response.

"Not only Orasus," the prince offered, "but those like him. Children who have yet to grow into manhood or womanhood, who have never seen the battlefield or raised a family, who, in many cases, have never tasted the joys of life and may have only seen sorrow. They are the ones most deserving of a future, Father," the sudden quiet of his voice alarmed him, as he realized that his paternal instincts took hold.

"Perhaps you know of what you speak," Aradmus conceded as a smug smile slithered in place. "I am very much selfish in that I care only what happens to you, but until the day comes where you have children you will never understand—"

"She bears my child," Raebon shouted over his father, eyes wide with rage and fists atremble. The smug expression of the king vanished instantly and the room fell silent. Tension thickened the air, and the anger of the king contributed to its sting as his eyes narrowed on his son.

"What did you just say," he demanded in a slow, menacing tone that sent a pulse of fear through Raebon's entire body. Nevertheless, the unapologetic prince stood tall and stabilized his shaking hands.

"As of three months ago, I have taken Miria, daughter of Forsaeus as my wife," he all but bragged, and as the irate king increasingly lost his composure the warrior prince continued. "In the time since, a child has been conceived." Aradmus' hate-filled glare mysteriously disappeared, and as his arms fell to his side his gray eyes hardened with his heart.

"So then this is what you have chosen," he spoke solemnly as his son's expression grew remorseful, "to lay with a whore and create an abomination." Aradmus exhaled as he momentarily closed his eyes. "I see now that there is no saving you."

"Father…" Raebon's voice trailed off as the claws of despair tightly wrapped around his heart and wrenched. He felt as if he, the hardened warrior prince, hero of the people of Alaedrea, were naught but a small boy suddenly abandoned in the wilderness by the only parent he had left.

"Where is she," asked the calloused king, who grew increasingly frustrated by his son's hesitation. "Where is she?!" The sting of the air intensified with his sudden burst of anger, and at that, whatever loyalty Raebon had to his father vanished.

"Somewhere safe," he responded as his eyes narrowed in spite. Aradmus chuckled, and as his eyes fell upon his son he pressed his palm against his forehead and laughed louder still.

"You think you can hide her from me," the king stated with the bite of condescension. He pulled out the Play as he grasped his son by the throat and hoisted him into the air. "Darkness, light, the very world in which we live, I can *become*! There is no limit to the manifestation of my presence or the assertion of my power. I will find her, my prodigal son. Whether or not you wish to help me." A loud burst echoed through the palace that drew the attention of the king. Raebon cracked a smile, as he realized that the seat of power occupied by his twisted savage of a parent had already begun to crumble.

"You may… want to get… started," wheezed the prince, and with a low growl the king released his grip and turned back toward the door. Raebon, who had fallen to his knees and greedily absorbed as much air as he could, desperately gripped the bed as he staggered back to his feet. The door slammed just before he could will himself through it.

"Under no circumstances is my son to leave this room," Aradmus ordered with a bitterness in his voice.

"Sir!" The guards shouted in compliance, and without delay the king exited the hall with twice the haste as when he had arrived.

"This is bad," Raebon muttered to himself as he pulled the Tale from his armor. He had to get to Miria before his father discovered her whereabouts. He pressed the tip of the small golden quill against the door and started to write.

"The foundations of the kingdom of Alaedrea shook, and as the Odelian enemy advanced against King Aradmus and his valiant forces, the Alaedreans trembled before their unprecedented might. Raebon, the crown prince and hero of the people had yet to arrive on the battlefield. They scrambled to hold the Odelians back, and though they fought bravely it was not long before they were overwhelmed. The forces of Romedor the Odelian king had slaughtered many in an effortless display, and messengers were dispatched by Aradmus' command to summon all other guards to the streets of Coraena where the battle raged on."

Raebon stowed the pen against his chest once again and patiently awaited the brief tale to come to fruition as he backed against the wall opposite the door. A chaotic boom resounded through the chamber, and the shouts that followed facilitated the exit of the guards that were supposed to keep watch over the rebellious prince. Raebon smiled as he ran for the door at full speed, and as he collided with the wooden fixture with unmitigated force it broke apart like a sheet of paper. He took a moment and surveyed the corridor, and it quickly became apparent that only he remained.

He ran through the winding path with his hand firmly wrapped around the hilt of his sword, and as he came to the foyer of the palace he watched the remainder of the king's knights run for the streets of Coraena. He dashed through the back of the palace as he had with Miria before, and ducked behind the shrubbery as the knights on horseback exited the stables with haste. The area was clear, and the dauntless prince rushed the stables to claim his signature black horse. The beast nudged him with its head, and with a smile he brushed his hand against its snout.

He quickly untied the reins and mounted its back, and in an instant, he was off. All around him the armies clashed. The metallic scent of blood filled the air, and the smoke that rose from the burning houses and shops darkened the sky. It was the very picture of horror, as soldiers and civilians alike lay slain in the streets, but there was little he could do for them now. He cracked the reins and drove his heels into the sides of the horse, and as it sped through the sea of combatants, he desperately prayed for Miria's safety.

An arrow hurdled through the air and lodged in the neck of Raebon's horse, and as it toppled forward, the prince leaped from its back to roll along the ground. He glanced back at his beloved steed, which now joined the ever-growing heap of corpses, and with a thunderous vociferation he turned his attentions to the direction from whence the projectile came. It took a moment, but the irate Raebon spotted the archer and chased through the forest after him. The shooter lined up another shot and pointed the tip of his arrow at the prince's head, and though he shot straight forward with sniper-adjacent accuracy, Raebon easily sidestepped the projectile and continued his advance. The face of the archer reflected his confusion as he withdrew two additional arrows from his quiver and lined them on his bowstring.

Prince Raebon withdrew his sword, and his white eyes glowed hot with bloodlust as he grew closer to his intended target.

"Do you really believe that your pathetic arrows would even scratch the surface of my skin," taunted the prince. The archer released his grip on the drawstring, but to his chagrin the prince dodged the first arrow while he sliced the other in half. "Your optimism is commendable, though wishful thinking will do little here." Raebon was mere feet away from the young warrior, who realized that the second he drew another arrow it would spell out his end. He trembled before the awe-inspiring presence of the prince, and as if on cue a squad of Odelian warriors emerged from the surrounding trees. "Oh look," Raebon cooed as a smirk as sadistic as his father's manifested on his face. He numbered them at five, saw that they were fully armed, and deduced that they were no threat at all to him. "You had friends…"

"Have," one of the soldiers corrected aggressively as he brandished his sword. Raebon guffawed at the audacity of the gaggle of fools but instantaneously became sober as he tossed his sword blade-first into the man's chest. The others looked on in horror, and Raebon watched as together they charged him. Two of the remaining four raised their blades while the others drove their swords toward him simultaneously, but before contact could be made the prince sidestepped and the oncoming blades penetrated the armor of the stationary assailants. The four of them together released the hilts of their blades. Two collapsed, dead as the first that Raebon had killed, and the remaining duo stood in awe of the powerhouse of a warrior between them.

They backed away from him with fear in their eyes, and the archer took aim again. He lined up his shot, but a single glare from the Alaedrean prince forced him to miss and hit one of his comrades. As the archer's unintentional target fell dead upon the ground, Raebon withdrew a dagger from his side and plunged it into the neck of the remaining Odelian soldier. The victim gripped the prince's arm as he fell to his knees, and with a sharp kick to the face the man's head snapped against the ground of the forest.

"Well," Raebon said to the lot of them as he collected his blades, slashed them through the air and sheathed them once again, "it would seem that you stand corrected." The archer thought to run, but his speed was far outmatched by that of the aggravated prince. Raebon slammed him against the nearest tree and gripped his throat with just enough pressure to properly display his seriousness.

"What are you," asked the foreigner, to which the prince tightened his grip and narrowed his glowing white eyes.

"There is a solid stone fortress not far from here. You and your men must have passed it in your advance upon the city," Prince Raebon began, and the terrified warrior rapidly nodded his head.

"Yes, yes, it was a safe house! King Romedor ordered it be destroyed and had the occupants taken as prisoner!" The prince's eyes widened with an even mixture of terror and anger.

"How long ago was this," the prince demanded, and steadily applied pressure to the sniveling archer that squirmed within his clutches.

"Not long," he wheezed as he gripped the prince's hand and desperately tried to pry it away from his windpipe. "You can still catch them… if you hurry."

"Thank you," he breathed as he dropped the soldier. The archer scrambled to get away, but the now frenzied prince immediately drove his sword into the small of his back and through his stomach. He rushed in the direction of the safe house, sword still drawn and more than prepared for battle. *Miria,* he thought as another pair of soldiers rushed him from either side. He ducked below the swing of their blades and in a single fluid motion cut through their legs. They toppled over, and though he thought to slaughter them all for their insulting attempt upon his life, he knew that time was short if he was ever to rescue his wife.

He took off yet again and worked to evade the low-hanging branches of the trees until the fatigue of his armored sprint began to take its toll. He paused for a moment and beat his fist against the ground as he caught his breath. A feminine scream ripped through the air, and his heartbeat pounded against his chest with the force of ten men. It was *her*.

"Miria!" The name escaped his lips before he could pull himself together, and just like that he powered himself through the trees yet again. *I will find her, my prodigal son.* Raebon heard the sinister voice of his father in his head, and though he worried for Miria's wellbeing, he resolved that none should ever have her but him.

He came to the place where the fortress had been and dropped to one knee as he gasped for air. His side ached from the work that it took to get him to this point, but he couldn't bring himself to stop. He scanned the safe house for his beloved, and watched as a pair of troops carried her unconscious body out of the building and loaded her into the lap of a knight on horseback. With a shout, the kidnapper cracked the reins and galloped off into the distance.

A furious Raebon ran through the thicket and instantly took to the back of a horse. The two soldiers who had previously carried his wife to her captor rushed to stop him, but with agility and grace the king's son launched himself from the horse's back to land between them, and in a revolutionary swipe decapitated them both. As their bodies fell lifeless upon the ground, he took to the back of the beast of burden once again and thrashed the reins with every ounce of animosity that coursed through him.

The horse was startled to life, and rapidly pursued that of the royal's enemy. Raebon could taste his blood, see the life slowly drain from his eyes, and as the images became more potent in his mind so did his desire to make the captor pay. The enemy, who had previously taken his time in his stride back to the Odelian camp, heard the exasperated roar of the Alaedreans' warrior prince and took notice of him. The belligerent ivory glare of the pursuer incited a fresh speed from his target, who repeatedly drove his heels into the sides of the horse.

Raebon thought for a moment to reach for the dagger at his side and throw it into the leg of the massive animal before him, but the toss of Miria's wind-blown hair quickly dissuaded him from the idea. He bit his lower lip with full force and tasted the frustration in his own blood as it dripped down his chin, but resolved to chase the man until the horses could go no further. But what was his plan after that? The second he was reunited with his beloved he would then be forced to flee from two warring nations, and because of his conquests on the battlefield there were few nations that would willingly grant him asylum.

And then there was the matter of Orasus. No matter how much she loved the prince, she could never be persuaded to leave without the little brother that she had protected for so long. Maybe they could… No, this was neither the time nor the place to concern himself with anyone other than his wife, who presently lay beyond his reach.

"Give her back," Raebon demanded as a flurry of violent thoughts swirled about within his head. He thrashed the reins yet again, and now rode alongside the malefactor that evaded him. "Give her back *now*!" The soldier jolted in utter terror as he gazed into Raebon's eyes, which had donned a solid white hue. The soldier blasted out of the forest and banked left, and though the prince followed he fell behind yet again. "I will destroy you," he roared as he raised his blood-covered blade into the air. The smell of meat over flame filtered into his nostrils, and with that he could tell that they drew near the Odelian camp. Miria stirred awake, and at the sight of the stranger that lingered over her she shrieked.

She reached for the blade at the knight's side, but with a great deal of effort he wrestled her hand away. For a moment his eyes met hers, and the golden sheen that all but mirrored the white luster of Raebon's sent chills down his spine. Nevertheless, he held her in place and barreled into the camp as the prince she loved followed behind.

"Prince Raebon approaches," the terrified knight shrieked. "Surround the enemy!" As Raebon's horse pounded into the camp, a horde of Odelian troops quickly advanced from all sides. The horse neighed in fear and Raebon reached for his sword but slowly retracted his hand as the Odelian soldiers drew their weapons in response. The prince ignored them all, as he was solely focused on his struggling wife. She resisted with everything she had, and as a result the knight that held her hostage raised his hands as if to strike her.

“Do it,” Raebon called from the other side of the clearing, “and I will crush you all with my bare hands!”

“There will be no need for that,” came a familiar voice from the prince’s side. “Bring her here.” Raebon watched as his wife was transported around the circle of warriors, and felt his blood boil when the bastard on the horse tossed her into the arms of his commander. She vehemently fought against him, but he forced a kiss despite her struggles. Raebon dismounted the horse and drew his blade, and though the congregation of soldiers prevented his advance, his subsequent roar attracted the attention of the man who harassed his wife. He turned around, and much to the horror of the animalistic prince, General Eulic flashed a devilish smile in the light of the fire. “Greetings, my prince.”

Chapter Eighteen

"Oh, come now," spoke the treacherous Eulic as he licked the side of Miria's face like the salivating dog that Raebon imagined him to be. "Does this really surprise you, Raebon?" His blue eyes lit with sickening euphoria as the face of his former prince twisted in disgust. "Is it so shocking that I, the esteemed general and dedicated knight, would betray the sniveling brat that belittled me and stole his beloved away?"

"I was never yours in the first place, Eulic—" Miria spat.

"You were always mine," the general shouted in return as his grip tightened on her arm. "The mistake was allowing you to believe you had a choice in the matter!"

"Is that because she chose me over you," taunted the warrior prince, "because she actually loves me? Are you really so small a man that you would betray an entire kingdom over a broken heart?" Eulic paused for a moment and slowly rose to hysterical laughter.

"You are truly unbelievable," he chortled as he locked eyes with Alaedrea's heir. "Yet again you berate me, though it is I who decides whether you live or die."

"How dare you threaten me," snapped the prince, "when it is I who brought you the many victories that established your esteem?"

"You *humiliated* me," yelled the general at the top of his lungs as he released Miria's arm to point at his former superior. The maiden turned from her captor and attempted to run, but before she could break away from the horror of the scene, the disgraced battler grabbed her by her hair and dragged her back to his side. "You've always humiliated me! You contradicted me before my troops, called my integrity and devotion into question in the public eye, stole Miria away from me," his voice momentarily softened, and the woman in his grasp screamed in pain and fear as his arms jerked about.

"Eulic," Raebon snarled. "Unhand my wife!" The very word caused the general's wounded heart to fester and his eyebrow began to twitch.

"Ah, but you see, she is mine now," teased the general, but as the words left his lips the air began to sting and the shadows within the camp coalesced before them both.

"Actually," came the voice of King Aradmus as he manifested from the shadows, "she belongs to me." The king, who slowly pulled the Play from his face, boldly stared into the eyes of the son who all but foamed at the mouth at his arrival. "I told you that I would find her, did I not?"

"You stay away from her," the irate Raebon demanded, and calloused Aradmus flashed a grin as he spread his arms.

"Ah, my dear son I ask you, where is the fun in that? After all the trouble I went through to stage today's events, you wish me to merely stay my blade and walk away?" Raebon growled, and as he raised his sword above his head the king snapped his fingers. "Bind him." The foreign soldiers that had surrounded Raebon since his arrival quickly swarmed him and slammed him against the ground. Miria called out his name in distress, and General Eulic smiled with devilish delight. "Now… it seems as if something is missing…" Aradmus again snapped his fingers, and with an eerie smile on his face he returned to his mask.

"What are you about to do," the grounded warrior questioned with white ferocity in his glare as he thrashed about in an effort to free himself. Aradmus turned to the empty space between Raebon and Eulic, and with arms spread out he manipulated the shadows.

"I am going to teach you the penalty for your actions," he said with an air of delight. Every eye in the camp turned to the two orbs of solidified darkness that appeared in the clearing, and in mere moments the shadows gave way to reveal two figures bound by their hands. They fell upon the ground, and as they groaned Raebon and Miria came to know them as Sorin and Orasus. “You see, my son,” the sadistic king began again as he drew the sword from his waist, “when someone of your position defies your king, they threaten the very structure of the society in which we live. Anarchy tends to follow, and before long all that one ever held dear tends to fall prey to the madness produced by a single act of rebellion. In fact, it is often the case that the insurrectionist is forced to watch as those most precious to him perish. A fitting reprimand for your rebellion, is it not?” Raebon and Miria froze as their hearts leapt into their throats, and together they watched as the king drew near the boy.

Miria’s eyes became alight with rage as she kicked the general in the groin and made a break for her baby brother.

“Orasus,” she called desperately as she approached, but with a wave of his hand, Aradmus bound her by the shadows that he loved so much. She fought to break free with everything within her, but it was all for naught as the darkness gripped her ever tighter. She was forced to watch the tyrant revealed as he turned for her and brandished his sword.

“Would you like to be the first,” he asked her sadistically as he gently pressed the blade’s edge against the woman’s throat. “Or perhaps we should begin with the abomination within you... there is no end to all the possibilities.”

“Wait,” spoke the general, who gripped his groin and pushed himself back to his feet. “Do not kill her. I… I love her…”

“You *love* her,” the king repeated with an air of humor in his voice. “You, the one whose very idea this was, he who harbored deepest hatred and animosity for the rebellious son and the wayward wench what tempted him, profess feelings for her while the curse rests in your grip? Ridiculous.” The king returned his attention to the woman paralyzed by his darkness and methodically waved his blade between their faces.

“Stop!” It was General Eulic who shouted it, and as he approached the object of his misguided affections he revealed the Earth in the palm of his hand. Aradmus’ full attentions rested on the soldier now, though it was unclear if it was from intrigue, aggression or amusement. He swung his sword downward and prepared for battle as the general spun the ivory orb of clay. The swirls of gold and silver around its surface glowed with the same intensity of Eulic’s blue eyes, and as the speed of the ball’s rotation increased it produced three clumps that bubbled on the ground before their master. They slowly lifted themselves up and defined themselves according to Eulic's will. There between the king and his former servant stood a trio of humanoid slime, each with a disturbing pair of white eyes.

"My, my," hummed the king with an air of intrigue. "What an interesting little trick…" The trio of White-Eyes charged the king with arms upraised. They thrust their lifted limbs forward, and to the surprise of all present their hands sharpened as the heads of spears. King Aradmus stepped back and faded into the shadows as the creatures passed, and reappeared behind the man that summoned them. Eulic turned, and at the sight of the monarch's descending blade he lifted the Earth. The clay expanded to block the blow, and as the sword of the king bounced off its hardened surface, its wielder went for a slash at the general's midsection.

Eulic blocked once again, but much to his concern there was no contact between the sword and the clay. The king looked down as his arms swung the brand, and a terrified Eulic followed his line of sight. The end of the sword slipped into a shadowy portal, and just as the general thought to ask where the king had sent it, his answer ripped through his midsection from behind.

Eulic's torso fell from his lower body, and the creatures that came to life at his discretion returned from the orb by which they were formed. Aradmus picked up the ball of clay, and with a gleam of delight in his eyes he placed it in the pocket of his cloak.

Sorin stirred to his hands and knees, still uncertain just what hell he'd been warped to this time, but at the sound of the king's footsteps he slightly turned and beheld the bisected body of his former master. He examined the whole of the terrain, and with every new horror he realized that this was nothing but reality.

"What is… what is going on here," the philosopher asked as his skin grew cold. Aradmus knelt at his side and gave a glance back at his son, who struggled so desperately to get free.

"It would appear that our mutual pawn has been removed from the game," the king whispered in response. He turned his attention back to Prince Raebon as he pressed his blood-soaked blade edge against the neck of Raebon's dearest friend. "Do you know why your friend will be the first to die, my son? I suppose it would be necessary to impart upon you the reality of the situation. The curse of which the general spoke," the king reached into the darkness and pulled out the blood-spattered roll of parchment that Sorin recognized all too well, “this curse, was written by your friend at my request, but no sooner than he handed it over to us did he feel remorse for what he had done.” Raebon writhed against the hands that held him with increased vigor as he grunted and roared like a wild beast. He dared not even look to Miria, as with every breath he took he was reminded that he had failed to keep his promise to her. “He tried to warn you, to save you before the words on this page could be read aloud and your iniquitous union be forever broken apart, but when he saw you, when he beheld the loving smiles upon your faces he instead returned to his former domicile and penned a counter-curse. And so, for his treason he must bear the consequences.”

“No!” The prince vociferated as the sword of the king separated Sorin’s head from his body. It rolled toward the prince, who stared into his best friend’s eyes as the hazel lights were glazed over by dull white. Tears stung Raebon’s eyes as he turned his head, but his father would not allow it.

“Make him watch,” the king commanded, and one of the soldiers that had the prince bound forced his head forward as the king approached the young Orasus. Miria screamed and cried as she pulled against the shadowy chains, but no matter how she tried to reach her precious baby brother, he remained far beyond her touch. Aradmus lifted his hand as he balled it into a fist, and the shadows that bound the prince's wife warped over her mouth and silenced her. Tears streamed down their faces as they were forced to watch the king hoist the barely conscious child by the collar of his shirt into the air.

"Father, stop this," Raebon begged as he jerked about and trembled from fatigue. "He is only a child!"

"And what kind of example has been set for him? Shall he grow older only to resent the crown and rebel against the king as the two of you have? Will he bring calamity on the nation that saw him raised and fed and cared for? No, the boy is the very seed of *risk*, planted by your own misdeeds. His blood is on your hands," Aradmus yelled as he plunged the end of his sword into the belly of the child. Orasus eyes opened one final time, and though he reached for the face of the king, his little arm fell limp.

Aradmus twisted his sword sideways and slashed it free of the boy's carcass and Miria broke into heavy sobs. Raebon's breath became heavy with disdain and the white glow of his eyes intensified as his father slowly approached his one and only love.

"You stay away from her," he demanded as he slowly powered up. Adrenaline coursed through his veins alongside the hatred and disgust, but as he pushed the soldiers off and regained his strength a sharp pain pierced his side. He collapsed, weakened yet again, and felt the warmth of his own blood spread within his armor. “Father, please… If someone had done this to Mother, then what would you have done to them? How would you have felt?” The king’s stride came to a halt as he turned to face his son. He laughed hysterically as he returned to his steady pace toward the woman that held Raebon’s heart.

“Oh, my dear son…” Aradmus’ voice trailed off as he leveled his sword with Miria’s abdomen. “How do you think your mother died?” Raebon’s tormented eyes grew wide with greater despair as his heart contorted under the sound of delight in his demon father’s voice. Without further hesitation, the monstrous king pierced the womb of his heir’s bride with a sinister smirk and a force that *almost* relieved him of his aggression. The tyrant waved his hand, and the gag of darkness that kept Miria quiet dissipated in an instant. She wailed as her blood spilled upon the grass, and fell to the ground with her arms wrapped around her waist. Aradmus’ eyes lit with devilish glee, and the twisted laugh of the would-be emperor echoed throughout the night sky. “Can you hear it, my son; the blissful sounds of sinners’ agony?”

"You are mad," Miria screamed, and with a slight push of his blade she, too, was skewered like the rest. Raebon felt his heart shatter like glass as her name escaped his lips. Her eyes trained on him as her heartbeat slowed, and silently she cried in fear of what her prince would suffer in the moments to come. Raebon's hand broke free, and through heavy emotion he reached for her.

"Do you see it now, my boy," questioned the father as he paced the ground, alive with the thrill of shedding blood. The last remnants of the royal family glared at each other, and as the pace of Raebon's breath quickened from the feeling of emptiness unimaginable, the king approached and slashed his sword through the air, ready to put an end to his child's deviance. "Do you now know the cost of rebellion? This is the fruit born of the tree that you planted, and it is still yet to become ripe!" He dug his blade into his son's shoulder and pinned him to the ground. The wounded cry of his baby boy did little to shake the heart of the merciless monarch, who unraveled the parchment and removed his mask. "Here is the culmination of your reward, my son, a curse more than deserving of one such as you." Through his anger, Raebon's body shimmered in golden light as his eyes donned a solid white hue. The twisted disposition of his father radiated a stinging heat, and the soldiers that bound the prince grew weaker as their very lives fed into the shadows of King Aradmus. As he watched his son Raebon thrash and rise through the pain of his wounds, he started to read aloud the Paradox Curse:

"The blade has dulled and glory passed,
And times come frighteningly fast
Where children cease to sing his praise
And long forgotten are the days
Where Raebon walked upon this earth
And slayed the dignity of his birth.
As the Kingdom Alaedrea falls
So Raebon must, too, heed death's call
As will that Temptress gone astray
Who made the King's son Lechery's slave.
The Lovers of dissociated class,
He a noble and she more crass
Are thrust henceforth through time and space
Forbidden to gaze upon the other's face
Unless the loving man should see
It is his writing that holds the key

To open doors shut in ages old
And reunite the Lovers' souls.
Forever more will they still rise,
As many times as they have died.
And when the earth blots out the sun
Will then this wretched game be done."

The final word was uttered, and in one last act of unprecedented cruelty, the father slayed the son with the sheer force of his darkness.

David awoke last within the shimmering silver plane as before. The notepad upon which he wrote their names before bore the entire account of their curse, and as he leafed through it all he gripped his chest from the pain.

"David," Nico spoke solemnly as he walked across the argent cloud. The philosopher hesitated to look upon the author's face, as the shame of his actions carried their weight steadily over the course of time. "I—"

"I'm sorry," interrupted the author, who now stood to his feet and pulled his friend into a warm embrace. "I couldn't protect you… Any of you… Your deaths were all my fault." He was badly shaken, and though Nico wanted to do something, he knew that he was incredibly limited.

“You have nothing to apologize for,” came an angelic feminine voice from behind him. David instantaneously released his best friend and turned to see the smiling face of his beloved Eva. He took her in his arms and held her tightly, and just like that he was calmed. “You did your best to try and save us. You chose to fight and struggle, even when it would have been easier to lay there and accept it. That’s why towards the end, I looked to you. I wanted the last thing my eyes beheld to be you.” He gently took her lips with his and ran his fingers through her dark brown hair. He pressed his hand against her stomach, and for a moment she pulled away. It was surreal to him, how they once again stood face to face, fully aware of who they were. His hand trembled, and though he hated his father for the things that he had done, David felt relief in the presence of what proved to be his real family. The lovers’ eyes locked in sincerity, and in his typical humor, Nico waved his hand between their faces.

“Guys, wake up,” he told them flatly. The couple glared at him, though they resisted the urge to smile.

“You’re so rude, you know that,” David said with an unintentional chuckle, and Nico threw up his hands.

"Look, I hate that I have to ruin your sappy romantic moment too, but let's not forget that we have a Shade to take out," the agent reminded them. David and Eva exchanged looks of terror, but Nico remained upbeat.

"You're right," Eva conceded with a huff. "So, do you have any more of those Paradox Keys just lying around or am I gonna have to go out there and fight the king in my own strength?"

"Actually," Nico responded with a curious upward inflection as he nervously clasped his hands together. Eva narrowed her eyes and grabbed him by his collar.

"Don't you dare suggest that I just hang back here while you boys go out and have all the fun," she cautioned, and Nico, nervous smile in place, put up his hands in an effort to soothe her.

"I wouldn't dream of it," he said, even though he had. "I was just gonna say that the remaining three Keys have been scattered across the world. Since I died along with you back then, they don't answer to me anymore so I would have to hunt them down myself in order to bring you one."

"Well isn't that lovely," she said with a sting of sarcasm.

"Don't worry," David told her as he massaged her shoulders. "You'll get your chance to make him pay." The terrible images crept into his mind, the blood, the blades, the dull white eyes devoid of the life that gave them color. *Sorin, Orasus, Miria, the unborn child...* David thought as his brown eyes returned to their original white and glowed with power unfathomable, *you will pay for them all.* With a wave of his hands, the silver plane swirled in on itself, and in an instant the Medieval Trio stood upon the rooftop of the hotel surrounded by the black of the night sky.

Chapter Nineteen

The devilish laughter of the Shade thundered through the city, and the clear skies up above grew increasingly clouded as the chilled air started to sting. David could feel the presence of his father as the wind swirled around the rooftop, and while his friend and beloved watched, he decidedly took a seat at the center.

"He's coming," the reincarnated prince whispered as his companions walked out to stand in front of him. "Nico, you're not fighting. If you get too involved with this then you'll end up dying. I know you want to help, but I'm not losing anyone this time around." Nico tossed the small red leather notebook to his best friend and smiled when he caught it.

"I, as the Guardian over the Key of the Paradox of Poem, hereby relinquish it to you along with the power that it contains." The formality with which Nico spoke caught the lovers off guard, and as they donned confused expressions he couldn't help but crack a smile.

"Thanks, but… why are you giving me this, exactly," David inquired in honest curiosity. Nico's eyes turned to the sky and patiently awaited the arrival of the demonic shadow.

"Think about it," Nico replied. "If I use my Paradox to help you win then as the moderator I'd die. That's not to say that you can't use your Paradox on me, though. That way, I'd be able to help and none of us have to keel over. Well, except your dear ol' dad, anyway."

"Sounds like a loophole worth trying," Eva mused with her arms folded. She brushed her dark brown hair out of her face and tucked it behind her ear. It was hard for her to stave off thoughts of Orasus' smiling face as they waited for the demon to show itself. She clenched the purple fabric of her turtleneck shift dress as she tried to remember happier times, but here, now, as the three of them prepared to fight against the beast that ended them once before, she just couldn't. David took notice of the tear that escaped her eye.

"Are you alright, Sweetie," David asked with concern in his tone that sounded foreign to them both after so long, and though Eva wanted to snap back with something witty to diffuse the tension of the moment, she shook her head.

"No," she admitted in all seriousness. He looked into her golden eyes and saw into the depths of her soul. He understood what it was that she felt, to be reunited with those she'd held dear, to once again run her fingers through Orasus' hair and sooth the boy to sleep, and then abruptly have to watch as the light left his eyes. "To be honest I just want this to be over."

David gave a low, barely audible hum as he opened the Poem before him and withdrew the Tale from his pocket.

"Nico, when you first gave me this Key, you told me that it could create or destroy entire universes, yes?" Nico looked back at his friend, who leafed through the pages of the notepad from before and felt the imprints of the pen on every one. It perplexed him how it flowed like a well-woven story, but it excited him all the same. Beyond his admiration of their shared history, however, David couldn't help but feel as though something was… missing.

"That's right," the manager responded.

"Then would it be possible for it to negate the abilities of the other Keys," David questioned further. Nico raised an eyebrow as he tapped a foot against the concrete tiles of the rooftop.

"Temporarily, I think, as long as it fits with the flow of the story. Why? What exactly are you planning?" David smirked at the inquiry as he applied the pen to the paper within the Poem.

"I might have a way for us to beat that forgotten king and end this," David announced, which tickled the ears of the grieving Eva. “The thing is, I’m gonna need the both of you to keep him busy while I write.” Eva’s entire demeanor softened as a sudden burst of hope ran through her.

“I’ll help in any way I can,” Nico agreed, “though you have to keep in mind that you’re the one who manages our Paradoxes. If you aren’t paying attention you could get me killed. I’m basically powerless now, after all.” Eva slapped him on the shoulder and flashed him a look. He rubbed the sore spot and marveled at what heavy hands she had for a woman with such a delicate frame.

“No pressure,” she spoke sarcastically as she rolled her eyes. She turned her attention to her beloved, who looked back over the events of their former lives and dragged his pen across another page. She had never seen him exercise his passion before, but she greatly admired the way his brow furrowed as his eyes dashed back and forth, how his ears twitched as if to hear the muses that spoke to his soul, how he bit his lower lip as second by second he grew increasingly ensnared by the sights, smells and sounds of the world in which his mind wandered.

“It’s almost time,” Nico informed them, and while David’s eyes remained fixated on the page, those of his companions shifted to the starless sky. “You needn’t hide anymore, Shade.”

Nico looked the two lovers over with a tinge of fear in his expression, but steeled himself to utter what he knew must come next. “They remember.” The world around them drained of all color as the sting of the air burned hotter. The laughter of the demon became wild with delight as the shadows formed a dark portal in the air above the roof’s edge, but what emerged from it was hardly the slender Shade to which the group had grown accustomed.

He stood clothed in armor from his neck down, and his unkempt white hair draped over the silver mask that was the Play. He stepped forward onto the platform that was the roof of the building and popped the knuckles on his massive hands. Aradmus, former king of Alaedrea and father of Raebon surveyed the collection of his enemies that sat before him.

“I have waited for this day for over a thousand years,” the king spoke with eerie elation in his voice. “Now at long last I get to destroy the two of you once and for all!”

“Good luck with that, you shady geezer,” Eva spat with a ravenous glare. His disgust with her became immediately visible.

“How dare you speak to your king in such a coarse manner,” he returned with just as much animosity.

"You're not a king anymore, Aradmus," Nico interjected in a stern tone. "You're just a bitter old man clinging to a bygone era, trying to reclaim a power that will never return." Aradmus' eyes became enlarged with rage as he moved forward to grip the agent's throat, but failed to penetrate the otherworldly force that protected it.

"What is…" The king started in total confusion as the new depth of his emotion brought with it a new level of searing pain.

"You're weak, old man, and like an old dog broken beyond repair, we're gonna have to put you down," David quipped with his solid white eyes still following the trail of words on the page. They glowed as he wrote, and a light emanated from each word that gave the illusion of literal flames at David's command. The king saw the lack of attention on the part of his son, and as his anger gave way to humor, the demon laughed.

"Your bold words do little to fool me, Raebon," Aradmus said as he opened his hand and the very blade that killed them all materialized, shrouded in darkness and pulsing with heat. He threateningly pointed it at the former prince, and though for a moment it frightened Eva to even witness the relic's rebirth, it angered her much more. "You fear me," King Aradmus continued, "so much so that you cannot stand to look up. No matter, I will ensure that your eyes never gaze upon me ever again!" He lunged for the impassioned author, and as he brought his sword sharply down over David's head a sharp jumping side kick by the volatile Eva shattered its entire blade. Aradmus was taken aback, and while his guard was down, Nico executed a leg sweep and watched as the head of his enemy snapped against the concrete tiles. Eva, still boiling over with rage followed up with a crushing elbow to his sternum that knocked out whatever air still circled within him.

David finally looked up at the person that once was his father and merely chortled in amusement.

"You actually think we're afraid of you," he started as his best friend and beloved took to his side and watched as the decrepit king staggered back to his feet. "You act as if your authority is supposed to mean something to us, but all you are is a vestige of hatred that has mistakenly been allowed to live over a thousand years. Since you're not smart enough to come to this conclusion on your own, I'll just tell you: you're not gonna last too much longer."

The king's eyes became the same sickening white as in his Shade form, and while he thought to attack them head on, he was forced to accept that they were right. He was old, and the slightest misstep would result in his unassailable failure. Nevertheless he clenched his fists, and the shadows that surrounded them all rushed to take his side.

"Fools," he exclaimed with his arms spread wide as the darkness cloaked him and his hands withered as before. "Night is my domain! As long as I control it I cannot be defeated!" David cut his eyes as his hand continued to dance across the paper in his lap.

"Who said you controlled *anything*," he inquired. The Shade slithered as a snake through the air, and as his son's companions rushed him, he extended his arms to them to warp their very perception of reality.

Eva fell to the ground, but Nico slowed in his stride as an unimaginable pressure descended upon his shoulders. He grunted as he exerted his full strength to move, and the Shade Aradmus sharpened his bony hand into a blade that mirrored the likeness of the one destroyed. The demon thrust his hands toward the slow-moving philosopher, but as a counter, David wrote and Nico subsequently spoke:

"Decrepit shadow, fall to fear

As you realize your end is near.
Displaced by time
With no real home,
Be blinded by darkness all your own."

The Shade screamed as his vision blurred, and with his bladed hand thrust forward grew surprised at the stark lack of fresh blood on his skin. He snarled in exasperation as he slashed his arm through the air, but little did he know that Nico had long moved out of the way. He picked Eva up from the ground and carried her on his shoulders.

"Nice going," commended the philosopher as he set the pianist down at her beloved's side. The blinded Shade removed the Play from his face, and instantly his form warped back to that of the King. In exchange for his fleshy sword he regained his sight, and in a burst of animalistic rage he charged his son, the servant and the sweetheart with alarming speed. "David," Nico rattled as the king sprinted across the rooftop. David's body glowed in a golden cloak as it had before his death in the Odelian camp, and with his father's every stride the writer became all the more entranced. Nico grew frantic as the belligerent king rapidly approached. "He's coming! David!" David smiled as he continued in his writing, and before Nico could think of what to do a powerful wave of words flowed through him and he spoke:

"Strong and sacred celestial light,
Flow from Heaven and Earth do strike
Upon the head of twisted king,
The crack of which will make men sing."

Lightning rained down from the blackened sky and struck at the feet of the king. Aradmus shifted right of the blast with surprising agility for a man of over a thousand, but his approach was hardly disrupted.

"Is that the best you can do, my son," taunted the king as shadows revolved around his hands. Another of heaven's lustrous arrows flung from the skies toward him, but with an upward thrust of his hands the shadows devoured the light. Aradmus looked at the author, now indifferent to the evasive philosopher or the unconscious pianist, and strode with absolute confidence as the lightning continued to strike. "I must give you your dues for the creativity that you have displayed, but nevertheless," he uttered in deepened tone as he deflected an oncoming blast, "I am beyond your skill." David still said nothing as he poured his thoughts upon the page. Images flashed through his mind and sounds filtered through his ears that transcended the very boundaries of reality. "Answer me," grumbled the king as thunder cracked loudly up above. "Answer me!"

Rain fell from the clouded sky that chilled the air incinerated by the fury of the Shade. David's eyes momentarily fell to Eva, who remained motionless on the ground next to him. His hand became all the more fervent, and the smell of mystical ink penetrated his nostrils and plunged him deeper into the realms of literature. He swayed back and forth as the thud of his father's heavy footsteps resounded about the improper battlefield, and as he steadily lost himself, his beloved Eva became found.

She stirred back to life, and as Aradmus reached for the puppeteer that was his son, she kicked the aggressor's knee with the force of an angry horse. He stumbled forward, but before her former king could rightly hit the ground Eva pushed backwards and drove her knees into his chin. Aradmus flipped backwards into the air as Eva's feet planted on the ground, but then the king disappeared into the shadows once more. Eva carefully cast her gaze in all directions as she prepared for his assault.

“Behind you,” Nico shouted as a jaggedly clawed hand reached for her through the darkness. He ran for her and leaped into the air with elbow raised, and out of shock she ducked in time enough to avoid the servant/master collision. Nico’s elbow connected with the forehead of the king, and as the former Poet rolled back to his feet and donned a ready fighting stance the elder Aradmus slid on his back against the concrete.

“Watch where you’re flying,” Eva demanded as she dusted off her clothes.

“Jeez,” Nico mumbled as he scratched his head, “This is the thanks I get for saving your life. You’d think *I* was the one who just tried to kill you.” She completely ignored him as the hairs on her arms began to stand on end. Her heartbeat escalated, and as she exhaled a sudden cool swept over the arena. Her amber eyes glistened from the glow of David’s body, and with the angelic orbs trained on her enemy she measured the king as he picked himself back up.

He turned around, and she rushed him at maximum speed with her arm extended to take his throat. He ducked the blow and grabbed her hair, and with unprecedented force he pulled her backwards as he drove his knee into her spine. Her breath escaped her on impact, but with borrowed momentum she gripped his head as she continued to roll and drove his face into the concrete tile. She landed on her feet, and with attitude pushed her hair out of her face yet again.

Aradmus laughed repugnantly as he donned his mask, and once more did his appearance change. He slithered through the air above, and with malevolence in his eyes he pulled the ivory ball of clay that was the Earth from his shadowy cloak. He knew this formation would be impossible to break without assistance. Raebon controlled the battle with every word he penned, and Miria and Sorin fell under his protection so long as he was allowed to maintain focus. He had to clear a path to his son and take him out before this fight grew even more complicated, and with the reemergence of the Earth, the devilish monarch was sure he had found a way. Eva and Nico watched as the ball began to convulse and divide, and as the bubbling lumps took their shapes, the two of them were caught off guard entirely.

Eva's eyes filled with tears as Orasus, bloody and impaled, appeared in spades before her very eyes. She fell speechless, and in disgusted horror she backed away as the dolls approached. Nico offered his comfort for only moment, as his beloved Sierra, multiplied by the dark powers of the king, glided towards him with her hand on her belly. The images of Sierra smiled at him, and though he knew it was an illusion, that these figures were just some trick that his enemy had presented him with, his heart jumped to his throat at the very sight of her. Nico stood back to back with Eva as the bleeding clones of her little brother closed in and stared at the false images of his wife with confusion.

"You let me die, sister," spoke the clones in eerie unison as their small feet tread further. Eva poised to strike despite the fear, but the lack of intimidation that they displayed rattled her more than she cared to admit. She looked back at her beloved, whose eyes narrowed on the page as he slashed the quill aggressively. Both of the author's companions suddenly became emboldened, and with a wave of Nico's hand the living sculptures returned to the sphere of clay that birthed them.

"What is this," demanded the Shade as he slithered around the air.

"Eva," Nico called as he crouched down and tied his fingers together. She ran for him instinctively and he vaulted her into the air. The Shade Aradmus fell victim to the brunt force of her shoulder in his abdomen, and much to his dismay the Play behind which he hid dropped from his face. The pair descended to the platform with a crash, but Eva quickly removed herself from the body of the beast.

The king's temper flared, and the chilled winds stung the flesh of all that dared war against him. In blinding speed, he rushed his former servant and kicked him sharply in the temple. Nico's sleek black hair flopped about as he rolled across the ground and scraped the edge of the hotel rooftop. Eva charged the object of her hatred only to receive a punch to the gut that brought her to her knees. The king delivered a crushing kick to her side, and like the philosopher before her she slid against the rocky slab until her back hit the clear glass barricade.

"I have had more than enough of this," Aradmus roared as he hastily strode for his mutinous child who sat comfortably engulfed in the flow of the story. He found that his mask lay just inches from the writer, and as he picked it up a series of dark portals opened on all sides of them. "Blow into the wind." As the words escaped the king's mouth, an innumerable series of arms shot forth from the atmospheric openings and rapidly wrapped around the author. The demon listened with delight as the sound of the scratching quill against the paper ceased, and relished in Eva's wounded cries as he stretched out a hand.

The shadows pulsed as a pet under the touch of its master, and as the Alaedrean king closed his grip, his dark extensions wound tighter around his son.

“Let him go,” Eva cried as she powered herself back to her feet. She gripped her side as she stumbled forward while Nico groaned in the distance.

“And if I decide against it,” the nightmare king provoked as he tightened the shadows further. He turned his head slightly to look at her, and much to his surprise her body glowed with silver light. She rushed him with speed that exceeded his own, and before he could respond she’d twisted his arm behind his back. Aradmus lurched to the side under the pressure of the hold, but immediately attempted a backhand strike with his free arm. Eva released, and as the torque from the assault twisted the king’s entire body she swept his legs out from under him. He descended, and as he approached the ground he watched in awe as she lifted her leg and drove it into his side. Her eyes became solid gold, and without delay she kicked him in his chest and sent him rolling across the terrain.

Furious, Aradmus extended both of his hands towards her, and as the many shadows reached for her, she evaded with grace and agility. She quickly closed the gap, but as she moved to crush his chest with an elbow he narrowly jumped away from her. He slammed his hand against the glass guard that surrounded the edge of the rooftop and shattered it entirely, and as a result of his fury he charged her now. They went for a punch simultaneously, and as their fists collided the force of the impact sent a shockwave through the building that shattered its every window. Aradmus kicked at her head and Eva tossed her body in the direction in which the kick moved to evade. She landed, hunched over and eyes as sharp as a tiger on the prowl, and with every ounce of hatred she felt she drove her open hand into and through the chest of the king.

His mask fell from his face one final time and landed at his feet, and as the shadows faded and his armor split, Aradmus grabbed her by her arm.

"You look a bit surprised," Eva cooed as her lips curled into a smile. Aradmus' face radiated disgust and indignation, but as the blood fell from the hole in his chest and back, he was powerless to even reach for the vessel that prolonged his life.

"How did you…" he mumbled. "You have no Paradox… So how?!"

"Simple. I've waited a thousand years for this moment," Eva replied as she kicked his abdomen to free her arm. He gasped one final time as his blood poured out upon the ground, and the victorious pianist drove the heel of her foot into his neck. "I wasn't gonna let it pass me by."

“You are one terrifying woman when you want to be,” Nico laughed as he stood back up. He coughed as he gripped his chest. “Ugh, is it possible to break a lung? Because I think mine is shattered to bits.”

“Do you ever stop joking,” came David’s weary voice rang over the now silent rooftop. He fell backwards as he lifted the notepad and quill into the air. He breathed a sigh of relief, because with the final period in place, the story of the Paradox Curse had finally ended.

Chapter Twenty

A year had passed since Aradmus' defeat, and the horrors of the curse still manifested in David's nightmares from time to time. He was thankful, though, that the beauty of the time before had overtaken his reality. He looked into the shimmering sunset and basked in the final warmth of its light. The breeze was gentle and more than welcome as he waited in his sharp tuxedo with his best friend by his side. He met the eyes of the minister, who smiled at him with Bible in hand, and smiled back. Torrie stood on the other side, dressed in a soft yellow dress that was complemented greatly by the waning lights of the summer sun and radiated the same amber of Eva's eyes. Though she glared at him suspiciously, he couldn't help but smile as he tightly clasped his hands together and looked out toward the ocean.

The white sands of the beach turned orange, and the ebbing waves of the sea glistened in the rays of light. The seagulls sang as they flapped their wings overhead, and David felt, for the first time in this life or the ones he'd led before, truly at peace.

"You nervous," Nico asked him, but he shook his head.

"Nah," said the prince as his knees knocked together. Nico took notice, and both of them laughed.

"It's alright. You survived having me as your best friend, got stabbed in the shoulder and battled a thousand-year-old demon for supremacy, so I think you can handle this," Nico rattled off. The minister and Torrie both stared at them with expressions of disbelief. Nico smiled as he waved at them. "Inside joke."

"You really do joke too much, babe," came the voice of his wife, Sierra. The boys turned their attention to her and the energetic baby in her arms.

"There's my girl," mused the philosopher as he reached over and kissed his bride. He looked her over and whistled at the stunning crimson dress that tightly embraced her petite form and accentuated every curve. He stroked her raven-colored hair and felt his heart melt as her dark blue eyes softened and her ruby lips lifted into a smile. His son glared at him, and with infantile force struck his father in the head. Nico laughed as he poked the little boy in the forehead. "I see you, too, squirt. How could I forget my little Phil?"

"My nephew has a lot of attitude, doesn't he," David spoke in his best baby voice, and with a tickle the child laughed.

“He gets it from Eva, honestly,” Sierra told him with a chuckle. “Honestly it keeps things interesting around the house.”

“I can only imagine,” David mused as he kissed the baby on his forehead. Sierra took her seat towards the front of the tent and patiently they waited for her arrival. David looked down to check his watch. Eva was cutting it close, and though he knew that there was no real rush he was just eager. This was as much his day as it was hers.

“Don’t worry, sweetheart,” Torrie said with a giggle. “She’ll be here. Eva’s too bold to chicken out, so don’t even worry about it.” David took a deep breath and closed his eyes.

“Thank you, Torrie,” he offered, and she flashed him a look.

“You just make sure that you uphold your end of the bargain, Mr. Super Sexy Author.” Everyone fell silent, even the baby, and all eyes fell upon quirky maid of honor. “I… said that last part out loud, didn’t I?”

“Yeah,” David responded with a chuckle. “But it eased the suspense so I’m grateful. And thank you for the compliment.”

The organist abruptly began to play, and as the guests rose, all eyes focused on the center aisle. She stood there, garbed in purest white, with the sun in her eyes and all of nature at her mercy. She strode upon the rose petals that led to the altar, and as the wind picked up they spiraled around her in graceful dance. She was the envy of beauty itself, and with every step she took he loved her even more. The lights of the sky dimmed now and, with its final shimmers, kissed her already perfect skin.

It was almost as it had been in the forest those centuries ago, but what had once been done in the darkness was now displayed in the light, and as he fell bewitched by her very presence he knew that even after a thousand years, his heart would always belong to her.

She gracefully took her place at the altar, opposite the only person she knew to protect her with his whole being, and as the audience of Sierra and baby Phillip took their seats, the bride and groom stared lovingly into each other's eyes.

"We are gathered here today," began the minister with deepest sincerity, "to celebrate the love of David Masters and Eva Gallows, and to unite them in holy matrimony. There is no truer expression of love than this: to bind one's life together with another, fully embracing the flaws of the other and choosing them daily in spite of themselves. Love is patient, after all, and it is kind. It does not envy, it does not boast, it isn't proud. It doesn't dishonor others, isn't self-seeking, isn't easily angered, and it keeps no record of wrongs. Love, children, does not delight in evil but rejoices with the truth. It always protects, always trusts, always hopes, always perseveres. Love never fails. Do you understand this, or seek to understand it if you do not?"

"We do," they said simultaneously, and the minister joined in their joyful smiles.

"Then if you have any vows, you may say them now," he said, and took a step back. David and Eva stared at each other for just a moment longer, but she decided to go first.

"David," she started, but paused as she struggled to hold back the tears. "I walked through my entire life believing that all I had was my music. I was terrified, for reasons I could never figure out, of drawing close to anyone. But when I met you, when we spoke about our passions and explored each other's minds I felt… I felt at peace, like I never had before. That's why no matter what, whether it be sickness or fighting, whether we struggle to make ends meet or lose everything we have, I choose to stand by your side. I love you, David, and I always will." Sierra pulled a tissue from her purse and wiped her eyes, as the words that Eva spoke reminded her of what she'd said to Nico a few years prior.

"Eva…" his now permanently white eyes became stern for the first time in a millennium, and instantly she found herself arrested by his gaze. "Before I met you, I longed for adventure. I was constantly searching for something much greater than what I was living through at the time. My life had become so cyclical that I became disgusted with the constant write, travel, sign, repeat, write, travel, sign, repeat, and it just became so frustrating, because despite the successes that I'd experienced from living out my passion, or the fans I'd gained doing what I loved or the amazing places I'd been enabled to see, I didn't have anyone to share it with besides the knucklehead that's standing behind me." Nico made a face, and the baby in the audience laughed happily. "But then, in the middle of the mundanity I met you and I was stunned, because I'd never witnessed someone so bold, brilliant and vivacious in all my life. It's something I'm still getting used to, to be honest. I'd spent my entire life wrapped up in a story, writing about adventures I'd never have to make up for the ones I couldn't find, but after everything we've been through together already, I realize now that I couldn't have ever written a better adventure than you. Eva, my excitement and my comfort, I love you with everything I have and more, and…" he leaned in to whisper to her, and as he flashed a grin he told her, "I will never allow for your suffering again." He backed away from her, and as the tears streamed down her face he wiped them away with a brush of his hands. "This, I promise you." The minister looked upon them through misty eyes as he clutched the Bible in his hands for dear life.

"David," he spoke, "do you take Miss Eva to be your lawfully wedded wife, to have and to hold, in sickness and in health, till death do you part?"

"I do," the author assured him with no hesitation, and his beautiful bride did what she could to restrain her cry. The clergyman shifted his attention to her.

"Eva, do you take David to be your lawfully wedded husband, to have and to hold, in sickness and in health, till death do you part?"

"I do," she said excitedly as she rapidly shook her head.

"Then, by the powers vested in me, I now pronounce you man and wife," the preacher concluded. "You may now kiss the bride." David and Eva looked upon each other with joy, and as the fears of the past drifted away with the distant tide and the noise of their surroundings drowned out, their lips locked, and they knew that it was here where their story would truly begin.

About the Author

Jordan Hampton is an African-American author. He was born February 3rd, 1994 in Memphis, Tennessee to Cheryl and (the late) DeWayne Hampton. Between the years 1999 and 2007, he lived in Darmstadt, Germany with his family as a result of his mother's military stationing. While there, he was exposed to an assortment of cultures, their storytelling, and their histories, and this exposure to varied cultures has facilitated an interest in global storytelling, however it might manifest. In 2014, he received his license to preach the Gospel of Jesus Christ, and he does his best to relate Christian themes through his works.

www.ingramcontent.com/pod-product-compliance
Lightning Source LLC
Chambersburg PA
CBHW060810310726
48980CB00002B/292
9780692164457